SISTERS OF SHILOH

SISTERS
OF SHILOH

Kathy *and* Becky Hepinstall

Houghton Mifflin Harcourt
BOSTON   NEW YORK
2015

For information about permission to reproduce selections from this book, write to Permissions, Houghton Mifflin Harcourt Publishing Company, 215 Park Avenue South, New York, New York 10003.

www.hmhco.com

Library of Congress Cataloging-in-Publication Data is available.
ISBN 978-0-544-40000-9

Book design by Brian Moore

Printed in the United States of America
DOC 10 9 8 7 6 5 4 3 2 1

To our brother and sister, Randy and Margie

SISTERS OF SHILOH

Libby waited for her dead husband in the woods, her breath making clouds in the cold night air. Her hair was cut short above her ears, and her neck was cold. Her wool uniform itched. She had not slept in two days. She leaned against a bay tree as the fog moved through the woods. She closed her eyes and began to drift. She heard the crackle of a footstep and opened her eyes. The fog cleared and Arden stood in front of her, pale and somber, the red stain of his stomach wound still fresh and spreading out across his gray jacket.

She was exhausted from the march, and the sight of him no longer caused the shock and dread of the earlier encounters. She had resolved that there must be a realm, when the fractions of night and fog reached some magical equation, where the living and the dead could coexist. Arden, though, had grown increasingly moody and demanding.

"How many have you killed?" he asked.

Her fingers shook as she counted them. She had known the answer at noon but had forgotten it with the coming of dusk.

"Nine."

"Nine? Still?"

"I'm trying, Arden." She looked at the blood spreading over his shirt.

"And your sister. How many has she killed?"

"I don't know."

He leaned in close.

"You're a liar. You do know. And you know who else she killed, don't you?"

1855

Winchester, Virginia

They were sisters, the pretty one and the one who lived in her shadow, a pale, chip-toothed, uncertain girl who made too much noise while eating celery. They lived on the outskirts of Winchester, in a house owned by their father, a dentist by trade. The fields behind their property grew wild with evening primrose and goldenrod. Near the cornfield on the east side of their property stood an apple orchard, and it was here that golden Libby and chipped-toothed Josephine, Libby's elder by a year, made their sanctuary, taking refuge from everything: the yelps of children during tooth extractions, the peskiness of a little brother, the swift, severe gaze of a mother, general pangs, harsh sunlight, and chores.

The other children in town courted the affections of Libby, but she preferred the sweet mixture of orchard and sister, all that shade and adoration.

When Josephine was thirteen, a shadow trespassed on that filtered light. The family next door had moved from a small town near Fredericksburg called Shiloh, a young couple with three sons. The oldest was named Arden. He came strutting into the yard on a warm spring day, when the leaves in the orchard were curling tendrils, and the shadows hung dark, waiting for May to darken them into the black of an Angus bull. He wore a pair of corduroys and a shirt with a Western design; his hair was almost as light as Libby's and his face just as angular. His eyes gave off different inferences that depended on the angle of approach. Libby saw wildness and sweetness and a deep capacity for sorrow. Josephine saw arrogance and entitlement and a lack of respect for elder sisters.

Soon Arden's feet were swinging from the branches, and the quality of conversation was forced into a different season, one that incorporated boys. Now Indian talk pierced the orchard, fishing lore, legends, and brutal accounts of cats killing birds. Pirate stories and secret caves, the challenge of breaking a colt. Even the drifting scent changed from the faint lavender of girls to the sweat of a hot boy. Something was unnatural here, like a tree that fruits before it blooms. Josephine was gently elbowed out of the shade until she no longer entered the orchard at all but lurked at the perimeter.

She didn't understand how to be alone. She felt insubstantial, impermanent as silence in a room full of women. There was some kind of secret to making friends, and, denied this, she began to spend her time in her father's office. Children cried and teeth flew.

"Hand me the laudanum," her father said.

She watched him pour the opiate onto a spoon to numb a patient's pain. She imagined the bottle held to her own lips, pain declining, pleasure growing. The sweetness of a watermelon, the dreaminess of a summer afternoon, the cool water of a fishing hole, the softness of ferns.

Hostility toward the whole led to belligerence about the parts. His laugh. His haircut. The shape of his arms. The blue of his eyes. The way his pretty face resembled Libby's.

"You spend so much time with him," she complained to Libby. "How about me? I thought I was your best friend."

"Don't be silly. You can sit in the orchard with us anytime."

"That was our orchard!"

"Oh, Josephine. Orchards belong to everyone."

When Libby and Arden weren't in the orchard, they would disappear into the woods and stay gone for hours, returning with new secrets, certain stories exchanged, pebbles gathered, sparrow eggs rescued, snakes slain. The sight of the interloper drove Josephine to distraction. She had nightmares in which he fell from the branch of a tree or from the top of their house, grasping her sister's hand and pulling her down with him.

A year had passed. Autumn had arrived. The apples were heavy in the orchard, weighing down the limbs. Flowering weeds turned colors or withdrew their blooms. The sky was white in places, sweet blue in others.

Libby's illness began as a weariness, a desire for naps. Quickly it grew a fever, then chills. The orchard sat empty. Libby lay in a dim room, her face flushed and skin perspiring. Arden visited her at first, but when she grew worse, he could not look at her without bursting into tears, and Mrs. Beale sent him away.

"Get ahold of yourself, son. You aren't helping matters."

Despite the protestations of her mother, it was Josephine who took over, fetching teas and applying poultices, whispering, singing, telling her own tales, finally. She wiped down the floors with lavender water so that Libby could awaken to the fragrance of flowers. She brewed tea, heated soup on the fire in the kitchen. Her nursing skills defined her, made her whole again.

A framed tintype sat on the night table. Two little girls stared out from it, one with golden hair and the other with bright eyes and a contented smile. Their father had taken them down to the studio at the Taylor Hotel as a birthday present for Josephine a few years earlier. She couldn't help staring at it now and remembering those days when Libby was healthy and belonged to her.

They would speak to each other, sister to sister, Libby's voice dreamy and hot, a breeze coming through the open window, a pail of water on the nightstand, a gingham cloth dripping water on the floor.

"Hold still," Josephine said, as she applied the compress.

No sign of Arden, whom their mother would not let back in the house.

Apples fell, too ripe now for eating. One day the chickens got loose and spent the day in the orchard, eating the bruised flesh. Crows came to that harvest, as did raccoons and deer.

The corn had ripened. Stephen, the lazy younger brother, was supposed to have gathered the ears but spent his time chasing an elusive bullfrog down a winding creek, coming back with his pants wet up to the waist. He slogged into Libby's room, dripping water on the floor and corrupting the sweet air with the sweaty odor of his body.

"Get out," Josephine said.

"She's my sister, too."

"You're smelly. That can't be good for her."

Whispers from their parents' room.

"She's not getting any better," said their mother.

"I don't know what to do. I'm a dentist, for God's sakes. And that crazy old doctor hasn't helped a bit."

"There are better doctors in Richmond . . ."

"Richmond? How can she possibly make that trip?"

Fever moved through Libby's body. She shook with chills and soaked her sheets with perspiration. Symptoms in opposition and growing further apart, like the views of the North and South. She mumbled things that made no sense. The old doctor came again and stood by her bedside and saw the bad news like everyone else. When he put on his stethoscope, one knob fell out of his big ear and he didn't seem to notice. He pressed the metal disk against a vein throbbing in her neck.

As if prodded by the shaking hands of the doctor and the look on his face, Josephine's father went to town and returned with a pine coffin. He didn't sneak it in at night but dragged it purposefully off his wagon, across the yard, and into an old shed at the far end of the property. Josephine opened the window of Libby's room and watched him. The coffin made a rushing sound in the dry grass, thumping occasionally against a rock or a rake Stephen had left in the yard. Dogs ran up and sniffed it before they sidled away. Dr. Beale walked with a stiff and singular purpose, dragging the coffin right through the herb garden and between the stables. The horses poked their heads out and watched him disappear into the shed.

Mrs. Beale came into the room but didn't look out the window or at Libby. She searched the room for something neutral, settling on a silver tea strainer that drained brown liquid on a china saucer.

"She's not going to die," Josephine said. "I won't let her. Remember that dog with the infected leg? No one expected him to live, either. But I saved him."

Josephine had always thought of God as a vague fog that lived in the sky, someone who never bothered her and whose music was sweet. An insubstantial being that seemed to vanish when studied closely. But now she had no choice but to tremble and believe. The room was full of fever now, reeking like tidewater in which plants have died, and no amount of lavender could bury the smell. Libby's dreams grew frantic. She called out sometimes. She saw things in the room that did not include her family.

Josephine summoned her quiescent faith, which had not been visited since the days of the infected dog. She apologized for the long delay and prayed a desperate prayer that would have been high-pitched had it been spoken out loud. The wood planks of the floor hurt her knees. One shin pressed against the metal slats of the gravity vent; she felt a draft as her lips formed the words. The wool blanket that covered Libby's bed scratched Josephine's elbows. She finished the prayer and began it again, finished and began, wearing a groove down God's patience, no doubt, but the thought of life without Libby was less imaginable than even the hereafter. Josephine started again. She heard her mother's footsteps when she entered the room, and her sigh, and the sniff of hushed weeping. Her mother sat down on the bed, jostling Josephine's elbows.

No one knew the exact hour of the fever's breaking. It happened sometime during the night. Libby woke up that morning mumbling. By afternoon she whispered things that made sense. She had lost weight; her face was gaunt, filled with sickbed shadows. Josephine held her hand.

The old doctor came in and shook his head. "She's better," he announced, as though it weren't obvious. "There's no medical explanation. These are the ways of God."

His breath smelled of absinthe. He gathered his bag and left the room, his back stooping.

"I had such beautiful dreams," Libby said. "It felt as though years had passed."

"No. You've been sick about a week. I've been here the whole time. I even slept in here."

"And Arden?"

Josephine stiffened. "I don't know where he's been."

By early evening, Arden had heard the good news. He pulled a chair up to Libby's bed and played cards with her. "I thought I had lost you," he said. "I couldn't stand it. I haven't eaten in two days."

Josephine stood at the end of the bed and watched them play. The cards fanned out, shuffled, flew onto the bed one by one. Arden and Libby studied the cards, then each other.

"I'm going now," Josephine said.

They didn't hear her.

That night Libby was led downstairs, leaning on her father's arm. Her hands trembled, but she was able to sit with the family for dinner. Arden had been invited to eat with them. Libby picked at her food. Arden goaded her on. "Come on, come on, you're so thin. How can we play unless you get strong again?"

He had finally begun to nurse her, now that she was well.

Mrs. Beale looked down the table at Libby, her expression tentative and warm. "Arden is so glad to have you back," she said. "He was so worried about you. Weren't you, Arden?"

Josephine saw them together in the shadows of the orchard. It was dusk. They had been there all day with their secrets and were now emerging, hand in hand. She glided into shadows of her own. By that cover, she watched them kiss. And like something suddenly noticed in the world, a color or a scent, she saw the kisses everywhere. Lightning quick and furtive. Covered in shadows or sheltered by the blinding light of noon, they went unnoticed by the rest of the world. She tried to turn her eyes away, but the kisses seemed attracted by her torment. When she could not see them, she heard them. And when she could not hear them, she imagined them. She wondered if a kiss could live in her own mouth, or if she was broken beyond repair, not a girl or a boy but a ghost, offering nothing to the world but a glow and a rustling.

One day, as she was on her way to the dry goods store, at her mother's orders, to buy a bolt of cloth and some needles, she met Arden coming the other way. His hair was getting long; he needed a haircut. Certainly her father would never let her brother

Stephen's hair grow past his ears. His hair made him look even more girlish with his high cheekbones and delicate brow.

They stopped a few feet from one another, no greeting or wave. Just the stare of enemies.

"You've been spying on us," he said.

"No, I haven't."

"Yes, you have. You saw us kissing."

"Libby's too young for kissing."

"She's thirteen now. Maybe it's not that you think she's too young. Maybe it's that she's kissing me."

The sun was bright overhead. The coins in her hand felt sweaty. His voice was not angry. Just matter-of-fact.

"That's true," she said. "I can think of better boys for her to kiss."

"You think about her too much. Where she goes, who she kisses. And I know why."

She didn't answer him. She tried to step around him, but he blocked her path. She went the other way, and he blocked her again. His eyes looked straight at her. There was no one on the road.

"It's because," he said, "you have no other friends, do you? Not a single one."

The statement burned inside her. She wanted to run away, but she knew he would catch her arm. Something about his voice told her he'd been waiting for the right moment to say these hurtful things, and he was going to force her to listen.

"And you are always alone," he added. "Because you are strange. You're not like Libby. You don't know how to talk to people. You have nothing interesting to say."

Josephine tried to deflect his words, not wanting him to see the hurt welling in her eyes. She looked at him directly and said coolly, "I do have interesting things to say. I just don't say them to you."

Arden took a small step forward, looking at her with intense, unblinking eyes. "You know what you need? You need a sweetheart. But you won't ever have one. You will never even get one kiss. No one will ever love you. You are invisible."

Josephine felt her face flush and a tiny hole form in her stomach, as though she'd been shot there. The cruelty in the remarks was the cool dispassion and the utter confidence with which they were spoken. It was true, sometimes she felt as though she were invisible, as though people drank in the sight of Libby and that was enough, that her place was in the shadows and her fate to be unseen. She stepped to the side of him and made her way to the store, trembling with rage and shame, the clenched coins digging into the flesh of her hand.

3

Dearest Lib,

We whipped that old peacock McClellan good in Richmond a few weeks back. The boys say he will lick his wounds and come right back at us. Now we are marching again, this time we hear another Yankee army is headed for Richmond again. I've heard so many stories this past year that never came about that I am never sure what to believe. But it doesn't matter, I suppose. I just march and fight and know that I am on the side of God.

The marches are so long and I am half-starved and bone-weary, but every night I look at the tintype of you I carry next to my heart, and I remember my purpose.

I wish I could draw strength from your latest letters, but they are so short. You talk of only town news and your difficulties with the Yankee occupations, and say little of your love or all I sacrifice for you.

You must always remember your devotion to me. Knowing you are waiting for me, and thinking only of me, keeps me strong in my fight for Southern rights.

Your husband,
Arden

4

September 1862

Libby stood at the back of the Beale property, near the barn and facing the new sun, letting its light focus on a letter from Arden. This latest had been written on a scrap of wallpaper. His supply of stationery must be running low, and on account of the Union embargo, she couldn't buy him any more.

> *We don't have proper shelter. Last week I had to sleep in a tent with eight men, Lib. Every time someone turned, we all woke up.*

She looked up from the letter and cast an irritated look at the brightening sky. It was time for another day. The passageways and pale rooms of the house were filling with light, smoke rising from chimneys. Coffee steaming, yellow flames crackling inside the stove, heating the bottom of a pot, and sending a bubble through a batch of fresh grits. Her father arranging his dental instruments.

After Arden had left for the war, she had moved out of the humble A-frame they had shared together on Kent Street and back under her father's roof. It was oddly comforting to once again be part of the family that had sheltered and adored her, although she had waited every day during the past year for some news of Arden or the movements of the Stonewall Brigade.

He had been desperate to join the Confederate army as soon as war broke not a month after their wedding, but he had taken a bad fall from their roof and broken his foot, and spent two months hobbling around on a cypress-wood crutch, reminding Libby at every opportunity that it was she who had hounded him to fix the shingles that day.

He had joined up that June of 1861 with the First Virginia Brigade under Thomas Jackson. It was during the Confederate victory at the Battle of Manassas that July when the brigade and its beloved commander earned the famous new name of Stonewall.

"There is no greater feeling, Lib," Arden wrote to her, "than to know that God fights beside you."

He had been an adamant supporter of Secession, and during the course of their courtship had slowly influenced Libby, whose family was moderate. One night three years before, they had met secretly late at night and talked over the news of John Brown's slave rebellion and the murders at Harpers Ferry, only thirty miles to the northeast of Winchester. Arden's warm breath touched her face as he spoke. His hand held hers.

In that darkness, they exchanged rumors: A dozen victims had been drawn and quartered; John Brown had eaten their flesh; slaves were rising up everywhere, holding secret meetings in an old cemetery at the edge of town. Arden had heard that the first sign of the uprising would be the discovery of all the dogs in Winchester piled in a heap at the edge of town, their throats cut. Even families like the Beales who owned no slaves would not be spared. Revenge would trade color for color; whites would die for no other crime than being white. At that very moment, John Brown's disciples were trying to free him from jail before his execution.

"Every one of those murderous slaves should be executed, too," he had said.

"But were they not fighting for their freedom? Slavery is wrong, Arden. My father's always said that and I agree."

"You are missing the point, as always," he had said with a sigh. "If you would take the time to educate yourself, you would see quite clearly what any smart person could—this is about the cold-blooded slaughter of innocent white people. These murderous Negroes who would gladly kill you and your family, even though you own no slaves. Is that what you think is justice?"

"No, no, of course not, Arden."

Libby had reached out and touched his hand, finding it cool and steady. He was ready for the war.

Now Libby returned to the letter, reading it again slowly. The words made Arden's experience so clear that she felt the mud in his boots and tasted the salt pork in his mouth. Transported to some dark clearing, she lay in a tent packed with soldiers and smelled the broth that half a dozen odors make.

Libby's love for her husband had only deepened since his departure. Once, in late summer, when his brigade had bivouacked near Winchester, he had received a pass from his lieutenant and come to see her. Together they had gone back to the little house they had once shared as man and wife, bursting into it hurriedly, straight to the bedroom, where they had made love on the pencil-post bed in a room frozen in time, under the motionless gravity clock, among the odor that neglected houses put off after many months. Arden's clean-shaven face hovered above her, his eyes looking down, full of war fever and husband fever, and she felt terrified for a moment, that there was no Libby anymore, that she would collapse into his beliefs and his fervor and his boyhood and his birth. She loved him that much, in a way that made no space for herself, as though he were a full glass of tea and she was the piece of ice that would cause an overspill onto the tablecloth.

She read the letter again. A breeze dried her moving lips. She had arrived at that same troubling paragraph.

My rifle no longer shoots straight, half the time. I think the barrel warped. I keep telling the captain I need a new rifle. He says if my gun shoots straight half the time, those are pretty good odds.

Sacrifice was the duty of every Virginian. The preacher at the Methodist church on Braddock Street had said as much, in a shrill voice that did not lower during Yankee occupations of their town. The right to secede was written into the Bible, or at least implied in the Gospels, and God's approving smile started at the northern border of Virginia and extended all the way to the southern coast. Perspiration ran down the minister's face. He wiped it away with the back of his hand until the cuff of his sleeve wore a faint yellow stain. As his sermons grew longer and louder, the congregation noticed that his shirt had a strange bulge. When the Yankee provost marshal had him searched, the bulge turned out to be the socks of his dead son.

Libby looked up at the clouds and took a deep breath. She heard the chickens rustling in their coop, imagined them gossiping about the brightening sky. She put her hair behind her ear, but a breeze came out of nowhere and undid the fix. A snort came from the direction of the stables, where a bay stallion had spotted her and was looking for a treat. She threw him a distracted look and returned to the paragraph about the defective rifle. She knew why the captain would not replace it: their regiment had no spares. The Southern troops were ill fitted in every way. Unlike the Union army, they didn't have sutler wagons or new shoes, and they had been reduced to stripping their dead enemies of clothing and supplies. Occasionally, they could find luxuries like tinned lobster in the haversacks of corpses.

The horse snorted again.

She folded the letter and stood breathing in the odor of straw and manure, and another sweet fragrance she could not identify. She walked toward the stables, passing the grave of a Yankee soldier who had died at their house the previous spring, after the occupying army and its new provost marshal forced the citizens to take in their wounded men. This Yankee had been shot in the leg. Despite the amputation done by a field surgeon, by the time he was carried into the Beale house, the wound was infected and leaking green pus. It sent out the overwhelming odor of rot, leaking through the halls and the gravity vents, drifting into cold fireplaces, infiltrating curtains and even soap. Anyone entering the sick room had to first stuff their nostrils with cotton balls soaked with camphor.

Dr. Beale had made an honest attempt to nurse the man back to health, but he was only a dentist. One night the dying man's screams woke up the family, and when they rushed into the room, he smiled at them and said he'd been playing chess and had trapped the rival king. Within an hour, he was dead. The house was scrubbed down with homemade soap and vinegar, but the pungent smell remained for days, moving into the backyard through open windows and settling on the profusion of yarrow growing out of the soldier's grave. Within a week, the yarrow had disappeared, and no other weeds replaced it. The Beales implored the Confederate soldiers to dig up the corpse once Winchester was retaken, but no one paid them any mind. Unwelcome bodies were buried everywhere, and there wasn't enough manpower to do anything about it.

That damn Yankee shouldn't be in your family's backyard, Arden had complained in one of his letters. *The minute I come home, I'm going to dig up that son of a bitch.*

When Libby reached the horse, whose name was Ralph, she stroked his mane while he nosed the front pocket of her dress, still holding out hope for his old treat of peanut brittle.

"I'm sorry," she told him. "We have no sugar. And we have no peanuts."

The horse seemed to understand, then kicked the stall door.

"Blame the Yankees," Libby said.

Josephine made her bed and then paused to watch her sister reading Arden's letter in the backyard. At twenty years old, her cheekbones had hollowed and her freckles had begun to fade. She felt ready for courtship at last. But the men were gone.

At least the war had swept Arden away, and she had Libby to herself—except when the letters came, and her sister withdrew to a world of stark good and evil, where Arden lived and fought. Another letter had arrived. Sunlight came through the window. Josephine squinted and shaded her eyes. Outside, Libby paused by the bare spot in the lawn where the Yankee was buried. Her disgust was evident in the language of her body. Once, during a hot day the previous June, Josephine had seen Libby gargle lemonade and then spit it on the grave.

Just a few weeks ago, she had nearly attacked Julia Caldwell, a young woman from a pro-Union family, accusing her of spying for the Yankees. Josephine had the sense that Libby's increasingly virulent pro-Southern views were not hers at all, really, but something directly appropriated from those of her husband. Josephine had to strain to remember a time when Libby had her own opinions and her own dreams. She wondered if, one night as she slept, Arden's favorite color had leapt into her, replacing her own, and if that pattern repeated on subsequent nights—his preferential horse breed, spices, season, hymns, and faith.

What Arden had done to Libby's God made her resent him most. That deity, shaped and formed under the tutelage of her gentle father, was a fair, benevolent God whose strict expectations regarding the Ten Commandments were tempered by an all-consuming adoration of all His children. Arden had darkened and narrowed the eyes of this God, added rage to His purpose and gave Him a taste for Yankee blood. His God—now her God—was unloving and out for revenge.

When Josephine had heard Arden was finally off to fight, her first thought—so insistent and so piercing she could not dismiss it—was the possibility that Arden could be killed and removed from their lives forever. She banished this thought sternly, but over the passing months it returned in different forms. Lately she had taken to forcing herself to pray for Arden, though through gritted teeth, her knees on the floor, her elbows on the bed, and her hands clasped together so hard that her fingernails bit into the flesh below her knuckles.

She glanced out the window again. Libby was walking away from the barn, the horse stretching his head out of his stall watching her.

"Josephine!"

She jumped. Her father was calling her from downstairs.

"Come here. I need you."

She glanced out at Libby one more time before leaving the bedroom and starting downstairs. She barely remembered when her father's dental office had served as the family parlor. Years ago he had pulled all the rosewood furniture out of the room and taken down the gilded paintings of men rowing boats. He had dragged the Malaysian rug to another room and given the settee to a neighbor. Only the wallpaper remained, a French frosted-grape pattern that reminded Josephine of an easier time, when people had money and weren't reduced to scraping the floors of their smokehouses for salt. Dr. Beale worked in this room, a wingback chair for the patient and a stool for himself, as arthritis had affected his hips to the extent that he could not stand for very long periods of time. He also had a table to hold his instruments and the zinc tub he used to clean them. When he needed anesthetic, he bought laudanum from a neighbor who cultivated poppies.

When Josephine entered the office, she saw a towheaded boy who had backed into a far corner. His eyes were wild, and one cheek was puffed out as though full of taffy. He wore a pair of old pants and carpet shoes. His shirt was too small for him.

"What's the matter?" Josephine asked her father.

"I've got to pull his tooth. It's impacted."

The boy shook his head. "It doesn't hurt anymore. I want to go home."

Dr. Beale looked annoyed. "Come on, son. This won't hurt so bad. You can be brave, can't you? Think of all those brave soldiers out there. Isn't your brother riding with General Stuart? Don't you want to be like him?"

The boy's eyes changed as though he'd been nudged by his brother's spur. He moved a few feet from the corner and then stopped.

"Where's his mother?" asked Josephine.

"At the Taylor Hotel, passing out bandages."

"He's scared."

"Hold his hand."

The boy began to tremble as Josephine approached him. A tear ran down his face, and he quickly wiped it away. Josephine knelt beside him, the floor cold against her knees. She took his moist hand.

"It won't be so bad," she said. "We'll feel it together."

Dr. Beale gave the boy a spoonful of laudanum and waited until his pupils began to expand. Josephine felt his small hand slacken and warm. Dr. Beale opened the boy's mouth. He inserted a tooth key and began twisting the ivory handle. Josephine grimaced but could not look away.

The little boy's eyelids fluttered.

Josephine held her breath.

The boy screamed.

A tooth with black roots hit the wall.

Blood filled up the hole it left.

A rumor drifted around Winchester, tentative and wispy in the morning, turning darker by noon. The enemy was gathering in Maryland, a day's hard ride to the north. As the rumor traveled from house to house, no one could be sure whether to believe it or not. The local newspaper had stopped operating, as had the telegraph that once ran along the Baltimore and Ohio Railroad, leaving only word of mouth and the *Baltimore Sun,* neither of which could be trusted.

The youngest member of the Beale family, Stephen, had heard the rumor in the afternoon and was riding home through the empty out-lots, the hooves of his horse thundering against the ground, gnats rising out of the goldenrod. His father had told him to fix the roof of the stable, but instead he had taken one of the horses and left to investigate the ruins of Fort Garibaldi, a Union stronghold destroyed by its own army in early September. An officer had gone back to check on the fuse of the powder magazine and had been blown into bits, much to the excitement of the local boys. The remains were gathered onto a sheet and buried, but Stephen's friends insisted that one foot had been overlooked and still lay on the ground. Stephen had an insatiable streak of morbid curiosity, and he felt compelled to see the grisly sight for himself. Although he searched the ruins of the fort all afternoon, he found no such foot, only a brass button and the blade of a pocketknife. On his way back to town, he passed the tollhouse on Strothers Lane. An old man waved him down and told him the news.

"That can't be true!" Stephen had said when he heard the number of Union soldiers.

"It's true, all right." The old man turned and looked in the direction of Sharpsburg. "General Longstreet ordered the Pipers off their farm. There's gonna be a hell of a fight, boy. A hell of a fight. That is, if it hasn't started already."

Stephen urged his horse on with pressure from his heels. That old man must be crazy. He couldn't even imagine so many Yankees in one place. A sea of blue, salted with gunpowder. The number terrified him and brought him guilty joy. Nothing made a boy seem older than the exclusive possession of news of the war. The wind was warm but goose bumps ran down his arms. He was carrying the rumor home, bound for the people innocent of it. He bent low down and urged the horse on, his shirttail pulling out a little further. Down through the out-lots they flew, the rumor pressing on his back, as he outrode it like a storm — his heart pounding, his face red, the heat leaving the earth slowly, the grass cooling. The terrifying number he'd heard multiplied in his head. He caught sight of his house in the distance and shouted encouragement to his horse. His shirttail had finally pulled loose from his trousers, allowing a winged insect to gain access to his bare back and sting him along his spine. He reached around with one hand and tried to squash the maddening insect, but he almost lost his balance and gave up, reduced to imagining his revenge once he got off that horse.

"Go, boy!" he shouted. "Go, go!"

Violet Beale had a meeting at the Methodist church that evening, and so dinner came early. The family sat at a gate-leg table eating pork and cabbage when the door burst open and Stephen ran into the living room, panting, his face bright red.

Dr. Beale looked up. "Stephen, what is it?"

In his exhaustion, Stephen pointed west instead of north. "Big battle coming! The Stonewall Brigade is headed to Sharpsburg, and so are a hundred and fifty thousand Yankees."

"A hundred and fifty thousand? That's impossible."

Stephen wiped the sweat from his face.

"That's what the old man in the tollhouse said."

"Arden is in the Stonewall Brigade," Libby said.

Stephen sat down and took off his hat. A dead mosquito fell on his father's plate.

"Arden will be fine," Josephine told Libby. "He is brave, and I imagine a very good shot."

Libby gave her a withering look. "You don't understand. Arden's gun is warped. But, then, you've always hated him. You probably hope he dies."

"Libby!" Mrs. Beale sat up straight. "There will be no talk like that in this house."

"I must go to him," Libby said. "Sharpsburg is not very far."

"You'll do no such thing!" Dr. Beale said.

But Josephine had noticed the look on Libby's face. And she knew once Libby had that look, no one could stop her. The family could pretend they had the authority, but they would fail.

"I have something for you," Libby whispered to Ralph, the bay stallion.

The sun had almost set, and the sky had turned the gray color of a storeroom. Libby had a cedar canteen, a confession, and a bribe.

"Ralph, I lied to you when I claimed to have no peanut brittle. Yesterday, a soldier sitting on the steps of the Taylor Hotel gave me a piece, because he said I was pretty, and it had been so long since he'd seen a pretty girl. I was going to send it to Arden. You understand, don't you? But now I'm going to give it to you, because I love you so much, and because you are going to be a really good boy and not buck me off when I try to ride you."

The horse gave her a look that said he made no deals. She took the peanut brittle out of her pocket, and his ears straightened. His big teeth nearly took off her fingers as he snatched the treat from her hand. Little pieces of it fell to the ground as he chewed it. After he finished, he pressed his muzzle against her, a gesture she took as a sign of gratefulness until she realized he was nosing her pocket in search of more candy.

"You greedy boy," she said. Her voice was calm, although her heart raced. She slipped the bridle over his muzzle and led him out the gate. She was just about to climb onto his back when she heard footsteps in the grass. She didn't bother to turn around. She knew who it was.

"Go away, Josephine."

"You can't do this. You can't just ride into a battle. It's crazy."

Libby hoisted herself onto Ralph's broad back and patted his neck. "You don't understand. You have never been in love."

Libby gathered the reins.

Josephine sighed. She didn't like riding horses. And she didn't want to ride toward 150,000 Yankees. But someone had to protect her crazy sister.

"I'm going with you."

"No, you'll stay here." She turned the horse to go.

"I'll scream for Mother and Father, right this minute," Josephine said calmly. "And you have heard my scream before. They will be out here in an instant."

Libby looked thoughtful, and Josephine knew she was judging the distance to the front gate, wondering if she could make her escape if Josephine were, in fact, to scream. Libby sighed, defeated. "I suppose you can go. But I don't know why. You hate Arden."

"I'm not going for Arden."

They rode up the Martinsburg Pike, Libby on the bay stallion and Josephine following on a sweet-tempered chestnut. As the sun set, the horses lengthened their pace. Not a soul passed them on the road. The landscape had been stripped clean of living things. The stars came out in a stunning pattern that stretched the universe over. They passed a series of farms, and some Mennonite wood lots. Josephine's thighs began to hurt from taking a man's position instead of riding sidesaddle, but the girls had no choice — sidesaddle was an easier, slower gait.

Hoofbeats and breath. The world so still and silent, it was

hard to believe a new sun would soon rile it into motion. She wondered if her parents had already discovered them gone, and if they were frantic with worry. Her back ached. Her hand was cramped from holding the reins. She found it hard to believe the number of Union soldiers rumored to be in Sharpsburg. Tall tales like that one had flown through Winchester since the start of the war. And yet she rode on, her legs rubbing raw, knowing she must protect her younger sister.

Josephine wished she could hate the enemy with the fervor of her sister, but although she resented, of course, their repeated occupations of Winchester, she had to claim a guilty love for the music of their regimental band and for the festive colors of the Zouave regiment, who had stolen their May cherries. She couldn't help but think of those young men with their strange accents and wonder if perhaps among them might be a man who would notice her.

The wounded Yankees in the Beale house had suffered terribly. The most handsome of them, the one who died, would tell her stories. His wounded stump frothed with gangrene and ruined his true scent and best laughter, but she found herself drawn to him nonetheless. One night she dreamed he was whole again and stood facing her in a patch of neutral ground. No bullets. No sorrow. No infection. Just the brief touching of their lips. A few days later the Yankee won an imaginary chess match and died. All summer, Josephine had stolen out in the dead of night to tend his grave. Love for a Yankee, hatred for the man her sister loved.

What a traitor she was.

5

The battle had started without them, raging fierce for one day, and was over before they could reach it. That day after no one could say yet who had won — the killing so terrible for all, and both sides trying to piece together the remains of their army. Lee's troops still sat north of the river, and both sides contemplated a renewed attack while they tended to the dead and wounded. The sisters had traveled all night and then bribed the Confederate pickets guarding the river. One of them had said, "Go back. I barely made it out of that battle, and you don't want to see what it looks like now. There are things on that field I can't describe."

Josephine touched Libby's arm. "Please, let's go home. There is nothing we can do."

"You go home. I am going to find Arden."

"It's dangerous. We could be killed!"

"Don't be so melodramatic. The battle is over."

Josephine knew that any further protests were useless, and she wasn't going to turn back without her sister. And so they pressed on, terrible visions in Josephine's head and a fear rising inside for what they might see. They crossed the river at the ford, then dismounted and led their horses down a road crowded with soldiers, ambulance wagons, and local farmers who rented out their own wagons to the keening families of the dead.

The bay stallion and the chestnut caught an odor as they neared the battlefield. They snorted, planted their hooves, and would go no farther. Sweet talk in the ear of Josephine's horse and threats in the ear of Libby's finally got the beasts moving again.

The tired, dusty soldiers who stopped to answer questions always pointed to the west. "Jackson's brigade? They fought in the woods across from the Miller farm and around a white church on that same side of the road. Or maybe it's a school. But it's white."

A hundred yards from the white church, they had no choice but to hitch their increasingly reluctant horses and walk the rest of the way. They reached the turnpike and looked down the road. The war entered their eyes before they could cover them. The real war, not the one they'd observed from Winchester.

The fields and farms past Sharpsburg lay under a blue sky, the full warmth of the September sun opening the petals of flowers and swelling the stomachs of soldiers. Blood ran down posts and crusted the fence line, coated the grass, and splattered a cornfield whose stalks had been razed by gunfire; famished soldiers had sickened themselves on the green corn and were vomiting right and left. Blood covered the wounded and dying as they writhed on the ground and begged for water. It tricked the eye with its colors: scarlet in places, orange in others, black and brown, gray in certain lights, purplish on dead Yankee's coats.

Josephine fought the urge to turn and run. Blood stained the sides of her boots, the hem of her long dress.

She turned and noticed Libby's face was pale, and concern for her little sister replaced that for herself. "Keep walking," Josephine said, touching her shoulder.

They passed a man's head lying in thistles and covered with ants. The smell of gunpowder and spoiling flesh hung in the air, punctuated by the neighing of loose horses and the cries of the wounded men. Shells had torn farm animals apart, and the flesh of burst pumpkins had slid down the sides of the walls. Burial details were trying to hack out graves in the rocky soil. Soldiers hung on the split-rail fences, killed on their way over the top and now frozen in gestures that varied in profundity. Face to the sky, head in the arms, one finger pointing, hands together as if in prayer, knees buckled, legs twisted, legs straight. A prankster had put a biscuit in a Yankee's open mouth. As the sisters watched, a Rebel soldier pulled it out and ate it.

They wandered in the wrong direction, directed by a confused Confederate sitting beside a fence. When they passed a sunken road, Josephine couldn't help but look at the piles of Rebel bodies that filled the road and stretched into the distance. Living men worked among the heap. One tried to use his rifle as a fulcrum to separate two corpses. She took Libby's arm. "Don't look," she hissed in her ear, and pulled her along.

Outside the white church, some of the soldiers who had escaped injury sat near the building, chewing tobacco, counting their unspent cartridges and cleaning their weapons, seemingly unconcerned about the carnage around them. Inside, field surgeons worked quietly. Stretcher-bearers carried the wounded into the church, whose walls were pockmarked with grapeshot. Outside an open window, a pile of amputated limbs crushed the wild grass. An arm flew out the window, landed on top of the pile, and rolled toward the bottom until it caught on the curled fingers of a disembodied hand.

Two stretcher-bearers carried a litter out to the field. Libby hurried up to them and asked, "Did the Stonewall Brigade fight around here?"

They nodded.

"Thirty-Third Regiment?" she asked.

"Got some boys here from the Thirty-Third," one said.

Libby tried to ask another question, but they were gone.

"I'll go into the church and see what I can find out," she told Josephine. She pointed to a field scattered with bodies and limestone rills. "You look over there."

"No, let's stay together."

"We'll never find Arden that way. There's too much ground to cover."

The sights in the church were worse than those on the battle-field. The doors had been taken off their hinges and laid across the pews to serve as operating tables. Blood-covered surgeons dressed wounds with cornhusks, sawed off limbs, and sewed wounds shut with hurried stitches. An exhausted-looking woman comforted a man who'd been shot in the thigh.

Libby tapped her shoulder.

"I need to find my husband," she said when the woman met her eyes. "He's in the Stonewall Brigade. Thirty-Third Regiment. D Company."

"I've treated men from the Thirty-Third here," the woman said. "That regiment took a lot of casualties."

"Have you seen a soldier named Arden Tanner?"

"Oh, sweetheart. I forget their names as soon as they tell me." She turned away and helped the man drink something out of a tin cup.

Libby walked among the pews, looking into the faces of the men. Some of them screamed, and some lay quietly under the spell of morphine.

She accidentally jostled the arm of a doctor.

"Get out of here!" he screamed.

Soldier by soldier, Josephine worked her way toward the West Woods, kneeling by bodies torn in pieces. Arms and legs gone, heads ripped off. One body was opened as though from a scal-pel, the flesh and muscle laid back to expose the lungs and the heart. Josephine saw that the heart was still beating, and sud-denly felt the ground rush up to meet her. She opened her eyes a few moments later, face-down in a patch of bloody grass. No one tried to help her. She stood up and kept going, determined not to faint again.

Throughout the afternoon, the odor of the dead grew more intense. She found a handkerchief caught up in the low branches of a locust tree and held the fabric over her nose to make breathing easier. The bodies of those who had died early in the battle had already begun to blacken and bloat, but the ones who had lingered into this day still had their natural features. Scattered among the older men were boys who looked too young for war, their adolescent beauty untroubled by beards or scars.

A man who had been shot in the chest stirred when she touched him.

"Emily, is that you?" he asked.

A bee landed on his sleeve. Josephine waved it away.

"Answer me, sweetheart."

"Yes. It's me," she said, because he seemed to want this Emily so badly.

He smiled. "I knew you'd come. Emily, hold my hand."

His palm was warm and callused.

"My sweet girl. Listen to me. There's a hundred and fifty dollars in the bank. I want you to buy a good horse, not some old scrub pony . . ."

His voice trailed off, then he took a breath and began again.

"And don't let that corn go bad. It's getting time. Make the boys help you."

"I will."

"Stay away from that bull, you hear me? That bull's crazy. I love you so much."

Josephine hesitated.

"I love you, too."

He held her hand tighter.

"Damned bull. Kiss me."

The man's lips were cracked. A rattle was growing in his

throat. She looked around to see if anyone was watching. Smoke and gore had blinded the world.

She leaned over and kissed him. But he spoke no more. She withdrew and looked at him. He was dead.

To distract herself, Libby thought of her favorite scents as she knelt down and peered at face after face. Cinnamon. Lavender. Lemon rinds. Even the harsh scent of lye could have hollowed out a breathing place. Black powder covered the skin, and the lips were black from biting cartridges. She had always been squeamish about the sight of blood. Now she could find something to make her shriek every second step, and this gout of horror left her bewildered, each image colliding with the next one: every possible variety of shocking wound, every pose of a dead man, every body part that could be separated, every sad story. She had seen a boy, a flag-bearer not past eleven or twelve, his skin the color of milk, scattered freckles, a death wince that revealed a chipped tooth. Her senses began to shut down, the wounds no longer shouted out a story but retreated into pattern, more of an explanation for the stillness of a body or the blankness of an eye. Her body felt cold, her hands and feet numb. And the stories and the wounds dwindled down to nothing, to just the task: not Arden, not Arden, not Arden.

Libby dropped to her knees, trembling. The battlefield went silent, and all its characters retreated back as though swept away by a gust of wind. The dead man had Arden's blond hair and high cheekbones, but his face was so black with gunpowder that Libby couldn't be sure of his identity. She took a breath and searched his pockets, finding a pint bottle filled with brown liquid. She unscrewed the cap, poured the pungent contents of the bottle onto her handkerchief and washed his face, the skin clearing from the whiskey bath until she saw the pale features of a stranger. Her body slumped in relief.

The dead man's eyes flew open, and he seized her wrist.

She gasped and tried to wrench herself free, but he tightened his grip, pulled her close, and pleaded, *"Write down my name!"*

The Union soldiers had tried to enter the West Woods but had been met with withering gunfire from the Stonewall Brigade and had fallen in a line. From a bird's-eye view, the position of their bodies suggested a tidiness of fate. The landscape, a testament to the limitations of shelter: dead men behind skinny trees or hunkered down behind outcroppings of limestone. It was late afternoon. An hour before, Josephine had left Libby searching at the edge of the woods and ventured alone farther within it. The birdsong had fallen from the trees, and the animals had vanished. All that remained were the fallen men. The dead had begun to bloat, and the wounded still waited for field surgeons, calling out in agony.

Josephine peered into face after face, beginning to believe that it was impossible to locate one particular soldier in such a large theater of chaos and death. But something caught her eye in the near distance, in the center of a circle of trees. A soldier lay on his back, his head resting on a log and his hat off to one side. She approached the man and dropped to one knee. She could not believe the good fortune, or the bad, of finding him after all these hours.

Arden.

He was still breathing, but he'd been shot in the lower belly; his intestines were pushing from the wound and covered with flies. She waved her hand frantically and the flies scattered.

He opened his eyes and studied her. "Josephine." His voice held no familiarity for her. He could have been saying her name or simply three syllables in a row that sounded similar. There was no love in his voice, no hatred. His lips trembled as he struggled to speak. "What are you doing here?"

"Libby and I came to find you."

"You are both mad," he mumbled. "Did you put Libby up to this?"

"Of course not. She came by her own stubborn will."

"Where is she?"

"Also in these woods somewhere."

Josephine craned her neck, searching for Libby through the dim woods. "Libby!" she shouted. "He's here! Come here, Libby!"

He touched her arm, stopping her.

"Wait." He closed his eyes as a wave of agony swept through him. He coughed and a line of blood ran from his mouth.

"How do I look?"

The question caught her by surprise. He was a ghastly sight: the fresh line of blood moving in a trail away from the corner of his mouth, the crusted blood of his stomach wound, the flies, the profusion of intestines — his condition would cause even a man to faint with horror and would have made Josephine faint had she not already seen worse sights all afternoon.

She forced herself to look into his eyes, still blue and still — for the moment — sharp with light.

"Fine," she said.

Libby thought she heard Josephine calling her.

"Josephine!" she called back, but got no answer. She had made it fifty yards into the woods and was standing near the dead body of a young Rebel she had already ascertained was not Arden. She sidestepped the corpse and began running in the direction of Josephine's voice, confused as to how to proceed.

"Josephine!" she called. "Where are you? Answer me, Josephine."

A terrible certainty had started up inside her. Some agonizing premonition that would not let go. She began to run deeper into the dim woods, past trees gouged with grapeshot, fallen branches, strewn haversacks, dead and dying men.

"Josephine! Josephine!"

She passed by a fallen soldier, and as she ran by, he grabbed her dress, halting her progress.

"Please, ma'am," the soldier said. "May I have some water?"

With all her strength, she wrenched her skirt free of his desperate grasp and ran on, increasingly frantic, her stomach in knots and the woods crackling beneath her feet.

Finally, up ahead, she saw the clearing and her sister and the fallen man. She knew it was Arden before she reached them. Josephine said nothing as she leaned down and took his hand. His lips were parted, his blue eyes wide open, staring at the sky between the leaves of the oak trees.

"Arden," Libby whispered.

"I'm sorry," Josephine said. Libby looked at her while her words sank in, noting, as though from a great, fuzzy distance, a fresh scrape on Josephine's cheek.

Libby returned her gaze to Arden, unable to believe the sight before her.

She ran her fingers through his hair, leaning down to kiss his face, his forehead and cheeks and brow. "Josephine, did he say anything?"

"Nothing." Her older sister's voice sounded strange, disembodied. As though this all was a dream from which only the trees would awaken.

Libby stroked her dead husband's face. "But his body is still warm." She touched the blood on the side of his mouth and showed Josephine her fingertips. "And, look, his blood is fresh!"

"I'm sorry," said Josephine. "He was dead when I found him."

6

Libby stuck her shovel into the earth, bending her knees to lift the load. The night was warm for September, and perspiration had soaked through her clothes. Josephine hovered a few feet away, pleading for her to please come back in the house. She had tried to stop her, making a lunge at the shovel handle, but Libby had roughly pushed her away, and she had retreated to the edge of the yard but continued to call to her.

"Libby, leave that Yankee's grave alone! What good will this do? Please stop! I'm begging you!"

Libby ignored her. A breeze moved through the orchard, and two ripe apples fell in unison. Stars of different variants shared the sky, some so bright as to hurt the eyes, others unremarkable.

Libby hadn't been able to bring Arden's body home. Anyone with a wagon who lived within a ten-mile radius had already been bribed. Near the Sunken Road, a Parrott shell had hit an apiary, and the riled-up bees had poured out onto the battlefield. Libby had seen the aftermath, all those furious bees, and imagined herself as one of them, her anger never dissipating into the love of nectar or flight. This was an anger that stayed, a buzzing restless heat. Libby lifted the shovel again, the motion causing a deep pain in her chest. The dirt flew over the top of the pile and landed in a patch of wild bergamot that grew by the split-rail fence. The grave was thigh-deep now. Three feet down, her shovel hit cloth. She dropped to her knees and scooped out the dirt with her bare hands as the form of a body took shape.

Libby's father and brother had been watching her work

through the back window of the house. Neither could sleep and so they stood there together, Stephen appropriating a regal posture and Dr. Beale re-cocking his arthritic hip each time it stiffened.

"You should sleep, son."

"It's too hot."

Dirt flew out of the grave in all directions. Finally Libby climbed out, holding on to a piece of winding-sheet and trying to tug the body after her.

"Stephen," said Dr. Beale, "you told me you buried that Yankee deep."

"I got tired."

Out in the yard, the winding-sheet had torn. Libby held a piece of it in her hand.

"What do you suppose she's going to do with him?" Dr. Beale asked.

"I don't know. Probably drag him to Julia Caldwell's yard."

Dr. Beale sighed. "Well, she can't pull that man out of the grave by herself. Go help her."

"*Help* her? You're not going to try to stop her?"

"You tell me, Stephen, why you think I can stop anything."

Arden's family held a memorial service for him in their back garden, under a lemon tree whose branches were empty. A row of cross vines bloomed orange along the back fence, bright and scentless like a sudden memory. The neighbors had brought over ginger cakes and cursed the war by shaking their heads. And the preacher from the First Baptist church, whose sanctuarial grounds were torn up with new graves, showed up with his Bible and tried his best. But his clothes were worn; his toes showed from the end of his shoes; his hair needed cutting.

To Libby, who said not a word but stood silently among the mourners, the preacher seemed much more suited to be a supplicant of God than a diplomat of His word, and the sight of him — Bible propped open under the light of early fall, eyes squinting through unbalanced spectacles — made her ache inside all the more, seeing in him a boy, a child, innocent in the world, vulnerable to the very things against which he claimed protection. She didn't cry. The very thought of it terrified her, as the thought of an impending labor terrifies a narrow-hipped woman. She was still so full of rage that the night before she had contemplated sneaking into town and burning down the medical building where John Brown's body was rumored to have been kept. But along with the rage now was an ever-growing exhaustion. She found herself nodding off and then jerking back to consciousness. And in those moments of quickly snatched sleep, she remembered him and he was real to her as though he were still alive: scent of the body, feeling of fabric, texture of oiled hair, shape of muscle under flesh, warmth of neck, roughness of a scrape on his arm. His lips touching hers in the dimness of their room. The urgency of his voice in her ear, *We will win this war, Libby, and we will have many children* . . .

By the end of the service, she was almost too exhausted to stand. She went to her room, crawled into her bed, and stayed there. Her sister knocked on the door. Her plaintive voice came through the wood. "You have to eat. At least drink some beef broth."

Josephine wouldn't give up. She kept knocking.

Libby ignored the sound. A suspicion nagged her grief without explanation, like a pull in the fabric of a black coat. She was sure Josephine was keeping something from her.

Meanwhile, her older sister was growing frantic, recognizing that Libby was showing some of the symptoms she'd had when she nearly died years before, though she knew this time it wasn't blackwater fever: the refusal to eat, the torpor and the sleeping, the lifeless voice and dull eyes.

"Please, Mother," Josephine said, "don't let her die."

"She's not going to die," Violet assured her, as she applied witch hazel on a cotton ball to the slightly infected scrape on Josephine's cheek. "She's not the only one to lose someone in the war. Mrs. Fenley lost two sons on the same day."

But late at night, from her bedroom, the sound of the more worried and fragile woman Violet let herself be in the presence of her husband floated up through the gravity vent.

"This is not just grieving, William. This is something darker. I fear our daughter is going mad."

"Allow a few more days. Perhaps she will recover."

"I don't know what to do."

"She's a strong woman."

"No, Libby is fragile. Not of body, but of mind. Even when she was a small child, I worried about how she took things to heart."

After a week passed, Mrs. Beale made Libby get out of bed and took her to volunteer to help with the injured soldiers at the Taylor Hotel. Dr. Beale and Josephine argued that it was too soon, but Violet was adamant.

"She is not getting better. She can't just languish away. She has to be strong. And taking care of others will keep her mind off her own troubles."

"I'll go with her," said Josephine.

"No, we need you here. Let her do this alone."

Winchester had no shortage of men that September. The Confederate army had abandoned its bold plan to invade the North after the carnage at Sharpsburg and slipped back across the river into Virginia a few days later. Stragglers lined the streets and glutted the parlors of houses, distinguished by their sunburned skin, tattered clothes, wounds and lesions. They looked surprised. They had thought for sure they were going to whip those Yankees. Somehow they had not, nor had they died in battle and gone to their glory. Instead they became men they had never dreamed of being—shot and stabbed and broken and missing limbs, tormented by dysentery and rising fevers.

Yankees and chiggers and fate. They had lost to everything. Those who weren't bedridden moped around outside, no longer waiting for battle but news of one. They lounged outside the Taylor Hotel, which had been converted into a hospital, playing dominoes and whittling or staring into space, their vacant eyes matching those of the newest volunteer, Libby Tanner, who washed the floors and fetched bandages and cleaned instruments and barely spoke at all, dutiful, gentle—and, deep inside, somewhere else entirely.

Libby was soaking some instruments in a zinc tub, the water turning pink as flakes of clotted blood floated lazily to the surface, when she heard about the boy. She dried a Nélaton probe and listened as two volunteer nurses stood talking nearby. She had been here a few days and done a passable job, though sometimes, lost in dreamy grief, she had to be told twice to change a bed linen or fetch a curette. But at this very moment, she found herself quite alert and listening intently.

"Impossible," one of them was saying. "How could they not know? The boy is twelve!"

"I suppose they didn't care. He could hold a rifle, couldn't he? That's all that matters."

"Will he live?"

"Probably. But his right arm is gone below the elbow."

Libby listened as they continued to talk, so wrapped up in the conversation that the newly polished probe slid out of her loosened grip and dropped back into the water.

Due to his tender age, the boy had been taken from the main hall with its rows and rows of cots and sequestered in room 24 upstairs.

"But surely the doctors would have noticed how young he was during the medical exam?" one of the nurses asked.

The other one snorted. "I've assisted with those exams. They barely take their pulse."

Libby didn't know quite what plan or idea was forming within her. She opened the door to room 24 very quietly and found him propped up on pillows. His hair was dark and cut above the ears. His eyes were closed, his face pale and delicately featured. Libby eased up closer to him, listening to his shallow breaths, studying his face, and then taking in the bandages that covered the stump of his arm.

His eyes flew open. "What do you want?"

Libby thought fast. "I'm here to change your bandages."

"Bullshit. They were just changed. Leave me alone."

Libby sucked in her breath. She had never heard someone that young use that word, and with such defiance.

"Now, get out, get out!"

Cowed by the anger in the boy's voice, Libby was turning to go when he suddenly closed his eyes tight and let out a fierce groan, his body stiffening under the sheet.

Libby turned, moved closer again. "What's the matter?"

"What's the matter?" He groaned again. More tears slid from his eyes, which were still tightly closed. The knuckles on his remaining fist stood out white. "My goddamn arm hurts, that's what's the matter. It feels like it is still there. I can feel my wrist, my hand, my fingertips. Oh my God, I can't stand the pain."

"I'll get the nurse," Libby said, and rushed from the room. She summoned the first nurse she saw and, half an hour later, tiptoed up the stairs again and entered the room, where the boy now sat complacently, lids half-open. He gave Libby a sleepy, satisfied laudanum smile.

Libby sat on the edge of his cot.

"How did they possibly let you join the army?" she asked. "You are obviously younger than the official requirement."

He shook his head. "They didn't care. They need men, and a boy is close enough. They asked how old I was. I said eighteen."

"But didn't a doctor examine you?"

"He looked in my eyes and listened to my heart. He checked to make sure I had two front teeth so I could bite a cartridge. Then he said, 'Welcome to the Army of Northern Virginia.'"

"So they'll accept anyone?"

"They don't ask no questions, ma'am."

His voice had a certain dreamy politeness now. Gone were the swearing and the defiance. The laudanum he'd been given had taken effect.

Libby was fascinated. She desperately hoped they would not be interrupted. "But why did you join up?"

The boy's eyes focused slightly. "They killed my brother."

"Who?"

"The Yankees, that's who." His words were slurred but full of slow venom. "I loved my brother more than anything in the world. So I decided I would join the Rebels and kill eighteen Yankees, one for every year of his life."

"How many did you kill?"

He smiled, held up his remaining hand, showed her his five fingers. Slowly he curled them back down, then raised five more, then two.

"Twelve?"

"Kept count on a hickory stick. One notch for each Yank. Kept the stick in my haversack. Don't know what happened to it."

"And did you feel bad, killing men? Do you have regrets?"

"Oh, yes." He nodded slowly. "I regret that I only killed twelve before I was shot. I don't remember being hit. I woke up in the field hospital. They were sawing off my arm without no morphine."

The door opened behind Libby and she jumped.

A nurse entered, carrying a tray with a dark bottle on it. Her white apron bore spatters of blood. She shot Libby a severe look. "What are you doing here?"

"The boy needed his bandage changed."

"No, he did not. And you need to go."

The boy looked at Libby, his saucer eyes calm. "It was nice meeting you, ma'am," he said, and raised the stump of his arm to offer her an invisible hand, and so persuasive was his utter belief that Libby almost took it.

As she headed down the hallway, the words of the wounded boy came back to Libby: *They don't ask no questions.* Before she reached the bottom of the stairs, her outrageous plan was perfectly formed. It was mad, to be sure. But how mad was the war? How mad was the North's plan to take away the rights of the South? How mad was finding her husband still warm on a battlefield with his intestines spilling out when he was meant to come home alive?

Her new purpose drew the scattered parts of who she was back together. Someone watching her this past week would have seen a pale, thinning woman, barely substantial, like the ghosts all survivors become. Only the tangling of her hair animated her. Her quirks, her vagaries, blazes of temper, rock-hard loyalties, little hidden details of the self, were no longer attached to someone who found them endearing; they simply existed, grasping at something the way pine needles cling to a roof. But here, suddenly, she was whole again, consisting not of gauze or the misty fiber of a cloud, but pure granite. The perfect plan had dropped in her lap, something to marry her anger, her grief, and her love.

She threw herself into the first phase of her new quest: studying men.

"Stephen," she said that night, calling him from the hallway into her room, "Come here."

"What do you want?"

"Just come here."

She knitted her brow as she watched him stroll into the room. "Good," she said. "Now pick something up off the top of the dresser. Now untie your shoes and tie them again. Now brush the hair out of your face. Now shade your eyes and look out the window. Now put your hands in your pockets. Now sit down. Stand up. Lean over and pretend you're petting a dog. See that book on the shelf? Open it and turn the pages."

Stephen obeyed her until his impatience overtook his entertainment over the mysterious new game. "You're crazy," he said, and left the room.

Over the following days, she studied the gestures of the opposite sex, carefully noting the way they walked, handled sticks, lifted forks, fastened belt buckles, and turned doorknobs. She watched the tilt of her father's head, the way Stephen pulled at the collar of his Sunday shirt, spat on the ground, and flinched when his mother dug her nails in his arm.

She took careful note of the wounded soldiers who lounged around the Taylor Hotel. They leaned on rails, relaxed in doorways. Scratched their necks. They had a tendency to chuckle with their teeth locked and slap at mosquitoes with reckless force. They liked to throw things to each other . . . anything. Apples, dice, even a folded newspaper, taking the chance it would open and fly like a bird. Cards meant a lot to them, as did brandy. They rested on their haunches, chewed on grass, snorted and grunted for no reason at all, would not say a word for hours and then suddenly, defiantly, would sing an old camp song or laugh at the antics of a dog. The surgeons who came outside the hotel to smoke cigarettes took longer puffs when their smocks were bloody.

Without fail, the Quaker man who lived across the street looked up at the sky just before he answered his wife's beckoning screech. And Dr. Beale's eyes narrowed when he pulled a tooth.

And Arden. Of course, Arden. His long-strided walk. His hands swinging. The looseness of his spine and hips. The way his body changed when he hoisted himself onto the back of a horse. That dominance, that grace. The way he wet his fingertip and collected loose granules of sugar from a tabletop, or grabbed at a blade of grass to stick in his mouth, or idly peeled bark off a tree as he leaned against it. The natural world was his to paw and peel and lick and worry, like he owned it.

Twenty-one. The number of men who would pay for his death. As a woman, she loved the poetry in that equation; as a man, she loved the rage.

Her family — with the exception of Stephen, who was in his own world like any other fourteen-year-old boy — was greatly encouraged by Libby's new vitality.

"The color is coming back into your face!" Josephine exclaimed in a thrilled voice. "And you're eating!"

"See?" Mrs. Beale said. "No matter the burden, God gives us the strength to face it."

Libby only smiled. "Yes," she said, "He does."

That night, after everyone in the family had fallen asleep, Libby lit a kerosene lantern and stole out of the house and crept through the dark town to the little A-frame house she had shared with Arden before the war. The air was cold and carried an odor of sweet smoke, as though someone had been burning a fire using old pine needles as kindling.

She passed Arden's old house on the way to theirs. He had been the eldest son, the adored one, and she'd seen grief weigh down that family. Their speech was unhurried and dull, and they walked in and out of church as though walking were a great burden to be borne by survivors. The way the father pulled out and checked his pocket watch had slowed. And the sticks his brothers drew down split-rail fences made deliberate, somber slaps. Now they were probably all calling Arden's name slowly in their sleep. She knew how they all felt. Until she had met the young boy soldier with the missing arm, she had slowed too.

She reached the edge of town and stood before the house that had been bought with her dowry. So much more humble than the Hudson River Gothic Revival she'd grown up in, where every room had a chimney and a five-octave grand piano sat in the parlor. And yet she'd loved it here, waiting for Arden to come home from his job at the mill. She took a key out of her pocket and put it in the lock. Keys had not been necessary before the war. The town had felt safe, and even the deaths that arrived had done so with warning. Old people died in bed. Young people died of typhus. Women died in childbirth. But thousands of young men and boys did not die suddenly in the course of an afternoon, their bodies forming mountains.

She entered the house and moved through the rooms, letting the light of the lantern fall over what would never be seen again without a certain stabbing pain: the hobnailed cups still sitting on the gate-leg table, the smooth pine boards, the simple ascot curtains, and the pencil-post bed, perfectly made and waiting for their return.

She hunted in their chest of drawers until she found an old pair of his trousers. She recognized them by feel. Remembered how solid his knee once felt inside the pant leg as they rested in the shade. Now the pants were empty of that man. She moved on to the wardrobe, where she retrieved one of his shirts and his worn brogans. A pair of his old socks and her task was complete. She did not allow herself to touch the bed or run her fingers across the teeth of an old comb of his she found in a drawer. She could spend a year there remembering him. But she had work to do.

The next night, Libby stood in the backyard of her parents' house, her long hair wild around her shoulders, bathed in a midnight glow that did not come from the sky but from some angel activity or friction of leaves. She moved the knife from one hand to the other. Tonight she felt no pain, only a sweet kind of wistfulness in which memories are constant and soft. An open moon would have revealed pupils the size of marbles. Inside her father's study, a bottle of laudanum sat open on his desk. She had seen laudanum provide courage to men without legs and to children whose bloody teeth were being yanked out by her father's tooth key. Now she needed it for a bloodless operation that would begin her transformation from woman to man.

The knife flickered in the light when she moved it from one hand to the other.

"Arden," she said, and raised the knife.

The air in Josephine's room was warm but not hot, perfect for dreams that evoke visions of things so ordinary they can be found in a kitchen cupboard. She lay on her back, her hands folded across her chest, dreaming of eating horehound candy in the foyer of her house. Yellow dust drifted through the open window, moving into her nose and mouth when she took a breath. Her nightgown had tangled up under the covers. These small discomforts made her frown in her sleep.

She finished the candy but not the dream. She was walking up the stairs now, to the second landing. She heard the wounded Yankee soldier — the one who died of gangrene — calling her from his room. She opened his door and found him sitting up in bed, alive.

"Aren't you proud of me?" he asked.

"Proud of you? For what?"

"I killed him."

Josephine followed his gaze. Arden sat slumped in a chair, dead, his arm shattered, intestines protruding from his stomach wound. He opened his eyes.

"How do I look?"

Josephine's own scream awakened her. She sat up in bed, bathed in sweat and gasping. She heard footsteps coming down the hallway and stopping in front of her door. She drew the covers up to her chest.

"Who's there?" she asked, shaking, wishing she were still dreaming but knowing she was not.

The doorknob began to turn.

She reached over to the night table and fumbled for a match. She had just lit the kerosene lamp when the door opened and Arden walked into the room, wearing a shirt whose sleeves were too long for him and a pair of baggy trousers. He was gaunt and pale, but the flies were gone and the hole in his belly had disappeared. Her body shook violently. She tried to scream but couldn't.

"Arden," she gasped.

He sat down on the edge of her bed, the weight of his body pulling at her sheets. He leaned toward her, his pupils unnaturally large.

"No," he said, "it's Libby."

Libby sat on a wingchair and watched her sister strip the bed. Occasionally she would move her hand up and feel the results of her butcher-knife haircut. It was longer on one side. She would have to fix that.

"Look what you made me do!" Josephine said. "This is my only set of sheets."

"They'll dry."

Libby's voice perfectly mimicked that of her dead husband, but the laudanum she'd taken made Arden sound dreamy and forgiving.

"Where did you get those clothes?"

"They belonged to Arden when he was younger. He left them at our house when he joined the army."

"They're too big for you."

"I'll manage."

Josephine wadded up the sheets and put them on the washing stand. "You can't join the Stonewall Brigade. That's a crazy idea. You won't fool anyone."

"I fooled you."

"It's dark."

"Don't you remember the battlefield, Josephine? Some of those dead boys were so pretty. Such pale skin and such long eyelashes. They looked more like girls than we do. And I've been studying men. I know how to talk and walk and move just like they do. And I suppose I've studied Arden for years." Libby stood and stretched, pushing her hands toward the ceiling in a gesture perfectly copied from her dead husband.

Josephine looked horrified. "Do you want to die like Arden? On the battlefield, covered in flies?"

Libby felt a sudden surge of anger move through the laudanum haze like a spear through a cloud of butterflies. "You were probably happy that he died."

"Libby! That's a terrible thing to say. I did not wish his death."

"Liar," Libby whispered, knowing that the laudanum both softened her words and sharpened their effect.

"It doesn't matter whether I hated him or not. He's dead, and you won't change that by going to war. And even if you could, you are not well, Libby. If Arden were alive, he wouldn't want you to fight. He'd want you to be safe."

"How do you know what he would want? He'd be happy to know I'm out hunting Yankees. I'm going to kill twenty-one of them. One for every year of his life."

Josephine was eyeing her. "Your breasts look flat as a board."

Libby looked down. "I bound them with muslin. Arden always complained that they were too small. He'd be amused to find that their very size turned out to be of help to me."

"But the medical exams."

"I've heard of the medical exams. Someone told me they hold a candle to one ear, and if light does not come out the other ear, you pass."

Josephine didn't smile.

"But what about the call of nature?"

"Woods are all around."

"And your monthly flow?"

"I'll make do."

"Libby, you are not strong. You are crazy with grief. This is a mad scheme, and if on some miracle your deceit is accepted, you will get hurt. You do not know how to shoot a rifle or make a fire. You do not know anything except how to be a woman, and that will be of no use to you at all."

Josephine's words meant nothing to Libby. The laudanum ate them and left only their tone. "I'll write you, Josephine. Just like he wrote me."

Her sister shook her head and sighed. "I tried to help you. You've left me no choice." She opened her mouth, but Libby was on her in the blink of an eye, clapping a hand over her incipient scream.

"You call Mother and Father in here," Libby warned her, "and they'll try to keep me a prisoner in this house. But I will escape, sooner or later. You know I will. And when I return from the war, I will never speak to you again."

Libby dropped her hand, and Josephine let her breath out. "I would accept such a punishment if you returned from the war whole. But how can you? You aren't leaving whole. If you insist on going, I'm going with you."

"Of course you are not."

"Yes, I am. There is nothing you can say to make me not follow you."

Libby allowed herself a small smile.

"You're going to help me kill twenty-one Yankees?"

"No. I'm going to keep twenty-one Yankees from killing you."

October 4, 1862

Dear Mother and Father,

 Libby and I cannot stand by while courageous men like Arden lose their lives for our cause. We will serve our Confederacy the only way that we can, by finding a hospital in which to serve as nurses. We will return to you safely once this war is done.

Ever your loving daughter,
Josephine

October 6, 1862

Dear Sir,

Yours is but one hospital of many throughout Virginia I have written in search of my daughters, Libby Tanner and Josephine Beale, who left our home clandestinely to offer their help as nurses. We had reports that they may be bound for Richmond.

They are respectable young ladies, with character and virtue above reproach. Their zeal for our great Confederacy, coupled with my younger daughter's grief over the loss of her husband, has caused them a lapse in judgment, but their intentions are sincere.

I am certain that you can imagine the dreadful worry that grips a father's heart when the safety of his children is in question, particularly those of the timid gender. I would be forever in your debt if you could send me good news that they are with you and safe; and I will immediately travel to Richmond to collect them.

Cordially,

Dr. William Beale

They hid in an abandoned church a mile past the edge of town, practicing their craft and living off a loaf of bread and some dried pork Libby had taken from the smokehouse. The church had been taken over by the Union army, who laid planks across the pews to perform amputations after the Battle of Winchester. Afterward they had used it as a place of residence for one of the regiments. The Yankees had gotten drunk one night and wrecked it, breaking the windows and carving their names in the pulpit. The cross was chopped up into firewood. Their angry officers had banished the sinners from the church, and now it stood empty, even after Jackson's brigade had driven the Yankees out of town. No one wanted to sing and worship in a sanctuary that reeked of dried vomit and urine. Under that roof, the girls committed their own brand of sacrilege, speaking in lower registers and practicing the gestures of the opposite sex.

Libby seemed effortless in her role. Josephine had a bit more trouble.

"Drink from this canteen," Libby said. "No, not that way. Tilt your head. Throw your head back and gulp. Let some water spill out the sides. Men have no manners."

Josephine tried again. "Yes, that's more like it," Libby said approvingly, "Now, catch." A cartridge came sailing toward her face. Josephine threw her hands up to block it.

"No," Libby said, "men catch things fearlessly. Try again."

The amputations had left the stone floor as gory as a battlefield. More blood speckled the walls. A bladder bag filled with tobacco sat atop the pulpit, and a mound of unused cartridges made a pile in the far corner. The women slept on pillows made of discarded haversacks and played with a deck of cards that was missing all of its queens.

When Libby was satisfied with Josephine's training, she made her cast off her dress in favor of Stephen's clothes. Libby had found them laid out to be washed the night the girls left home, and so it was these filthy clothes that Josephine had to wear. Josephine felt repulsed as she put on her brother's clothes and his mud-covered brogans, which had not been allowed inside the house but now seemed to fit perfectly inside this fetid church.

Libby inspected her.

"They fit about right," she said at last.

"They smell bad," Josephine said.

"We may as well get used to it. We won't be able to bathe and groom ourselves, not for a long time."

Josephine was grateful for the nod of approval, even though she felt wretched and ugly and stripped of nearly everything that made her feminine. She had never felt pretty. And now all the things she'd done to try and be more attractive were being stripped from her—the lace, the dress, the grosgrain ribbon. The cream she rubbed into her skin to make it soft and smooth. Every attempt to be a young woman had been stamped out now. She had never felt so ugly, so undesirable to the men whose attentions she had desperately hoped for. All she had left was her light, long hair, the same hair she had spent hours washing, preening, brushing and fixing. She felt tears start in the corners of her eyes when Libby picked up the knife.

"Are you sure you are willing to do this?" Libby asked.

Josephine stood miserable in her brother's clothes, the shoes heavy on her feet, her body sweating, her chest bound in muslin so as to flatten any hint of breasts. Her breasts were larger than Libby's, and the deception took more muslin and tighter binding.

"Is there nothing I can say to persuade you to stop this madness and go home?" Josephine asked.

"You know the answer."

"Then cut my hair," she ordered, as the first tears ran down her face. She stood perfectly still as Libby took a hank and began sawing. The freed strands dropped on the bloodstained floor. Light and a partial breeze came through the broken window.

Josephine wiped her eyes. "Keep going."

When they left that ruined church, Josephine left a pile of her long hair, her dress, and her name. She was now Joseph, and Libby was Thomas. She was glad she had no mirror to reflect back what she had become.

October 1862

Bunker Hill, Virginia

He was a shabby, bearded figure, wearing an old slouch hat and taking bad posture in the saddle. The buttons of his jacket had been torn off by female admirers for souvenirs; strands of his pony's tail had been yanked out for the same reason. He had a wide forehead and the shape of his lower face seemed to grow narrower over time. There was something comical about his visage: the nose, eyes, and mouth a Calvinist trio, but the ears a joke passed down a marching line. At the Virginia Military Institute, where he had been a professor, students drew caricatures of his enormous feet on the blackboards. Now those same students rushed into battle shouting his name.

Some thought him mad. He wouldn't eat pepper because he believed it made his right leg weak, sometimes held one arm straight up to balance himself, and liked to suck on lemons during battle. His wrinkled uniform made him half-general, half-wretch. He didn't send letters on certain days of the week, for fear they might be in transit on a Sunday.

He was Stonewall Jackson, and those who thought he simply obeyed the will of General Lee were wrong. He had buried his first wife and two babies, sinking the spade under God's direction. He took his orders from a wet Bible that lay in a leaky tent. The caress of the New Testament, the puncture wound of the Old. He had moved his brigade to Bunker Hill, restoring his troops to health and making plans he neglected to share. The Valley Pike loomed, macadamized and packed on each side with crushed limestone.

Bunker Hill was tantalizingly close to Winchester, a town dear to Jackson's heart. He had set up headquarters there the winter before, in a T-shaped house near the top of Braddock Street. The bachelor who owned the house had been incapacitated at Manassas, a minor discomfort when compared to the incredible fortune of having Jackson under his roof.

Jackson's wife, Anna, had come to Winchester to meet him, and they had stayed together at the manse of a Presbyterian minister. The Jacksons slept in the upstairs bedroom at the northeast corner of the house. At night, when they were alone, Anna touched his hands and ran her fingertips over his face. One night they closed the door after a dinner of roast beef, corn bread, and buttermilk. He lit the fire and undressed her. His finesse with the buttons spoke of much practice. Outside, frost hung in the trees. The persimmons on the ground were hard as stones. Cattle stood in the fallen snow. The windows rattled.

Naked and glowing by firelight, Jackson's pleasant-faced wife transformed into something so beautiful it took his breath away. Their time together would torture him later. Worse than exhaustion, hunger, or the smell of death would be the memory of her body beneath him, warming every part of him. Chest to chest, belly to belly. He moved his lips from her cheek to her mouth, then down her neck. In the backyard, a branch broke off a dogwood tree, fell onto the roof, and then slid down the house, scraping against it like the bristle of a beard. The fire crackled and sent sparks up the chimney.

"Thomas," she said, "I'm afraid."

"You have no reason to be."

"I don't want you to die. I couldn't bear it."

"Other wives do."

"I don't care what other wives do."

"If I die, it is God's will."

The bed creaked. The headboard tapped the wall. In a room nearby, Jackson's staff were sleeping. They heard the sounds and opened their eyes. Impossible. Sex was the joy of mortal men. When she left Winchester, Anna was pregnant with his child.

Bunker Hill was busy. Four drills a day, ninety minutes each. In between the drills, the soldiers wrote letters, boiled rye coffee, and played checkers. They were a sad-looking lot, badly dressed and hungry and weary of war. Some of them coughed persistently, and some had rose-colored spots on their skin that turned white at the press of a finger. Lice tormented them, making popping sounds when the clothing they infested was held over a campfire. So many soldiers had died or deserted. Thousands of wounded lingered in Winchester, nursed by the local women and crammed into hospitals converted from schools, churches, and even the courthouse.

The South needed reinforcements. Boys too young, men too old.

The camp had been set up in an orderly grid, the parade grounds on the opposite side of the officers' quarters, supply wagons parked in the middle. The sisters stood outside the surgeon's tent, two sweating frauds who felt weak in the knees at the thought of being examined. Another man came out of the surgeon's tent. The sisters moved forward in line. The day was hot for early October, the late afternoon sunlight still so fierce it seemed to penetrate their clothes and reveal their true figures to the world. Sweat dripped down Josephine's face. She wiped it away with her fingertips. Libby noticed the feminine gesture and looked at her in disapproval.

"Wipe with the back of your hand," she admonished in a

whisper. "And then fling the sweat away, even if there isn't any, and make a face like you're annoyed."

"I can't remember all this."

"Men aren't ladylike. That's all you need to know."

"We will never get past the doctor."

"He won't suspect us. The soldiers who go into that tent leave quickly. The doctor can't be looking very closely."

Josephine took a deep breath and felt the binding stretch across her breasts.

Finally they were ushered in by a harried-looking recruiting officer.

"What are your names?" the doctor asked.

"I'm Thomas Holden," Libby said. She pointed to Josephine. "And this is my cousin, Joseph Holden."

"You boys from Winchester?"

"No. Shiloh."

"Shiloh? Shiloh's not a town. It's a battle."

Josephine thought she might faint from the anxiety. Libby had decided on the name "Shiloh" to honor Arden's hometown.

"Shiloh is near Fredericksburg," Libby shot back. "I think I should know where I'm from."

"What are you two boys doing all the way out here, then?"

"Joseph's folks died when we were kids, and he came to live with us. My pa didn't want us in the war, so he moved us west after First Manassas. Pa died last month, so we came to join up," Libby said.

Josephine was impressed not only with the arrogant, calm way her sister spoke, but with the register of her voice. Had she not known Libby was female, she could have sworn an insolent young man stood in her place.

The doctor looked Libby up and down. "You and your cousin are pretty small. You're the size of boys, not men."

"We may not be very tall, but we can fight just fine."

The doctor sighed and motioned to Josephine. "Come here, Joseph. I don't bite."

He took her hand. It seemed to cause him some suspicion. Perhaps the palms were too soft or the knuckles too delicate. He looked her square in the face with a you-don't-fool-me expression that put a knot in her stomach.

"How old are you?"

The knot dissolved and then grew again as a different concern. Her gender wasn't in question after all. Only her age. Someone with her delicate features must have looked like a child.

Libby answered for her. "We're both eighteen."

The doctor exchanged looks with his assistant and sighed. "Well, I've been ordered to believe you. You got two arms and two legs, and that makes you soldier material. I guess you boys never think of your mothers and how they'd feel if you were killed. Either one of you ever had malaria or pneumonia?"

Libby spoke up again. "We're both healthy as horses."

"Measles? Typhoid?"

"No."

The doctor glared at Libby. "Your cousin speak at all?"

"Not much."

The doctor pressed the disk of his stethoscope against Josephine's chest. "Breathe. Now, again. Now hold out your palms."

Josephine held out her hands, and the doctor took them in his own, pressing on her fingers.

"Good color," he said. "You're not dead. Welcome to the Army of Northern Virginia."

The soldier who led them to their company wore spectacles and didn't have a hair on his head. He seemed bored, or tired. He was a thin man; his jacket hung off his frame, and his pants were too big for him. Libby and Josephine stumbled behind him, weighed down with their guns and gear and uniforms.

He carried a half-whittled stick and used it to gesture at the supply wagon. "You need anything, ask them. They don't got nothing."

"I thought we were going to get Enfields," Libby said.

"Sorry. Converted flintlocks are all we got, for the moment. And we don't got any shoes. You two are lucky you have shoes of your own. A lot of the men are barefoot."

No one stirred in the camp, but in the distance could be heard music and sharp commands.

"What's happening over there?" Josephine asked.

"Dress parade. That's what we do every day at six o'clock. We've got to look good. Of course, our general looks like hell. That's a god's prerogative." He pointed his stick again without breaking his stride. "Over there is what they call the sinks. That's where you answer the call of nature. Only, no one wants to go over there. Take a deep breath through your nose and you'll notice why. I think the boys dug the trench too shallow. Most everyone goes to the woods. More privacy, and the cardinal flowers are lovely this time of year. You know, there's an unwritten rule between Confederates and Yankees never to kill an enemy soldier while he's relieving himself. But don't count on that. Rules are made to be broken."

"Where do we bathe?" asked Josephine.

"There's a river yonder, on the other side of those trees and down a slope, if you can get to it through the blackberry vines and the scrub trees. Funny, most of the fellows don't make much of an effort. Then when winter comes, some of them stop bathing till spring. They hate the cold water. They turn into cats in December."

He stopped in front of a small tent. "This is all you got right now for shelter. This and your oilcloths. You should be grateful. Most everyone else don't got nothing but the cold hard ground. Two boys from your company stole this tent from a dead Yankee a week before they died themselves at Second Manassas. Then two other boys got it. They went down at Sharpsburg. No one else wants to use it. Too superstitious, I guess. But you don't believe in that foolishness, do you?"

"Of course not," Libby said.

Josephine eyed the tent.

"We get a lot of our supplies from dead Yankees, in fact," the man continued. "Blankets, haversacks, brandy, good socks. Sometimes we find dried beef." He swept his arm around. "This is your company. D as in dog. You'll be fighting alongside boys from Harrisonburg, Charlestown, and Winchester."

Libby and Josephine exchanged glances.

"No, never mind," he corrected himself. "We don't got any Winchester boys anymore. Six of 'em got killed, two got wounded, and the other two deserted. You boys ain't gonna desert, are you?"

"Deserters are cowards," Libby said. "They should all be hanged."

"We don't string up deserters. We shoot 'em, if General Jackson's in the mood. You can never tell with him." A gust of wind came up, and his pants flapped soundlessly against his legs. He winced and took his glasses off and rubbed his right eye with the back of his sleeve, noticed it was dusty as well, and pulled a handkerchief from his pocket to finish the job. "Damned dust," he said. "I never get used to it."

The sun went down. The tent darkened. The light of campfires glowed through cotton twilling. Libby heard voices and dogs barking. Her stomach was a knot of fear. She did not know if the man in her was ready or would simply devolve into womanly gestures or girlish tears. She recalled the walk of Arden as he strolled down an unpaved street with his hands in his pockets, the vision so clear that it tore at her heart and she was forced to blink it away. Libby's new woolen trousers scratched her legs. Her shell jacket was too wide in the shoulders and her belt was too loose, although she had cinched it to the very last hole.

Josephine sat next to her, tying and retying her shoes. The laces groaned as she tightened them.

"This is crazy, Libby. This will never work. We will be found out and sent home."

"We passed the inspection."

"They didn't care who we were. They just need men. And we aren't men."

"Stop saying you aren't a man. You have to believe you are. Think like one. Speak like one. Dream like one."

"I don't want to be a man."

"Then, go home."

They heard a voice outside calling hello. A lean young man appeared at one opening of their tent, his sand-colored hair illuminated by his lantern. The light made their muskets shine.

"I'm Wesley Abeline," he said. "Who are you?"

"I'm Thomas," Libby said. "And this is Joseph. We're cousins."

Wesley reached into the tent to shake their hands. Libby made sure her grip was strong and was rewarded with a slight wince from Wesley.

"Where you from?" he asked.

"Shiloh."

"Shiloh the battle?"

"No, Shiloh, near Fredericksburg."

"We used to have an aunt who lived in Fredericksburg. She had a pet hen. It would eat salamanders out of her hand. Now come on out. You're about to miss supper."

Campfires were blazing, sputtering, and crackling, the flames just as yellow as in peacetime. Some soldiers cooked meat on bayonets. Arden had tasted that meat. He had sat among men like these, heard this music, smelled this smoke. Libby had to force herself from imagining him watching her as she went by. Those eyes would have known her. She forced her shoulders straight and walked in a measured step. Josephine looked around as though absorbing every detail, and Libby wished a little more for Josephine's curiosity, a genderless trait that would raise no suspicions.

Wesley led them to a campfire where three men sat on ammunition boxes and ate soup out of tin cups. Wesley made the introductions.

Floyd had snow-white hair and an expressive brow. He seemed too old to fight, but his handshake was firm. Lewis was small and hard-eyed. He was Wesley's brother, it turned out, but didn't have his light skin or easy laugh. Matthew was the most striking of the three. Instead of a shell jacket, he wore a buckskin shirt. One side of his hat was pinned up, and a red feather was stuck in the fold. He took off his hat and revealed a head of blond hair, cut shingle-style.

Libby tried to imitate their gestures as she shook each man's hand. Any second, she feared, one would stare at her closely and say: *You do not belong here.* But no one said these things. They believed that the Southern cause was true, that Stonewall Jackson was God, and that all soldiers were men.

"Floyd's our ancient drummer boy," Wesley said. "He showed up after the Battle of Kernstown, looking for his son."

"His name was Robert," the old man said. "I found him dead in a patch of morning glory. You know, most dead bodies just look dead. But Robert was different. His face looked like marble. So handsome. Not as handsome as Matthew's, but his borders on pretty. No offense, Matthew."

Wesley said, "You know, Floyd, maybe when they shoot you, you'll be handsome for once."

"And maybe when they shoot you, you won't be a smart-ass. Now shut your mouth, vermin. What was I just saying? Oh, yes. I never thought my boy was much for looks, but any woman in the world would have fallen in love with him right then and there. Some sweet girl was waiting for him at home, all set to marry him after the war, but the fact that you love someone don't affect fate one bit. I wanted to fight in Robert's place. But they said I was too old, even for this desperate army, and they made me the drummer boy."

"The drummer dinosaur," Wesley said.

Floyd gave him a sideways look of contempt. "I might be old, but I can pound out the orders. The call to dress parade, forward march, attack — they each have their distinct cadence, and I am faithful to it."

"What happened to the old drummer boy?" Josephine asked. "Was he killed?"

Wesley shook his head. "Naw. His mother showed up and told us he wasn't but eight years old, and dragged him away by the ear. I swear that boy looked twelve." Wesley gestured to Floyd.

"So now we've got the oldest drummer boy in the Southern army. God, does he make a racket!"

"I play the drum better than you play that horrible guitar. I could make a better sound with a chalkboard and the fang of a rattlesnake."

The sullen man, Lewis, finished his soup with a definitive gulp, set his tin cup down next to his feet, and began to scratch his face with the side of his spoon. The metal rasped against his whiskers as his eyes traveled from Josephine to Libby. He pressed the spoon harder, and a patch of skin on his cheek began to flush in the firelight.

"So, boys," Lewis said, "you ready to fight?"

"I'm ready," Libby said.

"You are, huh? Well, what is your level of commitment?"

"Come on, Lewis," Wesley said. "They just got here. They don't need your die-hard Rebel talk."

"All I want to know is, are the new boys here for the South, or are they here for adventure, or to impress some girl, or what have you?"

"I would die for the Southern cause," Libby said, "but I'd rather kill for it."

"All right," Wesley said. "There's your answer, Lewis. Did they give you boys your tin cups? Good. Hand 'em over. And sit down."

He walked away and returned a few minutes later and handed them their steaming cups.

"Soup's good tonight," he said.

Josephine blew on her soup cautiously. Libby took a sip and looked up, puzzled. Something wasn't quite right. Her tongue turned to fire. Her face flushed. Tears ran out of her eyes.

"Wesley," Floyd said, "you didn't pull that red pepper trick on the new boys, did you?"

"Ah, I'm sorry," said Wesley, handing Libby a cup of water. "It's just something we do to welcome the new recruits."

Libby threw the water in his face.

"Hey!" he said.

Libby tackled him. He fell over backward, and she jumped on top of him and raised a fist to punch him in the face. She felt others rising to stop her, grasping at her arm, pulling her off him, but she struggled ferociously, a terrible rage just waiting for the right battle, the right insult, the right spice, to open the door.

The camp had filled with quiet sounds, soldiers praying in whispers, ashes floating off old fires, quill pens scratching on palimpsest. The pickets fidgeted out in the woods.

The sisters had removed their belts and coats, and now lay with their trousers rolled up at the cuffs. Their shirtsleeves were so long, they covered their hands.

"These clothes don't fit," Josephine said.

"Neither do mine. I'm going to steal the pants off the first Yankee I shoot on the battlefield."

Josephine didn't answer. She had not told Libby yet that she would never kill an enemy soldier. She unbuttoned her shirt and pulled at the cotton binding. Some tiny varmint had gotten under the cloth and was biting the flesh of her breast.

The shadow of a mosquito loomed against the cotton twilling. Perhaps it was the last mosquito left in the world, now that summer had ended. One last drink of blood to toast the others. Josephine wiggled her fingers at the little beast, whose hum died in response.

"We did good tonight, didn't we?" Libby asked.

"You need to hold your temper."

"I wasn't talking about that. I was talking about our disguises. No one suspected a thing."

Josephine hugged her chest and watched the winged shadow still dancing across the tent. "They looked right at me and didn't see me at all."

When Libby first woke, several moments passed before the linen sheets of her old bed dissolved into the Spartan textures of her oilcloth and the bare ground. Other realities followed. She was in the army. She was a man. It was the middle of the night. And her bladder was full, aching in a way that wouldn't wait for morning. She was fearful of the darkness and wanted to wake Josephine, but she was sleeping so soundly that Libby decided to go alone, despite her misgivings.

The other soldiers of her company lay out in the open, near the low campfires, their breathing raspy and slow. They slept in pairs, sharing oil blankets under the cool skies.

Wesley and Lewis were curled up together, their faces peaceful under starlight. Matthew and Floyd took less intimate positions on their backs and a foot apart. Floyd slept with a folded handkerchief over his chest, an eccentricity whose origins were unknown. Libby turned between two officers' tents and crept past a pair of ambulance wagons into the field that bordered the woods.

High grass brushed her legs and made a swooshing sound that evoked memories of the cornfield back home. She reached the edge of the woods, catching the fragrance of wintergreen plants and the ammonia scent of urine. The lantern caught the bold design of a spider web, and she walked around it, eyeing the black spider in the center. She stepped on something that could have been an old snakeskin or the dried remains of ironweed, but did not lower her lantern to look.

She ducked behind an oak tree, hanging the lantern on a low limb so that its light fell from her waist to the ground. She sniffed at the air and realized someone else with an aching bladder had already found this spot. She had no desire, though, to look further. She pulled down her trousers, backed up to the tree, and sank into a crouching position, bracing her back against the trunk and holding her shirttail out of the way. She tried to hurry, but her bladder would not be rushed. She waited, trembling, alert for any sound beyond the splash of urine against the leaves of the forest floor.

She heard something. A footstep or the fall of an acorn loosened by the wind. Her throat went dry. She stopped the flow and listened. A definite series of footsteps now, creeping up so fast that she did not have time to react, but remained in her position with her sex bared as suddenly she was looking into a man's face. The lantern light caught his wild eyes as he stared at her.

She couldn't help herself. She screamed. He screamed too.

She fell over as he ran away, still screaming, in the direction of the camp. She managed to pull up her pants. Her fingers shook as she buttoned them. Voices rose in the distance, curses and urgent calls for the guards. She crept out of the woods and back through the field toward a gathering clamor. She hid behind an ambulance wagon and listened.

"They're killing me. They're killing me!"

She peered out from behind the wagon. Half a dozen soldiers were trying to pin down the crazy man's arms and legs, but he fought them ferociously. Other soldiers were gathering.

"We're going to die! All of us!"

The lieutenant, a short, chubby man whose uniform fit him tightly, came rushing up to the struggling group. "Private Abraham! You will be quiet now!"

But the man would not be silenced. "They're coming! They're coming! Oh God, they're here!"

• • •

"Private Abraham goes through spells," Floyd explained the next morning as he rolled up his mackinaw blanket. "The man's got nostalgia. That's the medical term. All of a sudden, he'll start screaming for no reason at all. Claims people are coming to kill him or a pack of wild dogs has broken loose. Once in a while, he'll think he's sinking in quicksand. He used to be a regular fellow. Last summer he was trying to reload his musket, when a Yankee shell took the head off the man standing next to him. Half the man's face ended up sliding down his neck. Private Abraham didn't speak for three days, and after that . . . well, you see what happens."

"Why don't they send him home?" Josephine asked.

"He won't go. He's still a good soldier, and Old Jack would let a billy goat fight if he could hold a gun."

Floyd began to rummage through his haversack and didn't speak again until he'd found his folding toothbrush and held it to the light.

"Years ago, there was a man from my town who fought at Churubusco. When he came back home, he didn't have no foot, and he was crazy as a loon. His family had to put bars over his window and chain him to his bed."

"What did they do with Private Abraham last night?" Libby asked.

"Ah, they threw him in the guardhouse. He's always fine in the morning, like nothing ever happened."

"Really? He doesn't remember?"

"Who knows?"

Libby hadn't slept, too worried about exposing her gender to an insane man.

"This war makes everyone crazy," said Floyd. "Some more than others, of course."

• • •

Just as Floyd had promised, Private Abraham was at morning drill. His expression was calm, but he had the eyes of a man in a blood-exhausted state, when all colors are equal, and North and South form interchangeable pieces of a broken whole.

"He saw me last night," Libby whispered to Josephine. "The lantern was shining right on me. He knows I'm a woman."

"Don't worry. He wasn't himself."

But on the way back to the campsite, Private Abraham caught up to them and pulled on Libby's elbow to stop her.

"Excuse me," he said, his voice formal and sane now by the light of day. "I believe we met last night."

"No, we didn't," Libby replied, her heart pounding. "You must be mistaken. I was in my tent all night."

He gazed at her in a way that meant inner processes were sorting through his memory and testing it against her declaration. "I'm sorry," he said at last. "I suppose it was someone else." His shoelaces had come unlaced. He walked away without tying them.

"Thank goodness," Josephine said. "He believed you."

"No, he didn't. He knows."

"Why do you think so?"

"When he took my elbow, he cradled it lightly with two fingers and a thumb. One man doesn't do that to another."

Libby and Josephine played dominoes on the uneven ground as Floyd practiced his rhythms. Libby's nervousness over the encounter with Private Abraham had left her preoccupied; she had just tried to join a two-dotted domino with a one-dotted one. Josephine pointed at the violation and Libby tried again.

A bugle sounded and Floyd stopped drumming.

"What's that, Floyd?" Libby asked.

Floyd listened for a moment. His face darkened. He set his drum aside and said, "I was hoping it wouldn't come to this."

• • •

Josephine stood between Libby and Wesley. She had no idea why she'd been summoned here, to join the entire division in a three-sided formation; it was just another part of the army life she didn't understand and would have to learn. Twelve soldiers marched into the center of the waiting men. An officer barked an order, and they stretched out in a line and came to attention. Several minutes passed, but the men remained motionless. An oak leaf, prematurely yellow, blew into the scene and skittered across the line, landing in succession on a boot, a hat, and the barrel of a gun. It tickled a man's beard and then settled on his shoulder, balancing precariously. His hand shot up and seized the leaf, crumpling it and scattering the pieces to the wind.

A horse-drawn wagon came into sight and creaked toward the twelve men. A prisoner sat on the back of the wagon on a wooden coffin, his hands tied behind his back and his body shifting to keep its balance. He wore a white shirt, a butternut jacket, a pair of ragged gray trousers, and was barefoot.

The wagon stopped, and the man sat looking at the twelve men. The horses were more animated than the prisoner, betraying their nervousness with little snorts, their eyes big and troubled. The drivers of the wagon helped the man down, then slid the coffin out and set it down beside him. They propped open the lid and gestured for him to sit on the edge of the coffin. He obeyed after a slight hesitation. The drivers seemed relieved that their job was done. They climbed back onto their seats and shook the reins, and the wagon departed, leaving the man alone in the silence. Someone who saw his face out of context might assume him to be suffering the pains of an ordinary soldier on an ordinary day: the desire for a drink, the absence of a letter from home, the itch of a new chigger bite near the crease of the knee.

Another officer came forward to tie the blindfold. Thrice it came undone and fell away from his face, revealing by the third time an expression that had lost all its composure. Finally the handkerchief stayed in place. The provost marshal read from a piece of paper.

"Corporal Thaddeus Grant has been found guilty of desertion from B Company of the Twenty-Seventh Regiment and, by the penalties prescribed by the Confederate States of America, has been sentenced to death. A pardon request has been denied by President Jefferson Davis, and the punishment is to be carried out immediately."

A chaplain stepped forward and read a passage from the Bible, then spoke to the prisoner in a low voice. The prisoner ignored him, and the chaplain stepped away.

Josephine couldn't swallow. The wind shifted, carrying the odor of corn bread from the mess wagon and evoking a sudden memory of the freewoman cook of their childhood, stirring batter with a spoon.

The men on the firing squad looked frightened. Some of them moved their lips as if in prayer. The condemned man was shaking his head now. He almost fell back into the coffin before he caught his balance. Josephine watched his chest, imagining his beating heart. She felt an elbow in her side. Wesley nodded in the direction of the meadow. A horse and rider had appeared in the distance, the horse quite ordinary but the figure astride it unmistakable.

Stonewall Jackson.

Stripped of the clamor that usually greeted the sight of him, he seemed terrifying now. Had she touched his boot, her hand would blister. He was an angry king, his heart a crypt of dwindling mercies; he had ordered this execution. His was the bloodthirsty word.

An officer shouted an order. The firing squad brought their muskets to their shoulders.

"Aim! Fire!"

Josephine flinched at the deafening roar of the muskets. Her breath caught in her throat. The man on the coffin stiffened but did not fall.

"Oh God," Libby murmured. "They missed him."

Six scarlet patches appeared on his chest. He shivered as the wounds strained through the texture of his shirt.

He fell backward, and the men around the coffin slammed it shut, not even bothering to arrange his body into a pose, so that even his skeleton would speak of his shame.

Stonewall Jackson disappeared into the distance.

Josephine chased Libby through camp, pleading, "Come back! Come back!"

First the younger sister and then the elder one trampled a dead campfire and left black footprints across a poncho spread out on the ground for a game of chuck-a-luck.

Josephine was losing her breath.

"Wait! Wait!" She was too exhausted from running to hold her voice down in the manly register, and her words broke free into a girlish and desperate pitch. Libby plunged into the meadow and headed for the woods. Josephine drew in close, her breathing labored. Libby finally stopped and turned around.

"They killed him," Libby said, crying. "They killed him."

Josephine was so out of breath, she had to wait several moments before she could reply. "Just put it out of your mind. We're here now, and we need to be strong."

They heard footsteps in the meadow and turned to look.

Private Abraham marched alone, his gun resting on his shoulder, his feet moving in a perfect parade march. He went right past them without seeming to notice them at all. He reached the woods and disappeared in the shadows of the trees.

They both heard the gunshot at once.

They stared at each other, wide-eyed, then rushed into the woods. They found private Abraham sitting with his back against a poplar tree whose branches still shook. He cradled his musket in his arms, his legs straightening as his feet slid forward. A powder burn circled the wound under his chin. His lap was turning red. A bullet flattened by the top of his skull had entered the poplar at an angle; an insect with orange wings investigated the new hole.

11

Libby's deceit kept Arden near. His gestures and expressions — his voice, his walk, his laugh, his way of holding a fork, and his position of rest — were practiced and perfected. Kept alive that way. She felt protected from discovery, and not just because of her growing skills in her role as a man. Arden was with her, so close that it was hard, sometimes, to understand where she ended and he began. He grew more substantial as the days went by. Flashes of him came to her. Slivers of conversation, a quick, apple-size burst of laughter that seemed to drop from a tree. The sight of his wedding ring on his finger. A bruise on an arm, a lizard crawling down his shoulder.

Glimpses, fragments, pangs. At times she could almost believe that the afterlife and the present tense could merge on earth and heal the lonely. Not often but enough, like the equinox and its perfect balance of sun and moon. See a lightning bug flash in a frosted month, and you can believe that miracles exist on a human level too. She had dreams that she reached him on the battlefield, and he was still alive. Looking at her. Whispering, "Thank God, you're here. Help me, help me."

The dust descended, flying into noses and mouths, coating faces and boots and brass buttons. It penetrated the eyes and mixed with the sweat on the faces of the stragglers who trudged toward the camp. Men trained inside grayish clouds, responding to the choked commands of the lieutenant. When Wesley played his guitar around the fire, the dust settled on the veneer and gathered in the letters of his name, which his brother had carved into the wood.

An Indian summer had suddenly arrived, bringing the kind of weather that tempts soldiers to throw away their blankets and trench coats and then kick themselves later, in the dead of winter. Lice proliferated. The men stripped off their shirts and held them over a hickory fire, evoking memories of popping corn.

"Have a go at it," Floyd told the sisters. "Afterward, you can wear your shirt for a few hours before they crawl on you again. You're not shy, are you? If I can show off my sunken chest, then you can. All right, then, suit yourselves."

Josephine lay awake, scratching, more vexed by lice than the thought of battle, for the fighting seemed far away and the lice were right here among them, creeping through the grass, falling from the trees, moving through the buttonholes of trousers.

Pests and dust clouds weren't the only concerns. One of the men in F Company developed lesions on the back of his hand. The surgeon's diagnosis quickly permeated the ranks.

Variola.

Also known as smallpox. The soldier was quarantined from

the rest of the division. A nervous volunteer left his rations a short distance from his tent, and no one could get past the guards to visit him, should they care to. Those soldiers denied furloughs from the smallpox threat blamed the quarantined man and threw rocks at his tent poles.

The surgeon ordered precautions. Few needles were available, so the soldiers passed around scabs peeled by the doctors from the soldier's hand, inoculating each other with the tips of their knives. Josephine's arm hurt when she saluted her lieutenant.

Strange cravings came to Josephine at odd times of day for peppermint and marjoram, lemonade and hot chocolate. All the treats of both hot and cold weather mixed together. In her mind, she ate watermelon and washed it down with hot cider. She missed the smell of her own skin, once made sweet by a clam-shaped bar of soap that had dwindled all summer. The wrinkles of her uniform were filled with dust. And her oversize trousers rubbed a rash the size of a grapefruit on both of her thighs.

A mannish odor crept inside her clothes at night and stayed. Her voice learned its lower register. Her fingers and hips lost their grace. And whatever thready charms she had were no longer re-quired of her. They were only in the way, as heavy blankets were on a summer march. She had longed, all her life, to be noticed by a man. Now she had to actively plot, sweat, fight against it. Drill her invisibility into herself.

She felt terribly guilty about abandoning her parents. Al-though the note they'd left had briefly satisfied her, she knew that her parents must be desperate to receive further word from them. And yet she could not write them. What could she say? That they were not working in a hospital — worrisome enough, considering the diseases rampant in such places — but actually on the field of battle? She had terrible dreams about her mother and father, walking through the aftermath of a battle, among the dead and wounded, looking for their lost daughters.

She hid her tribulations from Libby, whose dreams had begun to worry her. Libby moaned in her sleep, perspired, and called out Arden's name. Josephine couldn't shake the feeling he was materializing somehow.

Which one of them had he come back to haunt?

On those days when Libby was caught up in herself, Josephine talked to Wesley Abeline. His easy laughter reminded her of the wounded Yankee soldier back in Winchester who had finally died in her house, and whose empty grave she imagined filling with water every time it rained, reflecting the birds in the sky.

Wesley's older brother, Lewis, had broken Wesley's arm once. Or so it was rumored. No one knew why, and no one wanted to ask. The story seemed strange to Josephine, since Lewis shadowed him constantly, attending to his every need. It was just another mystery in a war full of them.

One day, feeling lonely, she looked for Wesley and found him by a dead campfire, tuning his guitar. His sleeves were rolled up, his expression calm. He looked up at her and nodded.

"How are you doing, Joseph?"

Josephine hated her false name. Despised the way it pounded into her who she was now, stomping the name *Josephine* into the dirt like glowing ashes under the heel of a boot.

"I'm bored," she said in the lower voice she had begun to use without trying. She hated the voice, too, and wondered if her real voice would come back healthy after the war, or wounded, or dead.

"Well, that's the army, my friend," Wesley said. "Bored, bored, screaming, bored, bored, dead, bored forever."

"What is it like?"

"What is what like?"

"Battle."

He didn't speak for a few moments, instead twisting one of the pegs until a string told the truth and then going on to the next one. Finally he strummed twice and looked at her.

"It's the worst thing you can think of. It's terrible shooting a man. It's terrible being shot at. It's terrible watching your friends die, watching horses die. You crawl through blood. You can hear the bullets whistle, Joseph. You can hear them hitting people. And the screaming. The sound of a man screaming right in your ear. What's it all for?"

"Don't you want to beat the Yankees?"

"I don't want to beat no one. I want to go home."

She glanced at the bump in his arm where the skin was stretched over a crest of badly knit bone. Yet the bump looked soft, as though capable of flattening out under her fingers. Maybe he would escape from the war bearing that bump as his only injury. She wanted to ask him what had possessed Lewis to hit him, but her intuition told her to keep quiet.

Wesley followed her gaze and blushed. He stopped plucking at the strings and rolled his sleeves back down.

"Where's your cousin?" he asked.

"In his own world. Where's everyone else?"

"Oh, scattered around. Matthew's over yonder."

Josephine looked around and saw Matthew with his head lowered, writing furiously on scratch paper. He'd barely talked to her since her arrival. In fact, he barely spoke at all.

"He's at it again," Wesley said. "He ran out of stationery right after Kernstown. Then he ran out of wallpaper. Then he started ripping out pages of his novels and writing on the margins. He loves those novels, but I guess there's someone he loves more."

"A sweetheart?"

"He's crazy about her. Writes her every day. God knows what news he can dust off here."

Josephine envied this girl, imagining her reading the margins of the novel pages by a window, turning them three times to follow the love talk.

"We've all given up so much for this war," Josephine said, meaning she had.

Wesley had gone back to tuning but the F string, increasingly high and then perfect, seemed to agree with her. The dust cleared for a moment. Dress parade was coming soon.

Josephine watched Matthew's writing hand preserve some feverish thought. She turned to Wesley and said, "You got a girl back home?"

He nodded slowly, but she realized he was simply satisfied with the tune of the fifth string.

"No, I don't got a girl," he said at last. "But sometimes when we march through a town, they'll come and talk to us. Sometimes they're not too happy, because we're robbing their smokehouses. But they look so pretty, I want to kiss them, even the ones in Frederick who called us filthy Rebel dogs and dropped cantaloupes on our heads. I worry that they're all getting married, and by the time I come back home there won't be any left."

"There will still be plenty, I imagine."

"But who would love me? I'm not handsome like Matthew. I'm scrawny and I've got crooked toes."

"Women can surprise you. After all, one of them married Abraham Lincoln."

Wesley smiled slightly, then said, "Sometimes I want to make a deal with the Yankees. I want to say, 'Listen. I won't shoot you. You won't shoot me. We'll forget about this war and go find us some women.'"

"My cousin would kill you if he heard you say that," Josephine said.

"So would Lewis."

Wesley looked sideways at her.

"How 'bout you? You got a girl?"

Josephine hesitated, considering the question. "No," she said. "But when I get back home, I'll find someone." She had tried not to torture herself by imagining her homecoming, but like marjoram and chocolate, the thought evoked the heated pleasure of the out-of-reach craving. One day, if God were willing, she would slip off her uniform and put on a new slat bonnet. And new crinolines. And new shoes. The lice would carry away her uniform, and she would wave it farewell.

A breeze blew in, catching a dog in mid-step and moving its long ears forward. Wesley gave his guitar a final strum and tapped his carved name. "All done," he said.

"Play something."

"Nah."

"Be a sport."

"If you'll get off my back." But he smiled as he said this and began to strum, at first the discontinuous chords of rehearsal and then a song that favored neither Rebel nor Yankee, but lived independently by the side of a river, in a bank of bloodless ferns.

Josephine knew that something about her puzzled Wesley. A shadow would cross his face and then vanish, as though he could see her just for a fleeting moment before he saw Joseph again, just another boy in the Rebel cause, dusty, lice-eaten, hungry, and male. Josephine lived for those moments when she caught Wesley's glance by firelight or during sing-alongs or the interminable drills as the chubby lieutenant yelled at her mistakes.

"Private Holden! Do you understand *right face?*"

"Yes, sir!"

"Do you understand *left face?*"

"Yes, sir!"

"Then turn when everyone else turns, you idiot!"

Only Wesley's occasionally searching looks kept her from

completely losing herself and drowning in her maleness. She thought about him late at night, scratching herself in her tent, Libby dreaming by her side and sometimes crying in her sleep. She did not find him plain or scrawny at all, and found the angles of his face and the darkness of his eyes increasingly pleasing. She knew it was dangerous, feeling this way. One slip and she'd be out of the war and so would Libby, and Josephine was convinced that a broken quest would kill her sister, that all she was living for was revenge and that was the soup that kept her breathing. And so Josephine remained vigilant, talking to Wesley as she imagined a boy would, without fondness, without any appreciation for the sound of his voice or his laughter or the words of his songs, or for the desire in his heart to trade the war for a swimming hole.

She envied Libby for having been seen half-naked by the mad Private Abraham before his suicide, for this was an affirmation, a knowing and confirming, if demented, glimpse. Josephine could only make do with seeing herself, feeling herself, on certain furtive bathing trips in the river at night, running her hands over her naked body, her filthy clothes on the riverbank, free now of shell jacket and the binding cloth and the heaviness of a flintlock on her shoulder. Just herself, just a woman, breasts still there, skin and lips and the hair between her legs and what it guarded. Knee and shin and elbow. The delicate fingers of her hands. Her brow, cheek, neck. She ran her fingers through her hair and felt tears coming as the hair let her fingers go after the blink of an eye and there was no more hair left to caress. But it was soft hair, female hair.

She sank down into the slow-moving river, sat down on the silky bottom as the water flowed up to her breasts and the moonlight lay on the water. Beneath the surface she was real. When it grew too cold to bathe in the river, where could she find herself?

She had not yet seen the worst of the war, the middle of a battle, when anything soft is banished in favor of raw instinct and the will to survive. She had held the long, heavy bullets and couldn't imagine them cutting her flesh, tearing through her lie and gutting the truth. She imagined being buried where she fell, her secret preserved forever.

Was all of this her punishment for the wish for Arden's death? Or for what she'd done at Sharpsburg? In the panic of the moment, she had made a decision that seemed more right than wrong. But in the passing days and weeks, the rightness of it, like the woman in her, was starting to slip away. Perhaps it was a fiendish deed after all. She didn't know, and there was no one she could ask. Sometimes, as she watched her sister sleep, Libby would open her eyes and look at her with such a rank suspicion that Josephine was sure she knew. But then her gaze would soften and she would fall asleep again, breathing in, breathing out, and, during those brief, motionless pauses in between, look for all the world like her husband in his deathly repose.

Josephine would move away to the very edge of the tent, dragging her eyes away from Libby's face. If God had invented this torture to punish her, then He was a brilliant God indeed, twice the genius of Stonewall Jackson, and she never wished to meet Him.

The dust died down, but then a scourge of a different sort took its place that October. Rain fell from the sky in drops big as plum pits. It leaked through woolen uniforms, plastered hair against heads, and soaked the visage of Jefferson Davis off the backs of playing cards. Horses tried to buck off their riders when thunder rolled. Drills continued during pauses in the deluge, but the rain fell again. The lieutenant would look at the sky and shake his head in disgust. The soldiers huddled under their oilcloths and jury-rigged shelters out of canvas and the low branches of willow trees.

Poker and faro continued, as did cockfights, held in secret

places. Bloody rain flew off the wings of the birds as they fought in standing pools; the wind blew tinted water into the faces of the betting men. Once, the winning bird drowned the loser.

Dog-eared pamphlets of *Les Misérables* had been passed around Company D for weeks. Socialites were reading it in the cities, and cowboys out west. Even the farmers put down their newspapers and picked up the harrowing tale of Jean Valjean — prisoner, thief, fugitive, and consulate — a man whose fortunes rose and fell as often as those of the South. On rainy evenings, soldiers crowded into a Sibley tent and elected someone who was halfway literate to read aloud, usually Floyd, the most dramatic. He would clear his throat and the tale would begin, as the odors of the unbathed bodies in the tent faithfully approximated the smell of a hunted man's fear.

The rain slackened one night, but not so the chase. Javert, the obsessed police detective in *Les Misérables,* had learned of Jean Valjean's whereabouts and was rushing over to arrest him and send him back to the galleys, where he had been a slave. Jean Valjean saw an avenue of escape — a high wall that formed part of an old building. He himself was strong enough to scale the wall, but what would become of Cosette, the orphan girl he'd taken in and loved as his own?

The slush lamp fell to the ground, blackening the tent, and the shock of the broken-off tale evoked a collective gasp.

Floyd's voice accused the unknown culprit who lurked at arm's reach in the darkness. "What idiot knocked down the lamp?"

"Not me," said Wesley.

"Oh, I bet it was. You probably hit it with your dumb, ugly head."

"You hit it with your stupid old waving arm."

"Pipe down and find a candle."

• • •

Libby and Lewis stood picket in a copse of red oaks, two hundred yards removed from the argument about the fallen lamp. The rain had finally stopped, but they were both soaking wet. Water dripped off broad leaves that would have shown changing colors in the daytime.

"They're reading *Les Misérables* without us, I reckon," Lewis said.

"Probably," Libby said. "I sneaked ahead a few pages this morning, when no one was looking. Believe it or not, the French inspector—"

"Don't tell me."

The sky had cleared of the boil of night clouds, and Orion shone with the energy of the moon. Libby was thinking about Josephine. A memory kept coming back to her, one she wasn't quite sure was even real. She tried to push it from her mind. A drop of rain slid down her face.

She looked sideways at Lewis. She'd heard he was a brave fighter whose aim was true, but he was also a man of swinging moods, generous with hardtack rations but quick with his fists. When his brother played the guitar, Lewis would sit cross-legged next to him, his shoulders hunched and face intense, his coiled body resembling a wolf tied down by the tenuous rope of a song. Anyone who dared interrupt Wesley was subject to his brother's ominous stare.

Low, thin fog drifted through the saplings, and damp heaven light hung close to the ground, giving honeysuckle bushes the look of skulking monsters and making serpents out of fallen vines. Branches creaked and twigs snapped. The rain dripping from them was of different temperatures, warm and ice-cold. Lewis had pulled a two-foot dogwood sapling out of the ground, stripped it of its branches, and snaked it down the back of his shirt in search of chiggers or lice or some unnamed vermin that attacked on wet nights. He finally gave up, withdrew the sapling, and tossed it into a tangle of elderberry. "Rain's gonna come back. Give it thirty, forty minutes, and we'll be treading water again."

Libby saw a flashing light and raised her gun.

Lewis grabbed the barrel. "That ain't nothing. They call them things northern lights. God's way of teasing pickets. No one knows what makes them. All I know is that they've scared soldiers into blasting away at Yankees that ain't even there."

He ran his hand inside his coat and pulled out a rolled cornhusk. He unrolled it and applied a thin line of tobacco from a pouch around his neck, and then rolled the cigarette tight. She looked at him in surprise. Arden had always said that only sissies smoked cigarettes. Real men chewed tobacco or smoked a pipe.

Lewis put the cigarette against his nose and inhaled deeply. "You think I'm a girl for smoking these?" he asked, as though he'd read her mind.

"No."

He fished in his pockets for a match. "Well, let me tell you something. These ain't cigarettes. These are cigaritos. My father smoked 'em in the Mexican War, and there ain't nobody more man than him."

"My father was a colonel in the Mexican War," Libby said. "He rode with Robert E. Lee."

"So did mine, in fact he wanted to sign up this time, once he heard Lee was gonna be fighting. But he's too old, and besides he took a shot to the pelvis and can barely get around the house."

"My father wasn't wounded. But now that he's older, his hips are stiff. He can't even ride a horse."

"Well, our fathers best stay at home this time."

A gust of wind put out his cigarito. He swore and found another match while Libby set the stock of her gun on the ground, balanced the barrel in the crook of her arm, and rubbed her hands together.

"You're getting better handling that gun," Lewis said. "I gotta tell you, the first few days I thought you and your cousin were never gonna make it. But you boys have come a long way in a few weeks, 'specially you. And I know that you believe in the cause as much as I do."

Libby flushed with pride. Her approval of Lewis went up three notches.

"I just wish they'd let us target practice," she said. "It's strange to spend all day drilling and never fire your weapon."

"Well, you know, same old story. Not enough bullets." His cigarito went out again.

Another orb of light appeared in a thicket of poplar.

"Lewis, look!"

"Just like I told you, ain't nothing. You'll learn to tell the difference between nothing and something, but it'll take time, and meanwhile you might get killed. A friend of mine thought he shot a Yankee one night. Next morning, he found out he'd blown his own friend to kingdom come."

Lewis took a flask from his pocket, unscrewed the lid, and passed it to Libby. "Take a swig."

She put it to her lips and caught a whiff of brandy. She'd once tried it with Arden, back when they had first met. They'd gotten drunk and jumped in the haystacks for a while, then threw up in the stall of a bored palomino. This brew tasted thick and bitter, like the milk that oozes out of the veins of high weeds. It bit her hard in the stomach, and she broke out in a sweat that felt good in the cold.

She handed the flask back to him.

The light flashed on twice more and then faded into the mist.

"One time my friend and I got sick on this stuff," she said.

"Arden was his name. He lived next door. He died at Sharpsburg later on." She felt grateful for the chance to talk about him, to say his name.

Lewis shook his head. "Sharpsburg. I never saw nothing like it. Dead bodies everywhere, and men sitting in blood eating pumpkins. Everyone was starving. You didn't know whether you wanted to kill someone or pounce on an apple core."

"I'm here to avenge him. Gonna kill twenty-one Yankees, so help me God."

He took another long drink. "Twenty-one? Why that number?"

"That's how old Arden was when he died. I'm gonna kill a Yankee for every year he drew a breath. There are twenty-one Yankee mothers stirring chowder somewhere that don't even see me coming."

"Twenty-one Yankees," he murmured. "Hard to tell who you hit in battle with all that smoke and bullets flying around, but, hell, I suppose it's possible."

Something moved in the middle distance, and Lewis straightened up and squinted. He listened for a moment. "Ain't nothing. You know, if Wesley got killed, I would shoot every Yankee in the world, and everyone that's pulling for them, too. Like those bastards in Maryland who say they're not on any side. And if I die first, I'm gonna come back as a red-tailed hawk and protect him. They're fierce. They can take a man's eye out. And they've got that orange underbelly."

Something caught his attention. He raised his rifle and pulled the trigger. Someone fired back. The tree bark above Libby's head exploded.

"Shoot!" Lewis screamed at her as he reloaded.

She threw the rifle up to her shoulder and yanked on the trigger. The gunshot exploded in her ears. In the near distance, something heavy fell through the brush and onto the wet ground.

"God almighty," Lewis said. He finished loading his gun, took down the oil lantern from its perch on a branch, and motioned for her to follow him. "Shhhh," he whispered. "Be careful. There might be more. But it looks like they skedaddled."

The dead Yankee lay with his arms thrown out to either side, still clutching his rifle. The bullet had hit him cleanly in the face, and the hole it had made was the size of a child's fist. The crater was filling up with blood and then spilling down the cheekbones. One eye was gone, and the other was glassy. Clouds passed overhead and blackened the blood. It turned red again when the lantern light fell across it.

Lewis looked down at the dead man's gun and said, "Hot damn. That's a Spencer repeating rifle. Check his clothes for coffee. Go on, do it."

Libby opened the man's coat and felt around inside it, her hands trembling despite the warmth his body still exuded. Finally she withdrew a handful of coins and a pipe.

"That's all?" Lewis said. "And his shoes won't fit. Damn Yankee." He gestured toward the man.

"Well, anyway, there's number one for ya."

Libby vomited while walking back to camp and told Lewis it was the brandy. He nodded and said, "Well, its bad stuff, all right. Listen, don't you feel sorry for that Yankee bastard. He got what he deserved."

The soldiers gathered around Libby and slapped her on the back, and Floyd gave her a cup of coffee. Wesley took her hand and shook it hard.

"Congratulations. Got him before he got you."

"Right in the face," added Lewis.

Josephine was less sanguine when she ran to hug Libby, a girl's embrace, frantic and close.

"Stop it. Let go," Libby hissed in her ear.

She went to the tent and started to cry. Josephine tried to console her. "It's not your fault, Libby. You had to shoot him."

"I killed a man, Josephine."

"It was self-defense."

She wiped her eyes, but more tears came. "Half his face was gone. I did that."

She couldn't stop crying. She buried her face in her hands and wept inconsolably. Finally she heard Josephine's small voice.

"Libby," she said. "I wasn't going to tell you this, but maybe it will help you."

"What?" Libby managed.

"You're not the only one in the family to kill a Yankee."

Libby managed to stifle her sobs. She stared at Josephine through her tears. "What do you mean?"

"The Yankee soldier at our house, the one with gangrene?"

"Yes."

"Father killed him."

Libby stared at her, astonished. "What? He died of his wound."

"No, he didn't. The night the soldier died, soon after he was singing, I walked by the room. Father was inside the room. He was sitting on the side of the soldier's cot. He had a pillow pressed over his face. The soldier's arms were moving. I stood there and watched until the arms were still."

"But why?"

"Father said it was a mercy, that the soldier was in terrible pain and would have died anyway. He told me never to tell a soul. But now I'm telling you."

Libby felt a sudden surge of anger. "You waited all this time to tell me?"

"Father made me swear to secrecy!"

"What other secrets are you keeping from me?"

Josephine slept, but Libby could not. She lay in her rain-soaked clothes and shut her eyes, trying to think of something, anything, besides the sight of the gaping hole in the Yankee's face. Rampant changes were taking place in her body: sorrowing of soul, tenderness of breast; the unraveling of hard-earned masculinity, and even a slight twitch in the muscle of grudge. She tried to comfort herself, whispering to herself, "He would have killed me had I not shot him first. I hated that Yankee and I'm glad he's dead." Her lips moved as she repeated everything, only faster this time. The wound in the dead man's face drained of blood and then filled again. The air so warm between his body and his coat. The terrible moment replayed itself again and again. When she could stand no more, Libby turned to a solution of last resort, a memory she had never visited before, not even in dreams.

The lips of her husband were the color of a bisque doll, his forehead unwrinkled. His shell jacket was unbuttoned to reveal a wound that leaked intestines and swarmed with flies. They scattered when she waved her hands, but circled low and came back.

His hands were stiff with blood, so much blood that she couldn't see his fingernails, and his wedding ring was clotted with gore.

Libby felt the reassembling of hatred, a man's trait that called for a man's constitution. Her eyes turned flinty and her body stiffened. A hardening of heart and an influx of bile. She spoke to him, making no sound.

Arden, I remember a summer day when we were young and you were lying on your back in the grass, and all I can think of now is that nothing in the meadow told you that in five years you'd be dead. No clues at all. Not from the daisies or the clover or the birds or the wind. Not from the clouds or the dog whose ears you scratched. Not from God.

There were Yankee boys, then, in the North. Lying in meadows. Scratching dogs' ears. Time would pass and one day they would put on their shoes and come to find you.

Now I've come to find them.

October 17, 1862

Near Martinsburg, Virginia

Josephine saw the octagon house from where she stood on the tracks of the Baltimore and Ohio Railroad. The brigade had moved its camp to the area of Martinsburg and had begun the arduous task of sabotage. They tore up crossties, piled them together, and burned them. They heated rails and bent them around trees. They destroyed water tanks and bridges, all to stop the progress of General McClellan should he decide to venture into Virginia.

Josephine's first march had been entertaining at first, the men calling out jokes and insults and quoting *Les Misérables*. Most of the lines came from the main character, Jean Valjean, but some were snatched from the middle of a page, just because they seemed beautiful or strange.

His mother died of malpractice in a milk fever.

Gillenormand was a kind of twilight soul.

All extreme situations have their flashes, which sometimes make us blind, and sometimes illuminate us.

Songs shimmered through the ranks, their rhythm discontinuous against that of the route step. The men sang "Ida" or "The Girl I Left Behind," or simply chanted, "The devil is loose, the devil is loose" to the tune of reveille. Later in the day, the brigade grew tired and silent. The primrose was dead, as was the star thistle, but Josephine still noticed dandelions growing through the crushed limestone on the sides of the road. Many of the men still had no shoes. Wesley was wearing his brother's brogans, and halfway through the march, Lewis cut his foot on a piece of broken glass and had to limp the rest of the way. When the brigade stopped for the night, Libby and Josephine could not muster the energy to set up their tent or even take off their haversacks. They wrapped themselves in their oilcloths and fell asleep near the fire.

Josephine woke up in the middle of the night and looked over to where Wesley slept next to his brother. She sat up, studying his sleeping face. She had tried to march near him, always comforted by his cheerful voice, and she loved listening to him play his guitar around the campfire. But only now, with the entire camp asleep, could she indulge fully in the sight of him, and she drank it in.

Once the brigade arrived at the new location, the discomforts of the march were forgotten in the zeal of destruction, as soldiers took gleeful bets on how many chops it took to bring down a telegraph pole with an ax.

The octagon house sat to the east of the railroad. The branches of pine trees obscured Josephine's view of the roof and the rock fence hid the yard, but when she grew light-headed from the smoke of the crosstie fires, the house seemed to rotate, its windows glittering as it turned. To pass the time, she imagined decorating the interior, conjuring up ornamental rugs and furniture carved from exotic trees.

The crosstie fires sputtered with sparks. She looked at the house and added a grand piano to the parlor.

A bridge exploded. Fancy china and a spoiled cat.

The blade of an ax sank into a telegraph pole. Cordovan slippers. A velvet settee. Dried lilacs and teasel heads in a bull's-eye vase.

"Don't just stand there," Libby scolded. "The lieutenant is

coming. He'll yell at you." Libby's face was sunburned and her uniform was stained. Josephine still hadn't grown accustomed to the masculine register of her sister's false voice, or that of her own.

The lieutenant stopped in front of Josephine. The long march only seemed to have made him shorter. He came up to her collarbone, whereas a week ago she would have sworn he had made it to her chin.

"Private Holden!"

"Yes, sir!" Josephine looked down at the broad, sweaty face and the incongruous dimple.

"Is there something in the woods that fascinates you, Private Holden? The sight of the trees, perhaps; a bluebird sitting on a branch?"

"No, sir!"

"What if *everyone* stared into the woods? Would that intimidate the Union army, to see the entire Jackson brigade frozen in fascination over the antics of a bird? Would they surrender in their terror? Would George McClellan weep like a girl at the thought of being conquered by an *army of statues?*"

"No, sir!"

"Then get back to work!" The lieutenant spun on his heels and stalked away.

Matthew materialized by her side. "Don't worry about that lieutenant, Joseph. You know he's more bark than bite."

"My cousin's got a fire lit under his ass now," Libby said.

Josephine gave Libby a look. Her sister had taken up swearing and poker, too.

"Matthew's a good man," Libby said as he walked away. "His girl is lucky to have him."

Josephine didn't answer. She had discovered a jaw-dropping secret about him, one she didn't even have enough knowledge to fully understand. Matthew had gotten his hands on some new wallpaper, and that evening he'd started a letter, but the wind had pulled the first page away and carried it into the woods. Matthew sighed, lit a torch, and went to find the runaway love talk. He was gone for two hours and came back shaking his head. The next morning at dawn, Josephine went to look for it herself, ashamed and yet compelled.

She knew from experience that secrets hide themselves well and demand a meticulous search. It's not enough to kick at a holly bush. You must separate the branches and look inside, deep where no mockingbird has ventured. Don't just walk around a dead owl. Brush off the ants and lift its wings. And don't ignore logs and dormant honeysuckle. They know things.

When Josephine returned from the woods, the tips of her fingers were full of splinters, and a mob of chiggers had crawled on her shoes and up her legs. Soon they would burrow into her skin and cause her endless torment. But she had found the letter, a discovery that served as chamomile for the itch of a mystery.

The single page was full of love and promises, and talk of fingers running through hair. Near the bottom, Matthew had begun to write a fervent description of night falling. But that was not the part that caused such astonishment.

The letter had been written to a man.

She had heard of such men, but so obliquely as to leave her more confused. It seemed that certain men had something in them—something to do with love—which was quaintly different from other men. Imagine, she was told, a set of clay pipes with one turned sideways.

She had intended to give the letter back to Matthew, but now such a plan was out of the question. She had folded it up and put it in her haversack. Now, as she pried up the crossties with a crowbar, she could almost hear the letter crackling in her sack like a locust molting its shell.

• • •

Just before dawn, the sound of gunfire startled the sisters from sleep, their bodies stiffening under the oilcloth.

"Listen!" Libby whispered. "The pickets are firing!"

Josephine's hand found hers in the dark.

Another burst of gunfire. Their hands clasped tighter.

"I can't do this, Libby."

"Yes, you can. You must."

"Fall in!" The lieutenant's voice shrieked through their tent like a sudden gust of wind oriented at just the right angle for maximum force.

Wesley appeared out of nowhere at the front opening of their tent, already in uniform, his musket slung over one shoulder. Gone was the Wesley they knew. His eyes were dark, his face somber and slick with perspiration. The absence of his usual humor frightened them. He seemed to be guarding his best trait in the hope it wouldn't die with him.

"Let's go!" he ordered, pulling them out of their tent and helping them into their jackets, his hands shaking around the buttons. Men scrambled in the pale light, buckling on their leather cartridge boxes, checking their weapons, and tying their shoes. Some of them rifled through their knapsacks, removing dice, cards, and liquor so as not to die shackled to their glaring sins.

Libby and Josephine had no time to put on their shoes and had to carry them to the battle line that stretched through the thin woods, oak to birch to dogwood. Skirmishers ran out in front of them, disappearing into the gloom of the trees. Their fire intensified, then stopped, and an uneasy tension settled across the line of battle. They had been told to expect this, and that this period of ominous silence could last hours or even days.

The lieutenant approached the line, thrust a fist in the air, and shouted, "Death is the entrance into the great light!"

The soldiers recognized the line from *Les Misérables* and

whooped, and the lieutenant's face lit up. It darkened as gunfire crackled in the near distance.

The men wiped their faces and checked their weapons, and a tingling fear started at one end of the line and traveled to the other, caught a twitch, and came back again. They would have paid good money for mystical auguries foretelling their fate so they could just stop guessing. Many of them felt a sense of failure they couldn't quite define. Something they hadn't accomplished. Maybe it had to do with money or God, a stick half-whittled or a child unnamed, they didn't really know — but they didn't want to die without the answer. Some of the younger men had never touched a naked woman, and a false memory of such skin, so smooth, so soft, now brushed against their faces. As the fight approached them, they began to sweat and their stomachs cramped. One man threw up and blamed it on the fatback he'd eaten the night before.

Josephine's gun kept slipping out of her hand, and she could not catch her breath. The sound of the approaching fight terrified her, as did the silent plans of God.

"Don't take Libby," she whispered under her breath. "You know what I did. So take me, take me."

Libby peered into the woods from her own position. Matthew materialized at her side. He buckled her haversack, adjusted her belt, and moved her cartridge box around to the front of her body. All the while he hummed a little tune that sounded like "Hell Broke Loose in Georgia."

"Why did you fix the cartridge box like that?" Libby asked.

"Protects your stomach, somewhat." He walked away, still humming. Assistants of the quartermaster came around with ammunition. Libby put forty cartridges in the leather box at her waist and stuffed the rest in her pockets. She tore the cartridge paper with her teeth, tasting the acrid powder. The ramrod barely made a sound as it moved down the barrel. The wind was cold but sweat rolled down her sides, and she was conscious of the frailty of her body. Had Arden felt this way, in the green woods of Sharpsburg?

The firing had neared, and so had the screams of the wounded and dying. Her mouth went dry, and she could not control her trembling. War was for men, and she was a fraud.

"Aim low!" the lieutenant shouted.

Libby looked over at her sister, whose eyes fixed on her before they turned away. Josephine's gun was slipping around in her hands; at any moment it could shoot a foot or a branch or an angel. Wesley materialized. He took Josephine's weapon, wiped it with a cloth, and handed it back to her, leaning close and telling her something that seemed to calm her.

Floyd's drum started up and the order for forward march was barely heard over the din of the approaching gunfire. Libby's line began to move. Animals fled the opposite way. She felt as though she had no free will but was being drawn along by some mysterious force. The call of a bugle. The magnetism of grapeshot. Or Arden.

"Double time!"

Libby quickened her pace. Her uniform and haversack weighed her down, as did the full cartridges that bulged from her pockets, heavy as horseshoes. Her bayonet stuck in the wood of a poplar tree, and she had to stop and yank it out. The animals had vanished, driven by the same premonitions as the soldiers who had pinned letters to their loved ones on the inside of their jackets. Libby began to lose her breath.

Josephine ran a short distance away, keeping up with the others and holding her gun in the correct position. All of the training had finally kicked in, and Libby felt a rush of appreciation for the lieutenant, who had screamed her sister into soldierhood.

The line approached the edge of the forest, where the trees thinned and a haze of smoke filled the air. Dead bodies of Confederate skirmishers lay in her path. Some of them were still whole; others had been hit by shells and solid shot, and were missing arms or legs. She jumped the bodies and felt the squish of their scattered remains as she continued on. Flashes of blue uniforms were visible through the trees. Just before she burst from the forest, the soldiers running on either side of her faded into the light and the blue uniforms vanished, giving her the sense of a solitary, slow-motion run through a world that just happened to scream and burst. Her vision cleared again, though her head swam with a strange continuum of present and past. A branch cracked and fell, and Arden stirred molasses in his oatmeal, his hair in his face and his shirtsleeves unbuttoned. The scene faded and a new one appeared. Arden was struggling to land a fish. His fishing pole bent double, he lost his footing on the muddy bank and slid toward the water, laughing.

A wounded man crawled into a hawthorn bush.

Arden touched her face.

Something burned.

Arden kissed her throat.

She ran in an amber space of light. One last, small memory came to her with such intensity, its masculine smell banished all the others. Arden half-dressed, staring out the window in the bedroom of the house they'd shared so fleetingly. Sunlight coming through the window, Arden's bare back so smooth and muscular. His hands by his side, wedding ring on his finger. His full weight on one leg, because his foot was still broken from his fall off the roof. He said nothing but suddenly turned and looked at her, still propped up in their bed, smiled as he limped over to her, that smile saying it was time, once again, for an act once taboo but now sanctified by marriage. No war talk. Just her name.

"Hold your fire!" the lieutenant screamed. "Wait until they come in range!"

Libby tripped over a dead picket, stumbled, and then managed to right herself just before she burst out of the woods, where the smoke burned her nostrils and her dreamy senses sharpened, noise so deafening it meant nothing. The Rebel yell sounded, growing by the moment, full of deadly hope and false bravado and the split-second decision not to live forever. Libby found herself screaming it, too, as a Confederate battery fired and its shell exploded over the enemy line. Body parts flew through the air, taking the broad leaps of bullfrogs, and torsos turned into ground-dwelling creatures that writhed in the dirt.

"Fire!"

Pain tore through her right shoulder when she pulled the trigger. The bullet flew into a locust tree, and she stopped to reload. Rain had started falling around her, the drops moving the grass blades. She blinked and the rain turned to minie balls, whining, buzzing, mewing, imitating the cries of small and helpless creatures even as they mowed down soldiers on her right and left. The soldiers died without a sound except for the thump of their bodies striking the earth and the settling of their haversacks atop their sudden corpses. An owl flight of Confederate artillery shells broke the Yankee line, but it formed again a moment later. The cacophony paused for a split second, and Libby heard the sound of a single curse, so absent of God it seemed to come from the idea of war itself.

She stood, raised her musket, and took aim at a Yankee, but the bullet went over his head. The soldier next to her noticed what she'd done and shouted: "Aim low! Don't panic!"

As she paused to reload, she felt herself change from a frightened woman to a soldier facing down the same devil Arden had. She was Thomas Holden, a made-up name attached to a real fighter. And the force she represented was not the South; it was not gray or blue but the hot red of a woman compelled to live in a season full of ripening walnuts but empty of love.

The man next to her squinted down his barrel. Before he could fire, a whistling shell made a horrible thump in his chest and his rifle fell. Grapeshot tore the air above her head. A minie ball scorched past the lobe of her ear and hit someone behind her. She loaded and fired, loaded and fired, the gun growing hot in her hands, a voice inside her saying something about being alive, something about hatred, something about sassafras, something about a love that ends abruptly, something about what it means to feel jealousy and fear and loneliness, something about the faded light of a winter afternoon and the smell of pastureland and what it means to fight someone over all these things.

To the winner go the spoils, winner is alive, winner feels the worries and pains that are due later in the afternoon, later in the night.

She knelt in a bog that was dry earth before someone bled on it. The North took one step forward and two steps back, waltz of the temporary victory. A horse collapsed and someone screamed, *"Mother!"*

Bullets zinged past her, molten bees that could hollow out a cheek in their frantic search for nectar.

Her sister was surely nearby, somewhere in the smoke, but she did not answer when Libby called her name. As she fought, she grew wilder, growling as she ripped the cartridges with her teeth. Black powder colored her hands, her lips, her face, and the cuffs of her shirtsleeves. She pulled the trigger. Smoke settled in her mouth. She shot a man's arm off and tripped over someone's boot. She shouted a question to a nearby soldier, but his only answer was a thump and a wet spray from his direction all over her face; when she turned, half of him was gone. His warm brains coated her sleeve, but she did not change expression. No more fear now, no horror, only a hatred so immediate it could take the place of the breath in her lungs.

Sharp commands and terrible screaming, someone falling to her right.

A lone tree splintering.

The wild eyes of a loose horse.

Matthew fought a few yards in front of his line, impaling a Yankee on a bayonet, pulling it out, and forcing it into the throat of another.

The bluecoats were losing. They left their dead and wounded and retreated toward the railroad tracks, the Confederates in hot pursuit. As Libby ran, she felt that someone was missing, someone she loved but couldn't quite remember. This person might be here on the battlefield or back home in Winchester.

Her tongue had dried. The ache for water soaked the nub of herself, reaching the need for love, the wish to never be alone, wonderment about God, doubts and memories and unhealed abandonments. Her canteen was gone. She didn't know how much time had passed.

And someone was missing. In heaven, perhaps? No, not in heaven. Here on earth. That much she knew.

Her jaw ached, but she managed to tear another cartridge. As she continued forward, her shoes turned to anvils and the air was black with gunpowder.

Someone was missing.

Libby reached the railroad bed, tripped on a pile of charred crossties, and fell down the slope into a pile of dead and wounded Yankees, their bodies so soft beneath her.

She held tight to her gun as she struggled out of the pile. Her uniform was covered in the blood of her enemy. She had almost freed herself when someone grabbed her foot and held on tight. She screamed and pulled loose, ran a few steps, and fell on the ground, coughing in the smoke. She crawled forward. She touched the gray sleeve of a shell jacket and pulled on it but received no response. She moved her hands to the collar and shook a body that was heavy and limp. The smoke cleared and the empty eyes of the lieutenant stared back at her. Cold ashes from old crosstie fires coated the wound in his forehead.

She struggled to stand but couldn't. She covered her face and rocked back on her heels, screaming. A hand seized her shoulder. A stricken soldier was looming above her, eyes wide with horror. At last there was a name.

"Don't die, Libby. Please."

Josephine pulled at her clothes and then began to unbutton her jacket. "Where are you shot?"

Libby's throat was so dry she could barely speak. "Nowhere," she managed.

"Nowhere? There's blood all over you."

"Not my blood," she said, and looked around the battlefield. The dead and wounded littered the ground, both Union and Confederate. Next to her foot, the flowering head of a bent weed pulled out of a puddle of blood and straightened slowly.

"I'm not hurt," Libby said. "Are you?"

"I don't think so. What's wrong with your voice? It's all scratchy."

"I'm thirsty."

Libby accepted Josephine's canteen, unscrewed the cap, and took a long drink. Her throat hurt when she swallowed.

"The Yankees ran away," Josephine said. Her voice quavered when she spoke. "Most of them escaped, but some are making a stand."

The fight continued in the woods beyond the railroad. A

cannon was swung in the direction of the octagon house, and the windows exploded. The Confederates had surrounded the house. Another window exploded. Two Yankee soldiers fell out of it.

Libby again tried to get up and join the fight in the near distance, but she was too exhausted. She passed the canteen back to Josephine and said, "We survived. And I killed a bunch of Yankees. Where are the others?"

"I haven't seen anyone. Except Matthew." She lowered her eyes to a patch of clean ground. "He's dead."

"No."

"A shell hit him in the face." Josephine's voice had turned dreamy, a defense against tears.

"Oh God."

A horse came galloping toward them out of nowhere, eyes wild and mane on fire. It reached them so quickly that they could only cover their heads. The horse leaped over them and left the stunning smell of burned horsehair as it veered in the direction of the railroad.

"We have to find the others," Josephine said at last.

Libby remembered the dead lieutenant.

"I have some bad news," she said.

"What?"

Libby twisted around and pointed at his body.

Josephine drew in her breath.

"Josephine, he didn't feel a thing. They shot him clean."

"Is that supposed to make me feel better?"

The sisters crawled back to the lieutenant. His jacket was too small for him. Gravity had lengthened his jowls. His black lips were parted, revealing an equally black overbite. Josephine closed his eyes, unbuttoned his jacket, and searched his pockets, retrieving a photo of a little boy. "He's got the same dimple," she said, then turned the picture over to reveal big shaky letters, the kind children make before their fingers strengthen.

GEORGE

The firing stopped around the octagon house.

Libby said, "Here, take your gun." She picked it up by the barrel. Its temperature made her frown. "This barrel's cold. You didn't fire it, did you?"

"I don't remember."

"Josephine! If you don't kill the enemy, you're not helping win the war. You're not helping me. And you're putting us all at risk. I shot five Yankees, at least. Maybe six. But I'm going to count five, just to be fair."

Libby handed Josephine the gun. "I've got some cartridges left over. Tomorrow we'll sneak down to the river, and I'll teach you how to shoot. If anyone hears us, we'll say we ran into some Yankee pickets."

Josephine looked down at the dead lieutenant. "Are we just going to leave him here?"

"What else can we do?"

After the fight, the Confederate surgeons attended to the Confederates and let the Union men wait in agony. Grapeshot had gouged huge holes in the trees. A fire had started in a brush pile next to the railroad and burned an artillery limber.

The sisters found Wesley and Lewis in front of the octagon house.

"Where's Floyd?" Wesley asked.

Lewis spit a stream of tobacco juice on the ground. "I saw him boiling coffee next to that telegraph pole way over there."

"Matthew is dead," Josephine told them.

"Don't say that," Wesley said.

Lewis tore his slouch hat off and threw it against the granite wall bordering the yard. "Bastards!" He squatted down and covered his face.

Wesley watched him for several moments and then pulled him to his feet. "He's in a better place, Lewis."

"Better place, hell. He's dead."

"Let's go in the house. We might find some food."

Low azalea hedges bordered the path that led to the doorway. The odor of burned flesh hung in the air. Bodies lay propped against the granite wall and scattered all over the yard. One of the soldiers had collapsed trying to crawl out of the house; now he lay shadowed by the open door. He looked up at the Confederates as they filed past.

"Damned Rebels. You ain't got me yet."

"You shut your mouth," Lewis warned, "or I'll close this door on your head." He chewed his tobacco rapidly and then leaned down and spat the brown results in the man's face.

The foyer was beautiful, just as Josephine had imagined it, although a corpse hung off the second-floor balcony, red drops falling out of his open mouth and pooling on the floor. Artillery fire had destroyed the middle of the stairwell. Smoke spiraled up from the crater.

They went into the parlor, where the blood splattered on the drapes and floor had somehow missed the piano keys. Two soldiers lay tangled together, unmoving, their muskets by their sides.

The table in the kitchen had been wiped clean, and the word "Hello" was chalked on a black slate. The salt box was full. A corn grinder sat on the far shelf. The air smelled less like blood or smoke and more like cinnamon and yeast.

Wesley peered in a cupboard. "There ain't no food in here. Just the smell of food. The family must have took everything before they ran off. Selfish bastards. Let's go see what's on the second floor. They might have some money stashed in a drawer, and we can use it to buy something from the pie wagon on the next march."

"And I'll bet when these people skedaddled, they left some good shoes," Lewis said. "I'd hate to have to wear a dead Yankee's shoes."

The crater in the stairway was still smoking. They maneuvered around it as they climbed to the second floor. Other soldiers were checking the rooms.

"They're all dead up here," one said.

"We're looking for shoes," Lewis said.

"Suit yourself."

The rooms were spacious. Light filtered through the blackened curtains. Most of the dead were huddled near the shattered windows. One man still had a cartridge clenched between his teeth.

The room they entered next was clearly that of a girl. The wallpaper was a pink frost pattern, and two pier-glass mirrors caught the sunlight and directed it across the faces of a half-dozen dolls that sat propped against a shelf. Josephine opened the trunk at the foot of the bed and found more dolls. She retrieved one and held it to the light.

Lewis leaned his rifle against the wall. He picked up a tortoiseshell brush, pulled his shirttail loose, and scratched his stomach vigorously.

"We'll have to burn that brush," Wesley said. "No little girl should have to use that."

A chifforobe caught Libby's eye. She squinted and leaned her head to one side. She walked closer and squatted a few feet away. "Look," she said, pointing at a stream of blood trickling from the chifforobe.

Lewis dropped the brush and grabbed his rifle. "You come out of there," he said, pointing his rifle at the unseen prey. "You come out right now, or I'll blow you to kingdom come." He edged closer, moving at an angle in case the wounded man still had his gun.

"Be careful!" Wesley said.

Lewis yanked the door open. A great amount of blood sloshed out, followed by a soldier cradling a leg blown off at the knee. His face was twisted into terrible contortions. "Kill me. Please, I'm begging you. Kill me."

Lewis lowered his rifle. "You poor bastard," he said without sympathy.

Wesley took off his jacket and began to unbutton his shirt.

"What are you doing?" Josephine asked.

"Making a tourniquet. Now go find some help for this man."

Lewis moved his bare feet away from the spreading blood. He said, "Help for a Yankee? You're joking!"

"He's wounded, though," Libby said. Josephine nodded.

"What the hell difference does that make?" Lewis asked.

Wesley kept unbuttoning his shirt. "What if you were in his place? Or me? Joseph, go find the damn litter-bearers!"

The man had dropped his leg to hold the stump. "No! Kill me!"

Lewis seized his rifle by the barrel and swung it hard, smashing the stock against the man's head with a sickening thud. Blood ran down the Yankee's face.

"No!" Wesley cried.

The Yankee tried to shield himself, but Lewis hit him again. His head cracked open. He slumped over sideways to the floor and lay motionless but for the twitching of his arms.

Wesley stood wide-eyed, his shirt held together by one button. "My God, Lewis," he whispered.

Lewis wiped the stock of his gun on the bedspread. "That's for Matthew," he told the dead man.

• • •

Night fell. A subdued feeling hung in the air. Soldiers played cards and drank whiskey, their voices low, or sat by the light of a kerosene lantern, writing letters to the families of the men who had died. The burial detail had worked all day and into the night, growing sloppy in their exhaustion but making sure they dug deep enough. Bury a man too shallow and his body will exude a phosphorescent blue mist that lingers above his grave. That was the legend, at least.

Shocked to the bone from the loss of Matthew and the bludgeoning of the wounded man, Libby sat with the others, her cup of soup just a prop in her hands. She had managed to find some new clothes to replace her bloody ones: a pair of trousers, torn at the knee, and a white shirt that was too long in the sleeves.

Logs had been laid out in a U-shape around two corners of the campfire. Lewis stretched his feet toward the fire until his toes turned red by its light. He had found no shoes that would fit. Floyd stared off into space, tapping his drum distractedly.

Josephine had gone to bed early. Wesley hadn't spoken in hours. He folded a slab of hot bacon and put it between two cold pieces of hardtack. He bit down and the bacon oozed out the sides. He took the food out of his mouth and studied it, then showed Libby that his teeth had made no indentation in the flat biscuit. He pulled out the bacon and threw the biscuit in the fire.

Lewis said, "Hey, I would have eaten that. Why don't you play something? A little ballad for Matthew. Well? What's the matter, cat got your tongue?"

Wesley gave his brother a long, loveless stare, stood up, and walked away, leaving a heavy feeling in the air behind him. The others looked at their laps and didn't speak. Lewis rolled a cigarito and left it unlit. He glanced around at the others and put it back in his pocket. "I lost my temper. I was real upset about Matthew."

Floyd blew on his hands and started to drum again, but stopped himself. He curled his fingers and crossed his arms. "That ain't up to us to forgive. That's between you and God."

Lewis retrieved his cigarito, lit it, then sighed and threw it into the fire. The cornhusk blackened. "Well," he said in a darker tone, "at least I killed some Yankees today." He looked around the fire. His eyes rested on Libby. "Not like you."

"You're crazy," Libby said, her spine straightening. "I killed five of them. Maybe six." She held up her fingers as though they were witnesses.

"Like hell you did. You didn't kill nobody." Lewis stood and retrieved a musket from a trio that leaned together like the sticks of a teepee. The other muskets fell, but he ignored them. He walked back to the firelight and gave the musket to Libby. "This yours?"

She ran her hand along the stock and found her initials.

"Yes, it's mine."

"Let me show you something." He took the musket back, found a stick, and stuck it down the barrel, pushing it in and out. He turned the musket upside down. A great quantity of black powder poured out, along with some paper cartridges. Lewis kicked the resulting pile, and it smoked up the air.

"Well, look at that," he said. "Did you remember to put on the percussion cap each time you reloaded? Your gun wasn't firing, except maybe on the first shot, and I noticed you hit a tree with that one."

"God sakes," Floyd said. "It was his first fight. How good were you the first time?"

Lewis turned around to put the gun away. Libby leaped up and rushed at his back. He whirled around as she reached him. He dropped the gun and grabbed her by the collar.

"You want trouble?" he asked.

Libby struggled to free herself. "You're a bastard, Lewis! You smashed out the brains of a wounded man, and I bet you did break your own brother's arm!"

He sucked in his breath as though she'd punched him, but did not let go of her collar. He tightened his grip and pulled her closer. "Don't ever say that again about my brother, or you'll get what that Yankee got. I swear you will!" His voice shook and his eyes glittered, as though holding sunlight they had trapped at noon.

Floyd stood and held out his hands.

"Can you two stop it? Just stop."

Lewis had twisted her collar so tight, her throat had closed. The lack of oxygen produced a flush of sleepiness and a confusion about whom she was fighting and why.

"I said stop it!" Floyd said.

Lewis released her, and she sank to her knees. Floyd picked up Libby's gun, walked over to where the other guns lay, and arranged them so they leaned against each other. They fell in a heap and he tried again.

14

When Libby finally fell asleep, she dreamed she was back at the little Kent Street house in Winchester. The apples were gone, but the vines of stubborn jasmine were still blooming along the fence line. She and Arden sat on the cypress swing in their backyard and watched the dawn break and the sky take on sunfish colors, a confidence of hue. Arden leaned back against the swing and closed his eyes, revealing lids the color of lavender pebbles. Drops of morning dew clung to his face, each no bigger than the eye of a needle. In a few moments, the light would dry them.

His breathing deepened, and she wondered if he'd fallen asleep.

"Arden?" she asked.

"Mmmmm?"

"Did the Yankees kill me?"

He opened his eyes. "What in the world are you talking about? You look fine. Not a scratch on you. In fact, you don't seem quite as pale. Maybe war is good for you."

"Do you think I'm stupid? For jamming up my gun?"

"New recruits do that all the time. What bothers me is that I think you were happy about it. Happy that your gun jammed, and you didn't kill any Yankees."

"That's not true, Arden!"

He looked at her. "I'm wondering about you. Wondering if you care all that much about our cause."

"Of course I do! It means everything to me. You know that."

"At least you fired your weapon. Your sister did not."

"She was nervous."

"Or maybe she's a traitor."

"Don't call her that."

"It's true," Arden said. "You've been meaning to ask her about it. You know—about what you saw in the woods at Sharpsburg."

"I think my eyes were playing tricks on me. It was dark in those woods. Shadows moving. She could not have done what I imagined, Arden. I was mistaken. And, besides, you're not dead. You're alive."

"Sweetheart, if I'm alive, what's crawling on me?"

"Nothing."

"Oh, Libby."

He clapped his hands and the flies scattered.

October 19, 1862

Dear John,

I am a soldier in Matthew Sterling's company and found your name and address among his effects. I am deeply saddened to inform you that your gallant friend was lost while engaging the enemy near the town of Martinsburg.

A faction of Union troops surprised us one morning. Matthew was among the first to arise and prepare for battle, helping those less experienced than he with our gear and equipment. He was ever mindful and protective of his fellow soldiers, often placing himself in the clutches of danger whilst trying to protect our safety.

I was within sight of Matthew during the terrible fight and observed him bravely engaging the enemy when he was struck by a mortar shell. Although this may provide small comfort, please know that Matthew did not suffer, but was plucked from this life and delivered into God's hands in an instant.

You need have no uneasiness about his future state, for by the comments he made to me I could tell his faith was well founded and he feared no evil.

Pvt. Joseph Holden
Stonewall Brigade

The river next to the camp twisted through the lowlands, urging crayfish and colored leaves along as it flowed. Other leaves had been trapped by the bracken that lined the bank, gathering until they became like their own plant, made of every color imaginable. Minnows scattered in clear water as sunfish approached. The riverbed was furry with silt. It took a winding swipe and formed a pool.

A thicket of willow trees and scrub stood between the river and the greater woods, seemingly impermeable. But Libby and Josephine had discovered a path. They sat in a patch of yellow grass on the bank, watching shadows play across the pool in the river. They had taken off their shoes, rolled up their trousers, and dangled their bare feet in the river.

Libby rubbed her eyes. Lately her dreams had begun to extend themselves during early morning hours. A fog grown by twisted sleep would follow her around, and bits of the dream appeared where they should not: a nose, a buckle, a fingernail, a scar. And occasionally Arden's whole face, his eyes looking straight into hers. At first she had welcomed these visitations. But lately they had started to frighten her. Sometimes when she spoke, she heard his voice in her own, so distinctly. She wished for just one night's sleep without him. A dreamless rest. One day without the memory of him waking itself up to follow her around, because the memory no longer seemed a choice. He had once seemed so far away, in a heaven that existed somewhere past the farthest star. But now he was with her, in her clothes, in her ears and mouth and throat like the smoke from a campfire. She was not certain, anymore, which part of her uniform she inhabited. Did she only exist in a pocket or a fold, and was Arden back, taking up the rest? She wanted to tell her sister all this. Instead she said, "Do you think it is safe to bathe?"

Josephine didn't seem to hear her. She'd taken off her shell jacket and was sitting on it now, her eyes closed. Her belt was draped across a willow root. No hat, no gun, no haversack. She'd seemed weighed down by something these past weeks, and Libby wanted to ask her what was the matter. And still the nagging question in her own mind. That memory lacking resolution. It played itself out and started over again. She couldn't even say, with definition, that she'd seen anything at all.

She reached over and brushed a stray hair away from Josephine's face, a gesture of tenderness meant to brush away her troubled thoughts. Josephine opened her eyes and looked at her sleepily. "You know what? Sitting here, you'd never know a war was going on."

Libby started to tell her that war was a duty, but she decided against it. Such remonstrations seemed out of place here. Instead she balanced a dime of water on the top of her toe and flicked it at Josephine. Josephine responded in kind and giggled.

The sound of her giggle reminded Libby of another grudge, this one more immediate, and one she felt compelled to speak up about.

"That giggle," she said accusingly.

Josephine glanced at her. "What of it?"

"I heard you speaking to Wesley alone, just the two of you by the campfire. He told a joke and you giggled. Not like a man. Like a woman. A flirtatious woman."

"I did not."

"You did. You forget yourself when you're with him. You forget who you are supposed to be."

"I know who I'm supposed to be." Her sister's voice had turned a bit cold. "But when I'm with him, I remember who I am."

"You're Joseph."

"I'm Josephine!" she shouted, with a vehemence that startled her.

"Keep your voice low!"

"I'm Josephine," she repeated in a fierce whisper. "Libby, I've sacrificed quite a bit for you. But you will not take my name, or my feelings. I know what you are hinting about, and, yes, I like Wesley. I am drawn to him. If I didn't like him, I'd have nothing to remind myself that I am a woman."

"You are not here to be a woman. You are here to fight for your country."

"I'm here because you forced me to be here. And I'll be here when you come to your senses, but don't banish me from Wesley's company. He is the only one who keeps me sane in this army."

"You will give us away."

"I will not. Wesley looks at me and sees his friend. His male friend. It is the worst punishment for me, worse than you can imagine."

"Your suffering doesn't come close to mine," Libby said, her anger rising, "until you find Wesley dead on a battlefield."

They sat glaring at each other a minute, neither giving ground. Finally Josephine's eyes filled with tears. "You have Arden's memory. I have no one. I've never even had a proper kiss."

"Arden's memory is not always so pleasant."

"What do you mean?"

Libby said nothing more. Josephine stood up and began to unbutton her shirt.

"I hate these clothes," she said. "They are so heavy and so filthy."

She finished the buttons, removed her shirt and then freed herself of her trousers, her long johns and finally the winding-cloth around her breasts, and stood naked in a filter of sunlight and gloom. Her shoulders were square from the weeks of drilling, but softened by the V of her collarbone and the aureoles of her breasts.

Josephine looked down at herself. "It's strange. It's like seeing someone else's body."

"You're beautiful," Libby said.

"Of course I'm not."

"Yes, you are."

"You see me?"

"How can I not see you? You're standing right here."

Josephine gave her a long, searching look.

Josephine held her eyes for a moment longer but did not answer. She stepped into the water and kept going, her naked body submerging bit by bit until only her head remained dry. She took a breath and slid under the surface, reemerging in a different place, her hair soaking wet.

Libby got up and began to undress.

"Is it cold?" she asked.

"Yes."

Libby stepped into the river, feeling the bracing chill of the water. She stopped when the water reached her shoulders.

Josephine disappeared and came up ten yards away. She gave Libby one last look and glided into the shadows and a world of her own.

Alone now, Libby ran her hands down her face and the line of the jaw and the throat, her skin turning alabaster as her fingers approached the breastbone. Arden used to run his fingers down her throat. He'd move his mouth toward hers, his words slowing until his eyes closed, revealing blond lashes and spider-veined lids. Their lips would touch, gently and then with more pressure, until Libby felt the saliva on the inside of his bottom lip, that wetness provoking the clasping of their hands.

She continued moving her hands down her body to where the Y of her legs made a dowsing stick, touching the secret, the immutable evidence of fraud. She had done this, made the whole world her fool. Wouldn't Arden be proud of her now, although she had killed but one Yankee? She submerged fully and swam toward her sister smooth as a fish. Josephine came to meet her underwater, body pale and cheeks puffy with gathered breath. They stopped a few feet apart and lingered there, the need for oxygen beginning as a tickle.

They rose together, broke the surface, and laughed.

Libby did not know why she chose that moment to speak. It seemed as though some part of her was speaking in her place.

"That day at Sharpsburg, in the woods . . . you had a scratch down your cheek. You said it was caused by a passing vine . . ."

Josephine stopped laughing. She grew very still in the water as she listened.

"But there were no vines in those woods."

Libby stopped talking and let the question linger.

Her sister shrugged. "I don't know, Libby. Everything happened so fast. Perhaps I scraped my cheek on something else. A branch or a stick. I truly don't remember. What difference does it make?"

"It doesn't, I suppose," Libby said at last.

A thin school of minnows swam between them. Above their heads, a colored leaf fell to the water and moved slowly past them.

17

November 1862

Camp Baylor, near Bunker Hill, Virginia

Night came on so quickly — a magician's trick for a yawning audience. It was nearly three weeks into November. The air was chilly by day, colder by night, and still cold in the morning. The soldiers heated rye coffee and ate their meager breakfasts. Hardtack, molasses, sometimes eggs. Precious eggs. The pestilences that followed battles had set in: gangrene, pneumonia, strange fevers, nightmares. Lincoln had grown weary of McClellan's reluctance to re-engage the Confederates after Sharpsburg and replaced him with a new leader — one who promised to bring the fight to Robert E. Lee. Rumors of a long march to meet this General Burnside were swirling, although no one knew when this march would get under way and where it would take them.

When Josephine came up for picket duty with Wesley, she followed his direction and stuffed old newspapers inside her coat to keep warm. They stood in the forest, a torch flaring between them, heating Josephine's right arm and Wesley's left. Snow had fallen in flurries all day. A layer had formed on the ground and entombed fallen hickory nuts, giving the appearance of a miniature battlefield covered with graves. Josephine's breath made clouds that drifted through low-hanging cross vines. She had no doubt that, back at camp, the French police inspector was still chasing Jean Valjean, feeding his days to the fury of the quest.

As for herself, she was content to be in Wesley's company. On nights like this, the hours would go quickly before she reluctantly returned to her tent and a sister who seemed ever more removed. It was growing difficult to recognize her as the girl she used to be. Even the way she knitted her brows together was starting to resemble Arden's expression. Once, when Josephine followed her younger sister from a fair distance on the way to the woods, Libby's gait was indistinguishable from that of her dead husband. Since that afternoon in the river and Libby's strange and quiet accusation, the subject had been closed between them, and yet it lingered in the air. Josephine thought Libby believed her, but she could not be sure.

Wesley cradled his rifle lengthwise in his arms. From this angle, the rifle and his body formed the shape of a scarecrow, and the sight was such a welcome relief for the worries on Josephine's mind that she laughed. He looked at her and just smiled, evidently too cold to ascertain the source of the humor.

Earlier that evening, he had played his guitar by the fire. Perhaps his voice had been simply pretty once. If so, the last two years had changed it. Like Psalms, it held philosophies both lyrical and sad, and when he sang, the sorrows of his listeners achieved a crystal definition. Faces came into view that had been blurry for years, old wounds tore open, dead dogs caught sticks. Men caught glimpses of the boys they once had been, capable of cruelty to bullfrogs and garter snakes, the sudden clapping of their hands that ended a firefly's light, but not killers yet of men.

Wesley's face would change somewhere in the continuum of melodies. His smile would fade, and he would stop in mid-chord, close his eyes, and shake his head very slowly, then return to the song.

Amazing grace, how sweet the sound
That saved a wretch like me.

I once was lost, but now am found,
Was blind, but now I see.

His words became an endless apology fed to the stream of God's uncertain mercies. The memory of it now made Josephine shiver. A newspaper bundle shifted inside her coat.

"Hey, Joseph," Wesley said. "Look at that."

He pointed at something on the ground.

"What is it?"

"Don't be afraid, but an enemy turtle has infiltrated our post."

He picked it up and held it up to the light of the torch. The legs and arms had retracted, leaving only a shell. Its head had pulled back so far it wasn't visible at all. Josephine could see only a suction of darkness that warned away fingers. Wesley held the underside of the turtle to his mouth, inhaled, and then covered the shell with a long slow breath.

"What are you doing?"

"Warming it up."

Wesley set it on the ground and waited for the appendages to show themselves again. "How nice to be a turtle," he said. "You get to hide whenever you want, and nothing in this world could speed you up, even old Jackson." He turned the shell so that the hidden head faced away from camp. "I don't want him stumbling into Floyd or Lewis. They'd make soup out of him and wash him down with applejack." He nudged the turtle's shell with the tip of his shoe. "Go on, now. I just realized that I also want to make soup out of you and wash you down with applejack."

Josephine wanted to tell him that she felt like a tortoise in a shell, the shell of Joseph, and would welcome the blow of a hammer or the rasp of a saw.

Wesley was looking at her, smiling a little. "You know," he said, "that you and your cousin aren't fooling a soul."

She felt her stomach clench.

"What do you mean?"

"You're so young, you don't even shave. I say you're both probably sixteen or so. Lewis says fifteen if you're a day. So what is it? You can tell me. You know any secret of yours is safe with me."

Josephine slumped in relief. So that was it. Her true disguise was still safe. That blessing and that curse.

"Sixteen," Josephine said at last.

"Ha!" said Wesley. "I knew it." He punched her lightly on the arm. "Well, you're brave, all right. I ain't but twenty, and I only went 'cause everyone else was going."

He looked back down at the turtle, which remained hidden inside its shell. "Wish I had one of them shells," he said. "I'd hide in there and wait out the war. Ever think of hiding somewhere, Joseph, until the war is over?" He was looking at her intently, the same expression she'd caught him throwing at her during drills and around the fire. She was unsure of which answer to give. *I am hiding somewhere,* she thought.

"You don't have to answer me," Wesley said. "It's a dangerous question."

He watched the turtle pick up speed as it plodded through the pine straw toward the safety of the shadows.

"By hiding, do you mean deserting?" Josephine asked.

"I suppose."

"My cousin thinks deserters should all be shot. He says that if you leave the Southern cause, you're the worst kind of traitor."

"My brother says that, too. But plenty of folks are doing it. They go to Canada or hole up somewhere. If they get caught, well, you saw what can happen. But most of them don't get shot. They have to wear a barrel shirt or a sign that says 'Coward.'" He seemed to flinch at the word and then continued. "They brand some of them with a 'C' on the hip or the face. Of course, the one on the hip don't show. But if you get one on the face, you'll have a lot of explaining to do back home."

Wesley's eyes had changed, like the wounded men at the Taylor Hotel when the nurses' washcloths moved lower. He sat down under the dogwood tree and held his rifle across his lap. Somewhere in the branches, a whippoorwill called into the wind, haunting creatures to the west. The torch threw a caul of yellow light across his face. He spoke again. "Men desert for many reasons. Some need to get back to a sick wife or sick kids or sick crops. Some are just sick of the war. And some are afraid they might die in battle. So they're chicken, I guess."

He stood up by the torch, watching her as he spoke. "Joseph, what if a fellow isn't just afraid he might die, but sure that he will? Running seems like a choice of common sense, in that case. Don't you think?"

Josephine thought for a while. Heavy things seemed balanced on her answer.

"I suppose in that case, a man could be forgiven for running. I don't know. I get confused about this war."

Wesley's confession came out in a rush and bent the flame of the torch. "I ran once, Joseph. I deserted. Now you know. But I came back. Don't forget that." His voice ached, like the song he'd sung around the campfire. An endless apology directed at the past.

Josephine could only nod. Wesley's secret was juicy and broke like huckleberries between the teeth. And yet she tasted nothing. She wanted to move the torch so that only its softest light fell on him. Search the forest for gentle things to put in his pockets. And then have him search the forest for her.

"Tell me what happened. I won't tell anyone."

Wesley passed his hand over the torch, slowly enough to make him wince. "I've witnessed strange things. Men will die in battle without a single scratch on them. God just takes them whole. Farmers who live but half a mile from a fight won't hear a thing. Or you'll see lights in the woods not connected to nothing. Or a friend will tell you he saw a falling star and then die the next morning."

Josephine said, "Our cornfield back home was haunted by a ghost made of blue light."

"Yes, ghosts are everywhere. And once in a while, a man starts to feel like a ghost himself. It's an omen, you might call it. He knows he's about to meet his maker. My own uncle described that feeling in a letter he sent from out west, and the Comanche killed him the next day. The night before we fought at Mechanicsville, I got that feeling. I knew I was gonna die, sure as I know this torch is hot. So I ran away. The guards didn't even see me. They were too busy drinking brandy. I cut through the woods until I came to a deer path. I followed that for about two miles and then stopped. I turned around and went back."

"Why?"

"Don't know. I guess because I never was nothing before I joined the army. Just a blank. And the first color I turn ain't gonna be yellow. I'd rather be killed."

"But you weren't."

"True. I didn't die. But the feeling wasn't wrong. Feelings are never wrong, like God is never wrong. I didn't die because I didn't fight in that battle."

Josephine waited for the rest of the story. It would come out of its shell if she just left it alone for a while.

The torch had eaten a quarter ration of wood before he spoke again. "My arm was in a sling. That's why I didn't fight. Lewis broke it. Not because I deserted. He was the one who told me to run, even though he thinks deserters are lower than dogs. He just wanted this dog to live and breathe. When I came back, he was angry. He said, 'I gave the guards a good bottle of brandy for you. Now you get your ass out of here like we planned.'"

"I told Lewis I'd made my peace. He said, 'Suit yourself, you little jackass,' and before I could blink, he broke a board over my arm—my right arm, which connects to my right hand, which connects to my trigger finger. Floyd thought Lewis hit me out of plain meanness. That old man ran around the whole camp flapping his lips. There wasn't a damn thing I could say about it, not in my position. Lewis didn't say nothing either. So I ended up a coward of a different sort. A lighter shade of yellow. But yellow just the same."

He tucked in his pants with his free hand, a small act of appeasement for an unseen martinet. "I've got a letter folded up in my washing kit that explains the whole thing. It shows that Lewis broke my arm out of nothing but love. If I die in battle, I want you to read it out loud."

"I'll do that for you." She wanted to touch his face, run her fingers through his hair. Kiss the side of his face and his mouth. Go kiss his brother for saving him.

He turned around to spit, and she noticed the seat of his pants was stained from the wet ground. She stamped her feet to keep them warm.

Broad slats of torch light moved down the trunks of the trees. She inched forward so that the light included her. She wanted to roll up his sleeves, find that naked bump, and cover it with the tip of her finger so it would not hurt him. He was looking at her again. She wondered how far he could see. Confederate gray to the alabaster of her gender to the murky, vague color of her guilt. Perhaps he expected her to tell a secret of her own. Trade was common in the army, tobacco for flour, socks for gloves, typhoid for smallpox.

"I've got a secret," she said at last, having chosen the mildest of them.

"Go on, then. Tell me."

Josephine looked both ways, as though General Jackson might

be lurking among the trees, sucking cold lemons and sniffing out disloyalty. "I lied to my cousin. I told him I tried to shoot my gun, when really I didn't. I just couldn't do it."

"You're joking, right?"

"No."

Wesley stared at her and then laughed. He grabbed his stomach, locus of true hilarity, then almost bent double. "That's the craziest thing I ever heard."

She waited for him to stop laughing. "You yourself said you had nothing against the Yankees."

Finally he collected himself and straightened. "That's true. I don't. And I'd just as soon we all put down our weapons. I don't think neither side knew what they were signing up for, or they would have worked all this out beforehand. But listen, Joseph, if someone's gonna shoot at me, I'm gonna shoot back. If it's him or me, it's gonna be him, plain and simple."

"I understand what you're saying. I just don't have it in me to shoot a man."

"Why are you even here, then?"

"I have to protect my cousin."

"Seems to me like he can take care of himself."

"You don't know him very well."

"I just don't see how you're gonna protect him if you won't shoot your gun. And now I'm gonna worry about you. The other side's gonna take their shots, regardless of whether you do or not. And if the sergeant finds out, you'll get in big trouble. Court-martialed, probably."

"You won't tell on me, will you?"

"Of course not, Joseph." His voice had softened.

"Thank you."

He shook his head. "Well, if I ever desert again, I hope you're on the firing squad."

Wesley pulled the torch out of the swampy mud. It made a

sucking sound, startling the turtle that lingered in the shadows, and the tiny beast disappeared inside its shell.

He held his hand up to the flame.

"Are you cold, Joseph?"

"Yes."

"You know what's good in cold weather? Coffee. And I don't mean that rye garbage. I mean real coffee."

"Even if you had coffee, how would you heat it? We can't have fires."

"We have the torch. You hold your tin cup over the flame. It takes a while, but it's worth the trouble."

Josephine had never drunk coffee before joining the army, but in this cold weather, its warmth and kick were irresistible traits.

"Where would we get coffee?"

He glanced at her and smiled. "It's another secret. One I've never told anyone. What do you think? Can I trust your sixteen-year-old secret-keeping heart?"

She nodded.

"Then, follow me."

Wesley led her down a twisting trail, overgrown with bushes and thorns. Every now and then his feet would pull out of his oversize shoes, and he would have to stop and put them back on. The trail ended but Wesley kept walking. The ground was sloping downward. Josephine started to lose her balance and grabbed the cold branch of a tree to steady herself. "Are we allowed to go this far?" she asked nervously.

"Don't be silly. Of course not."

"Wesley . . ."

He put a finger to his lips and motioned her along. When they reached a small clearing, Wesley pushed her down behind a hedge. "Stay here," he ordered in a whisper, and kept walking. Josephine peeked around the hedge to watch him. He came to a narrow creek that flowed swiftly from the heavy rains.

"Hey, Yank!" he called into the darkness.

Josephine froze.

"Yank," Wesley hollered, "are you there? Or you already on your way back to New York, where you belong?"

A deep voice came out of the silence. "How about you, Reb? You knitting your surrender flag?"

"Sure I am. Out of your crinolines."

"You got any tobacco?"

"Sure enough. Got any coffee?"

"A little."

A soldier in a blue uniform emerged from the gloom. He trudged along slowly, his feet sinking deep in the muck and the leaves, stopping at his own side of the creek.

Josephine's mouth hung open.

The Yankee stared into the swollen creek. "I'm getting a little tired of this rain," he said.

"It's better than the dust, I guess," Wesley said.

"It's always some kind of hell, isn't it?"

"I got someone for you to meet." Wesley motioned to Josephine, who shrank back behind the bush.

"He's a new recruit," Wesley continued in a calm voice. "Our army's got plenty of them. If you could count the men in our army, you'd just give up."

"I'd just count the lice and divide by a thousand," said another voice. Josephine peeked out again. Now two Union soldiers stood side by side, their rifles resting in their arms. Their boots looked warm.

Wesley climbed back up the steep grade to Josephine's hiding place. "Don't be a spoilsport, Joseph. They're not gonna hurt you." He led her back down to the creek bed as she tried not to slip on the leaves. "This here's Joseph," Wesley said, putting a hand on her shoulder to steady her. "He is a fierce warrior. He can shoot the boil off a Yankee's ass at three hundred feet."

The first Yankee laughed. "He ain't but a boy. Give him a drum and let him beat on it."

"He'll beat on *you*."

Josephine shivered uncontrollably. Her knees were weak. She was afraid she would faint from her terror.

"Your friend speak at all?" asked the other Yankee.

"He's a man of few words." Wesley reached into his pocket, drew out a package of tobacco, and tossed it across the creek. One of the men caught it. The other withdrew a small sack from his pocket and tossed it back to Wesley, who opened it eagerly and stuck his nose down in it.

"Ahhhhh," he said. "Real coffee. Not rye, not cane seed, not chinquapin, not lizard eyes. I've got half a mind not to shoot you next fight."

The Yankees were dividing the tobacco. "You in for a little poker tonight, Reb?"

Wesley glanced at Josephine. "What do you reckon, Joseph?"

Josephine shook her head.

"Come on, Joseph. Trying to keep the Yanks from cheating will warm you up."

Josephine stared at their guns.

"Your guns make my friend nervous," Wesley said. "He's new to the army. Wonder if you can put them aside for a while?"

"Fine," said the Yankee. He and his friend set them up against a tree. "Now you do the same."

Wesley motioned for Josephine's gun. He laid their guns across a fallen log.

"There," he said to her. "No one is armed."

"But, Wesley . . ." Josephine pulled him close and whispered in his ear. "Are we allowed?"

"To play poker with the enemy? Of course not. That don't mean it's not done. I heard of some Tarheels who took a Union boy to town with them, introduced him to all the girls, and had him back to his unit before dawn."

Josephine hesitated. The Yankees still terrified her, as did the thought of what Libby would do if she ever found out. "This is our secret, Wesley, right?"

"No one else knows. Except Floyd. He don't like it, but he's not gonna tell anyone. He's a loyal old man."

"Come on," said the first Yankee impatiently.

"What do you say?" Wesley asked Josephine. "Are we gonna do it?"

Josephine nodded.

"Good," said the first Yankee. "Let's play."

18

Lewis's eyes blazed across the campfire. Libby stared back at him. A month had passed since their argument, but neither had forgotten it. Before their fight, Libby had begun to think of Lewis as a comrade, equally ferocious in his determination to win the war, but now he was just a harsh reminder that she hadn't killed a single man in battle or furthered the quest for a free Confederacy. She'd failed Arden. She'd failed the South. She looked at Lewis across the fire and wished him dead.

One night as she and Josephine lay together in their tent, her sister had told her to stop antagonizing him.

"He could hurt you."

"I don't care. I'll fight him any day. I'm stronger now." Libby spoke the truth. She had trained relentlessly, and now her muscles showed themselves when she flexed her arm. Her drilling had improved. But the torment of waiting had set in. She lay awake at night, her fingers poised for counting.

The brigade began to move, leaving behind a ghostly village that once was their campsite, pit fires still warm and graves by the edge of the woods. Stonewall Jackson had a plan in his head that he shared with no one, not even his staff. Perhaps he had whispered it into the ear of his sorrel, because the little beast seemed to know something. A wave of shimmering excitement ran through his men. They didn't know where they were going, but they knew they were heading toward the Yankees to continue their bloody sweep of victories. Confederate patriotism had reached a fevered pitch in the inactivity of camp. Rebel yells split the night. A captain had stepped in for the dead lieutenant, a passionate man who clenched his fist during morning drills and shouted, "We are the Stonewall Brigade, and we will win this war!"

His words fired up the soldiers, who started a bird swell of flying hats.

During the first few miles of the march, when the route step was fresh, the men sang songs and told jokes. Wesley and Floyd traded insults borrowed from *Les Misérables*.

"Marauder."

"Demon."

"Fruit thief."

"Wretch."

The army reached its first big river early in the afternoon. It was wide and flat, and its surface provided no distinction between its shallows and its deep holes. Local Union sympathizers had burned the bridge to stop the movement of the Rebel army. The soldiers leaned on their muskets and waited as the officers argued about the best place to cross. Floyd took off his drum and stretched his old back. "We'll be here the rest of the day, waiting for those idiots to make a decision," he said. "Get a bunch of officers together, and they can't even count the colors on a rooster."

A black man came down the road, the wheels of his pastry cart stirring up dust. Floyd bought an elderberry pie and frowned when he bit into it. "Where's the sugar in it? Isn't it supposed to be sweet?" He stopped his complaining and cocked his head. "It's the regimental band. What is so important about a river crossing that they need to bring the band out?"

The musicians gathered at the water's edge. A gust of wind blew the hat off the drummer boy and revealed his red curls. His drum was a truer shade of red, more like the color of a cherry, and he beat on it with a particular vitality, his feet planted and knees locked, his face flushing hot.

As the band reached the chorus of a marching song, a roar began down the line, growing in volume.

"Look!" Lewis shouted. "It's him!"

Stonewall Jackson appeared on his sorrel, riding with his feet high in the stirrups, acknowledging the deafening cheers by tipping his hat until it almost revealed his dark eyes. He stopped his horse at the river's edge and stared at the regimental band, whose members had grown sweaty despite the chill of the day. A lift of Jackson's finger killed the percussion, then the winds, then the flutes, and finally a single banjo. He allowed his horse to drink from the river, then rode over to his officers.

A boy in a straw hat who could not have been more than eight years old was fishing from the other bank. He caught a glimpse of Jackson and leaped to his feet, so distracted by the sight, he let the current pull on his line. His cane pole slid down the bank and bobbed in the water.

"General!"

The little boy pointed at a blue-green patch of river.

"Cross here! It's only two feet deep!"

Jackson saluted the boy, who drew himself up to his full height and returned the gesture, pulling off his hat and watching as the sorrel started into the river, water coming up to the general's stirrups and no higher. The horse took one more step and disappeared with its rider under the water. The little boy collapsed into hearty laughter, rolling back and forth on the bank and holding his stomach.

Jackson's sorrel surfaced, then the general himself, his slouch hat limp and streaming water. The horse swam back without him. It clamored up the bank and turned to stare at the little boy, who was still laughing. A soldier raised his musket and fired over the boy's head. The boy disappeared behind a barricade of jimson weed as a gust of wind caught his hat and blew it into the river. It landed gently, right side up, and floated out of sight.

The boy's disembodied voice rose up from his hiding place, gleeful and defiant. "Take that, you Rebel bastards!"

The brigade stood frozen. No one wanted to add to the great general's embarrassment by offering aid. In fact, they didn't want to acknowledge the incident at all. They lowered their eyes as Jackson swam to the edge of the river and hoisted out his awkward body, still wearing his slouch hat, which, due to his habit of pulling it down over his eyes, had stayed on his head. He stomped up the riverbank, dripping wet and leaving enormous footprints. The sorrel came back and nuzzled his shoulder. Jackson climbed on its back, and horse and rider galloped away, water sluicing out from under the saddle.

The army bivouacked near Strasburg the first night of the march. The sky was clear overhead, just the barest cloud drifting across in the opposite direction of the path taken by migratory birds. Dinner: salt pork, hardtack, and molasses too thick from the cold to spread. The wind blew harder. The sun had gone down. No stars. No campfires. Only a pitch-black sky and a frosted army that would not drip until the spring.

Libby and Josephine retired to their tent and curled up together under their oilcloths. All around them, pairs of men were doing the same, bodies as close as that of husband and wife, but bound by only a vow of warmth.

Libby shivered. "It's so cold," she said.

"Take my blanket."

"No."

"Please."

She shook her head.

Josephine rubbed Libby's arm. "Some of the men already have frostbite."

"I heard."

"Floyd says the worst of the weather is yet to come. He said he'd heard of soldiers freezing solid at their picket posts, still holding their guns. He says before this march is over, even the lice will be sleeping like spoons."

"Floyd is full of good news."

"I wish we could have a campfire," said Josephine.

"You know Old Jack won't let us. He's afraid the Yankees will learn our position."

They heard footsteps approaching. Wesley put his head in their tent. His oilcloth was wrapped around his shoulders, and his breath smoked the air.

"Your turn for picket duty," he said to Libby.

"Who's my partner?"

"Lewis. Try not to shoot each other."

He entered the tent as Libby exited, a feat that caused a temporary strain on the tent poles. After Libby's crunchy footsteps had faded, he said, "I wish those two would make up. What happened that night?"

"They both said things they shouldn't."

"They should remember they are on the same side. But it's not up to me to make them less stupid."

Josephine stuck a candle into a bayonet ring and lit the wick. Wesley held his hands to the tiny flame. He looked down as he spoke.

"Listen, Joseph, I got no one to keep me warm and neither do you. What do you say we sleep together until our boys come back from picket duty?"

"What happened to Floyd?"

"Ah, he found himself a friend."

"Who?"

"Remember that big farmer we passed on the road? Floyd took a look at the meat on his bones and offered him two dollars to sleep with him."

"That farmer looked warm, all right."

"So what do you say? I'm afraid I'll freeze to death before Lewis gets back."

The presence of Wesley had filled the tent with new odors. Spices from fires, pork grease, sweat, and something vaguely sweet. Molasses? Honeysuckle? Some ghostly fragrance out of nowhere. Josephine couldn't help but feel her hopes rise at the thought of being close to him.

"I'm cold, too," she said, trying to keep her voice neutral.

He took off his shoes, lifted her oilcloth, and crawled next to her. She turned on her side, and he put his arms around her and drew her to him, until her back was pressed against his chest and their legs were entangled. She shivered harder. His arms tightened.

"Don't worry," he said. "I'm like a campfire. Like the sun. Abilenes have hot blood. That's where Lewis gets his temper."

"You don't have one."

"I do. Comes out sometimes."

She felt his breath on her neck as he spoke. She'd been thinking of him, about how his arm had been broken out of love. It was just the kind of love you could expect out here, where decisions were harsh but necessary. He moved his arm, and she felt the hard knot where the bone had broken. He spoke in her ear again, something ordinary, but she barely listened, too busy reveling in the warmth and feel of his body.

She remembered once spying Arden and Libby lying in this same position in the meadow, no blanket between their bodies and the grass, no clouds in the sky, no breeze. A perfect day where the world turns blank, just for a moment, and lovers can live in a space with no distractions. Arden whispered something into Libby's ear. She did not reply but turned her eyes toward the direction of the woods, looking back into history, perhaps, or admiring a bird. All these secret, whispered things. Two people who fit together and left the rest of the world discontinuous.

She knew she was just another man to Wesley, but she couldn't help wondering if he had sniffed any clues on the back of her neck or felt any tension in the air of the tent, an inclination that she fitted him more perfectly than he knew.

"Wesley," she whispered, "are you asleep?"

He didn't answer. She could feel his steady breathing.

"Wesley," she said again, just to make sure, and then said his name one more time, in her own voice.

Libby and Lewis hadn't spoken all night. The tension between them made the sound of snapping branches hard on their nerves.

Libby couldn't feel her legs. The numbness had spread from her toes to her ankles and then crept higher as the hours passed. She struggled to stay awake. She hadn't been sleeping well. Arden still spoke to her in dreams; the dark tone in his voice troubled her and left her weary in the morning.

She exhaled a cloud of smoke. The forest turned mushy. Her gun slid out of position. As she approached the edge of sleep, a light flashed between the trees, her eyes flew open, and her body jerked and stiffened.

She raised her gun and fired.

There was no reaction in the inky blackness. No voices or returning fire.

Lewis snorted in derision. "There ain't no one out there. You're wasting your bullets firing at ghosts. You need twenty-one real men, don't you, to avenge your poor dead friend?"

Her eyes stung, but the tears didn't fall. She knelt and reloaded. The palm of her bare hand stuck to the freezing barrel. She gritted her teeth as she peeled her hand away.

Lewis spat in the snow. "You've killed one Yankee. And that was a lucky shot. Your dead friend—what did you say his name was? Arden?—is sitting up in heaven without nobody worth a damn to carry on his purpose."

Libby felt a sudden rage fill her. She stood and pointed her gun at him and suddenly found herself speaking to him in a voice that was even deeper than the one she constantly, vigilantly affected. "Say another word, and I'll shoot you."

"You don't even—"

She fired. The bullet whizzed past his ear, so close he cringed. He covered his ear and stared at her in disbelief.

"You're crazy," he whispered.

19

An artillery wagon had bogged down in the mud, blocking the road and halting the progress of the brigade. The men were told to rest, but Wesley and Josephine wandered off together, far enough that the swearing of the mule drivers was a hymn in the distance. The sky was the color of soaked hardtack, and under this sky the farms stretched out, fields in fallow, flowers dead, cows nibbling at stacks of hay.

Wesley swept his hand over the vista. "Just imagine living out here in the middle of nowhere. I could sit on my porch and play my guitar."

"What about the Southern cause?" Josephine said, mimicking the ardent tone of her sister with a small smile. "States' rights?"

"How about Wesley's rights? How about a chicken's right to boil in a pot? How about a blackberry's right to be made into brandy? Where are these famous states' rights we're fighting for? I've never met them. I'm not fighting for nothing, except my own good name. And sometimes I even wonder why I'm doing that."

They walked up a gentle rise. Wesley fell silent, and Josephine waited for him to speak again. She never knew what he was thinking about until he said it. Conversations with him were an adventure — sudden turns into religion, history, music, or the best way to draw the wild taste out of deer meat. He glanced at her and then looked away. His thoughtful stare had increased in duration and intensity as the march had progressed. A mystery lingered right under his nose. She had to fight the urge toward feminine gestures, natural when a man enters the space of a woman. She was, after all, a woman. She had checked for herself in the slow water of a river.

Wesley spoke again. "Lewis believes he's fighting for the South. But I think he just likes shooting things."

They had reached the top of the rise. He stopped there and gazed down at the farms below them. "I'm hungry, Joseph. Let's go get us some food."

"You mean, steal it?"

"Borrow it."

"We'll get shot."

"We'll be quiet."

The farmhouse sat in the middle of a huge plot of land, the field in fallow, skinny cows grazing. Apple and fig trees stood behind the house, their branches bare. A barn, an old shed, a smokehouse, and a field full of dry cornstalks completed the property.

"Where are the chickens?" Wesley whispered. "I want a chicken."

"How would we cook a chicken?"

"I don't care. I'll eat it raw. Follow me."

He crept down the hill. Josephine caught up with him, drawn by the adventure. It had just enough danger and just enough Wesley in it to spark her intrigue. Besides, she felt starved. She understood now why soldiers would pause in battle long enough to shoot a pig. Hunger, like Jackson, demanded to be served.

They entered the cornfield, moving through the stalks. When they reached the edge, Wesley hunched down and considered his plan.

"Whoever's in that house," he said, "has got to have food."

"You're one smart man, Wesley."

Wesley punched Josephine's arm, so hard she had to rub it.

Raccoon skins dried on the back porch. A bentwood chair faced the outbuildings. A pocketknife stuck straight out of the rail. Wood shavings littered the pine boards. "A whittler," Wesley whispered. "And he's old. Look at the birdseed scattered everywhere."

They approached the house, bending down low and darting forward, ever mindful of guns and dogs. Wesley peered into the window, pressing his forehead to the glass. "I don't see nobody. They must be upstairs." He shot Josephine a look of companionable sneakiness and turned the doorknob slowly. They entered a short passageway that led to the kitchen, which was spotless and smelled of bread. She pointed wordlessly at the hearth, where a fire was burning. He shrugged and opened a cupboard, pulling out a can.

"Oh, no," he whispered. "Condensed milk. I hate condensed milk. Then again, beggars can't be choosers." He stuffed the can in a pocket and kept looking, his efforts rewarded when he pulled out a jar of apple butter. "Look!" he whispered. He opened the jar and took a scoop that proved too ambitious when a clot of apple butter slid from his finger and landed on the table. He leaned over and licked it off, gathering some old cracker crumbs on his tongue in the process. He held the jar out to Josephine, and she tasted the treat. It flooded her with pleasure and a homesick feeling.

She heard a sound.

"What's that?" she asked.

"What?"

Sudden footsteps thundered down the stairs. An old man's voice called, "Who's there? Who's there?"

Wesley rushed Josephine out of the kitchen. She looked behind her and gasped. An old man in overalls stood at the end of the passageway and leveled his rifle.

"Run!" Wesley shouted.

They rushed out the back door and across the porch as the gun went off, then ran a zigzag pattern through the yard and took shelter behind the smokehouse. They caught their breath. Wesley peered around the corner.

"What's he doing?" she asked.

"He's reloading . . . now he's walking into the yard . . . damn, now he's coming this way."

Wesley tested the smokehouse door and found it unlocked. The smell of wood fires and cured meat filled up her nostrils as he pulled her inside and closed the door behind them. The floor was sticky with grease. Wesley pressed his nose to a crack between the boards and said, "He's looking in the shed now. If that old man goes in the direction of the cornfield, we'll bust out of here and run the other way, toward the fence."

The sun was positioned directly over the smokehouse, pouring its light down on them through the vents in the roof, illuminating the flayed carcasses of hogs and deer. Barrels lined the wall, and jars of crackling sat on a shelf above the barrels. She stepped backward into a pit of old hickory ashes. Her pulse fluttered and, despite the cold, her face was wet with perspiration. A little bit of battle fear had crept inside her, that feeling that comes from having no control over what happens next.

"Ah," Wesley said in relief, "the geezer's going back into the house. Too old for bloodshed, I guess."

Josephine wiped the sweat from her face.

"What happened to the apple butter?"

"I dropped it. I'm sorry." He gestured toward the carcasses. "Well, at least we got meat. And, oh, yes, canned milk. Let's see what's in those barrels. Maybe molasses. Maybe honey."

He pried off a lid with his pocketknife. Flour motes danced in the shafts of light. He grunted and moved on to the next barrel. "Oh, sweet God," he said after he'd eased the lid off. "This here's applejack, Joseph. If the boys back at camp knew there was a barrel full of applejack sitting here, they'd trample women and children to get to this farm."

Wesley poured the water out of his canteen and submerged it in the barrel, listening to the deep slugging sound with an expression of increasing contentment. When the applejack had filled his canteen, he toasted the carcass of a pig hanging nearby, threw back his head, and took several deep gulps. He paused to catch his breath. "You've got to try this," he said.

She shook her head.

"Just take a sip," he said. "It will warm you up."

He handed the canteen to her, and she tried a sip as he began hacking on the carcass of a pig with his pocketknife, freeing hunks of smoked meat. She tried another sip, then another, feeling the burn of deepening insouciance travel down her body, undoing things. War, hunger, cold, fear, various privations. Even touching her deep and terrible secret and at least dulling its knifing effect. She started to hand the canteen back to him, but stopped and took a gulp this time, letting the applejack travel down into her like a dove alighting on a field of battle. .

Wesley had his pockets full of smoked meat. He sat down with her, and they rested their backs against the wall, tearing into the meat and washing it down with applejack until it was gone. He stood up, somewhat unsteadily, and hacked off some more, and they repeated the process, trading the canteen back and forth until it was empty and he had to visit the barrel again for more.

Their filling stomachs and emptying canteen drew the sun closer until Josephine was no longer cold at all, but warm as though it were high summer. The influence of applejack had made her feel forgiven. Maybe she was innocent, after all, and subject not to a hellish punishment but to, perhaps, a continuous receipt of small good fortunes. Starting with the man who was looking at her now.

"You are a good friend," Wesley said. "As good as Floyd, even. I thought this war was gonna bring me nothing but misery. I never counted on meeting such good people."

He took off his jacket, and she almost took hers off as well, drunk enough to peel back the layers of clothing until a secret lived in the smokehouse. But she caught herself just in time. Slats of light moved across Wesley's face, revealing freckles. She felt warm and yet her breath still made a fog. The carcass Wesley had cut from swung slowly back and forth, a peaceful motion that imitated the rocking of a cradle.

"I think it's time to go back," she said.

"Oh, no, no." Wesley touched her arm. "Let's stay in here."

She rose and tried to regain her balance. Wesley did the same. His cheeks were flushed pink and his eyes were shining. One leg buckled and straightened.

"I don't want to go," he said. "I want to stay here with you. Things are so simple with you."

"Things are simple with you, too," she said. Her head was swimming. The hanging carcasses slowly rotated. The smokehouse smelled sweet, like peace. And there was Wesley. Smiling at her fondly, drunkenly. Looking for all the world like a boy just come back from a fishing trip or a wrestling match with his favorite dog.

"I want to stay in here, too," she said. "I want to never leave."

He stumbled, hitting the carcass of a pig. He looked at her as the pig swayed gently and then hung still.

"You don't belong in this war. You're too good. Can't even kill a man."

"You don't know everything about me, Wesley. I've done some things that would surprise you."

He laughed. "Like what? Slap a mosquito? Roll over in your sleep and crush a butterfly?" He touched the side of her face. "God," he said. "Even your face is smooth. How could that be?"

"You're drunk."

"So are you."

He moved toward her, so close that she could see flour motes in his eyelashes. Josephine looked in his eyes, and suddenly she reached her hands up to his face, pulled him down to her, and kissed him. He pressed his lips into hers, then pulled back in astonishment, his eyes wide, moving backward away from her, losing his balance, and stumbling against the smokehouse door. It flew open and he fell into the yard.

By midafternoon the ammunition wagons were fixed. The bugles had sounded. The men gathered up their weapons and began falling into rank. Libby cupped her hands to her face and called into the woods. "Joseph! Joseph! Joseph!"

Lewis's concern over Wesley had taken the form of an itch on his back. In his effort to scratch it, he had already contorted himself to the point that his shirttail had come out. He walked over to Libby and gazed out into the woods with her, still scratching. The two enemies stood together, bonded suddenly by their mutual fears.

Lewis spit some tobacco juice into the grass. "Where do you think they went?"

"I don't know. I went to fill my canteen, and when I came back, they were gone."

"You don't think the Yankees got them, do you?"

"Of course not," she said, but the question had already stung Lewis on the spot between his shoulders he couldn't quite reach. She watched him flailing at it, first reaching his hand over his shoulder and then up the small of his back, his escalating torment finally driving Libby to reach over and scratch between his shoulder blades. He turned and gave her a look of naked gratitude.

"You two come on," Floyd said. "We got to go. And where are those two peas in a pod?"

"They're missing."

"Missing?" The old drummer had spent the day asleep, his slouch hat under his head and his handkerchief folded on his chest. His brow began to contort as though it had a terrible itch of its own. "Wesley is missing?"

"And my cousin," Libby said.

Lewis pointed at the clearing, where two figures were stumbling into sight.

"Looky here," he said.

She squinted. "Are they drunk? They look drunk."

The three of them stood in silent disapproval as Josephine and Wesley, wobbling and leaning on each other for support, made their way up the small inclination to the place where they stood.

"Where have you two been?" Libby asked.

"In a smokehouse," Wesley said. He and Josephine burst into laughter, doubling over and slapping their thighs.

"Damn fools," said Lewis. "Could have been left behind. Could have been killed. We're about to move again. How are you two gonna march, all drunk and twist-legged?"

"March?" asked Wesley. "We're not marching. We're our own army, now. Not blue, not gray. We have no color. We are the army of the middle."

"Stop your babbling, you idiot," Floyd said. "Unless you'd like to wear a barrel shirt up that mountain pass."

"The army of the middle," Josephine repeated, whirling. All her masculine attributes had fallen off somewhere in the woods.

"Got you all something," Wesley said. "Gather round and reach in my haversack. Don't let anyone see you or there'll be a riot."

"What you got, boy?" Floyd said.

"Smoked ham."

"Oh, dear Lord, son. You are forgiven."

• • •

The sunlight waned as the army moved. Migrating hawks flew overhead. Wesley and Josephine sang a marching song.

"You two quit," Floyd said. "I can't stand your infernal singing any longer. Why don't you concentrate on keeping in step, you two applejack-soaked varmints?"

"Yeah." Lewis walked with his musket on one shoulder and Wesley's guitar hanging by its leather strap over the other. "Old man's right. Shut your mouths."

Wesley and Josephine paid no attention.

I hear the distant thunder-hum, Maryland!
The Old Line's bugle, fife and drum, Maryland!
She is not dead, nor deaf, nor dumb . . .

"I wish I was deaf," said Floyd.

"I apologize for my cousin," Libby said. "He has very little experience with liquor and has no tolerance of it."

"You know how Stonewall Jackson feels about liquor," Lewis said. "He won't touch a drop."

Josephine stopped singing. "Stonewall Jackson doesn't sound very fun. In fact, he seems rather boring."

Libby shook her head. "Joseph, don't talk that way about our general."

"His horse is ugly," Wesley said.

Lewis shot him a stern look. "You shut your mouth, boy, if you know what's good for you."

"Close up!" the sergeant commanded, and the line moved together.

For once, Josephine couldn't feel the chill in the air. The liquor had leveled the world until the war slid off of it, and she was free for the first time since the whole ugly thing had begun. She stumbled, fell, climbed to her feet, and fell again.

Floyd took her gun. Lewis handed Wesley's guitar to another soldier to carry, then picked her up and threw her over his shoulder. The Jackson Brigade was upside down, and the sky was mixing clouds until they lost their shape. She dangled over Lewis's shoulder, swinging back and forth in time to his perfect route step. She could not help smiling. For once she had not had to share a day with Jackson or Lee or even Jefferson Davis, for that matter. She had left the army and become a civilian and lived in a house full of smoke and meat and cracklings and sunlight and the company of a good man. Everyone should live this way. She arched her back and stretched her arms out. She could fly if she wanted. It all seemed so possible, the war so short and tiny and stunted, it would never seem mighty again.

Wesley in the smokehouse. Soft touch of his lips to hers, dance of flour motes. Electric current, a spark out of place. And because time loves the drunk and allows itself to be looped around happy things, she saw Wesley again and again, kissing her, backing up and starting over again, sunlight filtering through the air, his hands his eyes a kiss a kiss a kiss a kiss, sewn together into many kisses, oh yes, she had been kissed. Years from now people would discover the old shirtless man dead in his rocker, rifle cradled in his arms, and they would go outside, open up the smokehouse, and find this day.

Josephine had been there, not Joseph, not this false ghost of a man forced to live without lace. Josephine, who could go where she wanted and drink what she wanted and kiss whom she wanted and laugh at things that were not funny. Josephine, who fell out of line. Josephine, soldier of the middle.

She shut her eyes, but the starlight came into the tent and burned through her lids, finding her headache. She and Libby lay shivering together under their blankets. She was twice as cold as she had been the night before, her uniform twice as heavy. Gone was the laughter. Gone was the spinning sky. Gone was the sunlight, the freedom, the peace.

Gone was Josephine. Back was Joseph.

Libby had paused in her hushed, angry lecture, but then gained momentum again. "And you made me look foolish and our friends look foolish and the brigade look foolish, and you were just lucky the sergeant didn't happen by, and you didn't even know what you were saying, and you were acting girlish, and what if you'd given our secret away?"

"I'm sorry." Josephine shut her eyes tight in a vain attempt to block out starlight and sister. She didn't dare tell Libby about the kiss in the shed. She kept it to herself, along with the night she spent playing poker with the Yankee pickets, another secret crime.

"You need to keep your distance from Wesley," Libby said. "He gets you in trouble. And you need to stop looking at him so much. Do you know how much you look at him?"

The two women lay shivering, forced to share the heat of their own battle. The falling snow had accumulated enough to make a slight bulge in the ceiling of their tent. Josephine didn't know why she said the words. Perhaps only because they were true, and her little sister had once been someone who could hear true things and even say them back to her.

"I love him, Libby."

She expected Libby to fire back that loving a man in such circumstances was not only dangerous but futile, and when the response came, she was shocked by its gentleness and longing, as though the real Libby had both considered the remark and formed the answer, not this ever-hardening replica of Arden who usually inhabited her skin.

"I know."

. . .

The light was feminine. Pink and beige and lavender. Bare-chested, shoeless, shivering in the cold, Wesley knelt on the ground and fiddled with his haversack. His eyes were red. A hank of hair stuck straight out in a spike. He paused and smoothed it absently.

The sight of him burst Josephine's morning thoughts. Rolled blankets, cartridge belts, cold feet. All like motes of flour now, drifting toward the sky.

"Wesley," she said.

He looked up at her. "Hey, Joseph." His voice was flat. Without love or even recognition.

"Your head hurt?" she asked.

He shrugged. "A little." His spike of hair stood up, and he smoothed it down again as he looked at her with guarded eyes. "Listen, Joseph. I've heard about those kind of fellows. I'm not that kind of fellow, understand?"

It took a moment for his meaning to register. Josephine felt as though she'd been shot. Right now some sniper in the trees was gazing with satisfaction at the hole in her stomach. In the drunken hours that followed their time in the shed, she had not considered that the memory of the kiss, so lovely to her, was confusing and shameful to him. And why wouldn't it be? He couldn't see her and didn't know her. Her true self was lost like an acorn under the snow.

"I'm not that kind of fellow, either," she said. She backed away from him, stumbling over someone's iron spider and falling to the ground with a loud thump. He didn't move as she picked herself up. The pink light hurt her, as did its lavender streaks. She looked around the camp. Soldiers were hurrying, packing their haversacks, and rolling up their blankets. Nothing about the brigade or the world had changed since the day before. It was exactly as they'd left it. She didn't know if she could bear it anymore. She had emerged from the cold shell of her lie long enough to kiss the soldier she loved, and that moment had been so warm and true. She could not believe she was about to move down the macadam road away from it, leaving it behind. And she was filled with a certain after-battle kind of devastation, where the body stops to consider the depth of sorrow and the soul takes on an aching heaviness. Her companion was lost to her, not on a battlefield but in a smokehouse, not from a bullet but a kiss.

They marched twenty miles that day. She kept up listlessly, stone-bruised and brokenhearted. Wesley wouldn't look at her. He didn't join in on the marching songs or the jokes. Floyd told him he needed a haircut and a new face, too, then waited in vain for the counter-insult, like an old wolf listening for the returning howl of its pup.

"What's wrong with that boy?" Floyd asked Lewis.

Lewis shook his head. "He don't have no legs for liquor. Never has."

That night Wesley played the guitar and sang, face tense and eyes flat. And yet his voice still haunted his listeners, sending them to a private space where they had no skin. Josephine sat with the others. On this night, her mind went through all the losses and then rested on the new one.

20

It was barely December, but winter had already taken hold of the mountains. The wind howled. The mules lost their footing. Stirrups froze to boots. Men who awoke at dawn had to chip themselves out of a layer of ice. Toes and fingers turned black.

Josephine and Libby grew too thin for their pants and had to cut new holes in their belts. Their lips cracked. They walked on the rubber of feet gone numb and whispered together under their oilcloths, united in a common shiver. Separately they thought of their parents and ached for their company and their comfort, but the subject never passed between them.

One night a deserter was brought into camp, starved and halffrozen. He was spared execution, but the letter C was branded on his left hip, which turned red as they marked him.

Wesley stopped playing the guitar. His hands would have stuck to the strings.

Libby's skin turned pale, and the purple rings around her eyes grew darker. Her worried sister went from soldier to soldier, begging for dried meat or extra rations.

Floyd coughed.

The supply wagons bogged down in the slush. The hooves of mules split open. The teamsters applied dry calomel and caustics.

The pamphlets ran out after volume 3 of *Les Misérables,* leaving the soldiers to wonder what would befall Jean Valjean and Cosette, and themselves.

Josephine and Libby no longer needed to hoard rags or dart into the woods at odd hours. Their monthly flow had stopped.

Soldiers ate the leather of their shoelaces and the meat of dead horses. One man ate holly berries and died, and one shot a hawk and had to wrench it away from his friends.

Josephine caught Wesley's eye, and he looked away.

She had kissed a man. So had he.

Floyd coughed as he marched, as he ate, all night as he slept, his face drawn and chest heaving with the effort.

"You stop that, old man," Wesley said, and slept with his arms around him.

Lewis told his brother to stay away from him. "You're going to catch whatever he has."

"Don't be a bastard. He's cold."

One night Josephine woke up and found that Libby had vanished. She lit a torch and followed Libby's footsteps through the snow. She found her standing alone at the edge of the woods and took her by the arm. "Are you crazy?" she asked.

Libby's lips had no color.

"I heard his voice."

Waterfalls, pneumonia, clouds of breath, snow, ice. Mules straining. Men falling down dead, but not from bullets.

Wesley lay with his arms around Floyd, who had turned into a bony bag of heatless snores and unrelenting coughing. Floyd groaned in his sleep. Wesley hugged him tighter. This love he understood.

The Stonewall Brigade marched down into the Virginia Piedmont, toward Madison at the end of the first week of December. Rolling hills and farmland lay all around them, lulling them like the fields around Sharpsburg. Tall peaks rose behind them, the

Massanutten and the Blue Ridge Mountains. The men had been told their destination while crossing the Luray Valley.

Fredericksburg.

Now it was midnight, and the army was marching as they slept, one animal now, a conflicted beast who sometimes smiled in its slumber, sometimes screamed in it, sometimes coughed and sometimes cried, sometimes sang, sometimes hoped; eyes open, eyes closed, it did not wake. Anyone witness to the phenomenon would not believe it. Men could not sleep and stay in formation, weapons on their shoulders, mile after mile. And yet they did. The road behind them was scattered with hats that had fallen from their nodding heads, and they emanated an intimate hum, as twenty thousand men shared their dreams, equal sunlight, equal soup.

Certain local farmers claimed they saw translucent men among the ranks, those who still lived and breathed, but who were doomed nonetheless. When these farmers looked out their windows at the soldiers of D Company filing past, they saw this mixture of fate in the sleepwalkers, some whose bodies were starved and yet solid, and some more insubstantial, just a shape of blue mist.

The moon was full through the branches. Libby stood picket in the woods, listening for footsteps, her heart thudding. Black oak trees all around her. Sounds of night animals. Fog churning low, through palmetto and Boston fern. The other pickets were quiet in the darkness. Strange shadows crept forward and darted back when they touched her arms, responding to the heat of her body in the manner of reptiles. She froze, listening.

Did she hear footsteps? A branch cracked. She thought she saw a figure gliding among the trees.

"Halt!" she demanded in a quavering voice, but the figure had disappeared.

She heard footsteps again, and her body began to tremble. She put the gun to her shoulder, trying to steady the barrel.

"Who goes there?" Her stiff finger rested on the trigger.

The figure glided out from behind the tree and stood there, a black outline against the forest. It took a step toward her, then another.

"Stop, or I'll shoot, I'll shoot!"

One more step.

She shut her eyes and pulled the trigger with all her might. The explosion rocked the forest. When she opened her eyes the figure was still walking toward her. Frantically she tried to reload her gun, but the ramrod stuck in the barrel. A burst of moonlight fell down over the stranger, illuminating the handsome face, the dark eyes. A patch of blood grew on his stomach, spreading outward in the shape of a canteen. A group of fireflies spurted out of the wound, blinking off and on. Arden staggered, straightened up, moved closer.

"Libby," he said. "Do you not recognize your husband?"

"I've killed you, Arden."

"No, you haven't. You know who killed me."

"A Yankee."

"What did you see that day in the West Woods of Sharpsburg?"

"I saw many things. Things that could not be true."

"Libby." His face so close to hers, no smoke from his breath. "You saw it with your own eyes. Your sister killed me."

Libby woke up. Her feet were still moving, the road stretched out to Fredericksburg. No Arden. Just all the other soldiers, rows and rows of men, heads bowed, marching in their sleep.

21

December 1862

Fredericksburg, Virginia

Campfires roared. Bottles of liquor appeared magically. The brigade had reached Fredericksburg and was making frenzied use of the final hours before the battle. They had just spent a week at Guiney's Station, trying to restore themselves to fighting shape with fresh beef and warm fires. Members of F Company had been sent to Richmond to buy leather, and moccasins had appeared on the feet of shoeless men.

The impending battle had the same aroma as the skewered and sizzling meat. Soldiers drank whiskey by yellow light and traded actress cards of scantily clad young women. As the evening progressed, they grew raucous. Their eyes shone. Fire couldn't cure what the winter had done to them, any more than snow cures thirst. But they couldn't accept that. They wanted more heat, more. More sparks, more whiskey. The distant battle smelled good.

Confederate pickets tossed insults across the Rappahannock River and were insulted in return. An even trade. Like tobacco for coffee.

More rails were thrown on the fire, in violation of the rules set down by Stonewall Jackson. They had done nothing for weeks but march to another man's plan, freezing, starving, blood on the ice behind them as far as the eye could see, nothing but blind devotion moving them forward.

Dysentery, measles, typhus, pneumonia, frostbite.

And yet when their leader arrived at the camp, his men stood and cheered him, filled up with adoration the way they'd once been filled with Sunday lessons, satiated in this war of scarcity, the weeks and months of being almost well and almost calm and almost asleep and almost brave and almost home.

"Old Jack! Old Jack!"

He took off his hat and his sorrel horse pranced through the snow, its tail stripped thin by the souvenir-hunting women of Martinsburg. The regimental band struck up the music to a deafening volume, breaking ice from the limbs of evergreens. Jackson rode away, but the band kept playing. The spirited men began to dance. Lacking women, they paired off in couples, one taking the female role and one the male. The strong found each other, as did the weak. The vigorous pairs spun around and around until they grew dizzy. The frailest dancers barely turned. Those who could not stand up sat on logs and cheered the others. Those who could not speak lay in the hospital tent and turned their faces to the sound.

Libby's stomach had shrunk during the long march, and she had to stop eating after just a few strips of beef and some hardtack soaked in a cup of broth. But at least she was warm now. She sat on an ammunition box and watched the dancing men. They'd grown drunker as the night had progressed. Some of them had fallen down and crawled away. And yet there seemed more of them now.

A week of rest and warmth had cleared her senses. She was thinking about Josephine again, trying to bury that old, vague memory from the woods of Sharpsburg and yet reliving it again and again. She knew Josephine had never cared for Arden — had said as much many times — but could her sister, so gentle and kind, possibly be capable of such an act?

She looked up as Lewis approached. Her muscles coiled, but Lewis sat down next to her and stretched out his feet in a companionable gesture.

"I got some new moccasins," he said after a while.

"I see that."

He took a pint bottle out of his pocket and unscrewed the flask. "I think I got cheated on this hooch." He held the bottle up to the light. "It looks awful weak."

Libby glanced at the bottle and then went back to watching the dancers.

"Want a drink?" Lewis asked. "It's so watered down, a minnow could live in the damn stuff."

Libby shook her head.

They sat in silence for a bit. Lewis took a long gulp from his flask and then tapped his fingers against the glass. "I have a feeling you're gonna get some tomorrow," he said.

She looked at him, confused.

"Some what?"

"Yankees, I mean. Hell, maybe seven or eight."

Lewis took another gulp and swished it around before he swallowed.

Josephine stood by herself just outside the circle of swirling men and roaring fire and loud and raucous music from an increasingly drunken band. She had been largely alone on the march, Libby in her own world and Wesley close by but never close anymore. He was too kind to openly avoid her, but he kept to himself, speaking to her only when it would seem rude not to. His absence had been the worst part of the march, worse than the fear and hunger and pain. She wished she'd never met him, never cared about him, so that the privation could be evenly spread from one edge of the war to another. Misery from the beginning.

"Joseph."

Wesley's voice startled her. She had rehearsed a thousand things to say to him, one each more daring than the last, until she reached the height of her daydreamed confessions.

Wesley, I'm a woman. Now you understand everything.

"Joseph," he repeated.

The sound of two-thirds of her name was painful to her. A lie that one more syllable would make right.

She looked up. He cradled his guitar in his arms. It had frozen one night and thawed into a different instrument. She'd seen him tuning and retuning it, trying in vain to restore the old sound.

"Everybody's crazy tonight," he said, in a way that invited conversation.

She didn't know whether to feel angry or overjoyed. She touched the hot collar of her shirt. "Where have you been?" she asked, and realized, too late, that he may have taken her question in a larger context than she meant.

"Oh, I've been looking after Floyd. I brought him some soup and tried to play him a song, but this guitar is ruined from the cold. It's firewood now." He thumped it with his fingertips as though the hollow sound proved something to her.

"How is Floyd?" she asked.

"He's got a fever, and he's coughing up a storm. Crazy old man. What's he doing in this army, anyway?" Wesley looked out at the dancers. "Well, I'll be damned," he said, pointing into the swirling crowd. "My brother is dancing with your cousin."

"I thought they hated each other."

"Seems like everyone loves everyone tonight. And tomorrow we're gonna start killing each other without missing a step. What a war."

He held out his hand. "Let's dance."

"I can't dance."

"That's not stopping anyone else. Come on, Joseph, don't be a chicken."

The music blared. The fires crackled. Wesley and Josephine spun around and around, crashing into other dancers. The dancing warmed her own body, warmed his — she could feel it through his shirt, but she could not smile as he was smiling, nor laugh as he was laughing. The next battle was looming, and God could take anyone in the blink of an eye. Dancers and laughers and drinkers of whiskey and players of cards. And people burning with love.

Libby and Josephine lay behind their earthworks on a wooded hill that looked down on the flat plains stretching to the river. The Confederates were two lines deep, the Stonewall Brigade forming the second line. A heavy fog blanketed the plains, obscuring their sight, but for three hours they had been listening to the bustle of a terrible preparation somewhere underneath that mist. Wagons, bugles, drums. Artillery shells came soaring in from the direction of the river, exploding in treetops, and raining bark down on the Confederate lines.

"Missed me!" Wesley kept shouting.

Floyd had been too sick to join the battle. A drummer without his passion had stepped in for him. The sun was burning the mist away. Another few minutes would reveal what lay beneath their promontory. Josephine wasn't sure if she wanted to know what was coming. As a child, she had been taunted by the other children for covering her eyes when she heard stories of ghosts. *Cover your ears if you're afraid, ninny,* they said. But her visual imaginings had always seemed more frightening than the tales themselves.

Another shell whistled. She closed her eyes and saw darkness filled with an uneasy red static, an effect of the sunlight penetrating her lids. She waited. The shell burst a low branch, and she heard Wesley shout, "You're getting warmer, you sons of bitches!" She heard Libby breathing beside her and felt her sister's clarity of purpose. The night before, after the dance, Libby had sat up in the tent, staring at nothing and moving her lips. Josephine had awakened in the dead of night to find her in the same position.

Josephine opened her eyes and drew in her breath. A ghost story had been lurking out of sight, and the fog had just broken open to reveal the terrifying climax. An endless sea of Yankees moved away from the river and toward the Confederate earthworks. Bayonets by the thousands glinted in the sun. Batteries and ambulance wagons filled in the gaps between the blue coats. Josephine had never imagined so many soldiers, legions of them, marching in ranks of three. Regimental flags waved by the hundreds. All around her, Rebels were silently counting the flags, doing crude multiplications and shaking their heads.

"This isn't possible," Wesley said. "They must be playing tricks on us."

Josephine leaned close to her sister and whispered, "Libby, am I seeing things? There aren't that many Yankees, are there?"

Libby looked at her evenly. "Fire your gun."

The blue sea shimmered and advanced.

Libby's failure to kill a single Yankee in the last fight had tormented her the entire march, and now her only fear was that the great army before her was merely an illusion, and that it would disappear before she could begin to count the dead. Here was a grand opportunity for vengeance. A blue gift coming.

The Confederates had been ordered to hold their fire and let their artillery do their work. Shells from their batteries raked the left lines of the advancing troops, tearing out pieces of the beautiful parade. Stonewall Jackson sat watching the bombardment, seemingly unconcerned about the shells flying over his head. His sorrel snorted in bored contentment. Jackson's perfect faith kept him calm. The horse was just stupid.

The gray guns went quiet, sending up an after-cloud of smoke. The Federals regrouped and began their advance, encouraged by the certainty that they had destroyed the Confederate batteries. But they fell in Jackson's trap, and thus God's.

When they drew to within eight hundred yards of the earthworks, Jackson gave a signal, and artillery fire tore through the enemy. Union soldiers died in waves. A cannonball fell into their ranks, tearing off a man's head, blowing out the chest of someone behind him, and, at the lower end of the arc, severing the legs of the third man.

Battle flags fell. Blood collected in pools. Horses screamed and ambulance wagons overturned. Soon a new mist gathered over the heads of the armies, this one made of niter.

Throughout this bombardment, the Confederates along the earthworks had held their fire, but a sudden reversal of fortune let the Union soldiers regroup. They were charging now. The Rebels gripped their muskets.

"Don't shoot yet!" the captain screamed. "Wait for my signal. And don't be cowards! You are the men of the Stonewall Brigade! Do you want to live forever?"

Libby looked at her sister. "Fire your gun," she repeated. "Do you hear me, Josephine?"

Josephine put the rifle to her shoulder and touched the trigger, drew back, and then touched it again. "I hear you."

Union soldiers streamed through the trees, breaking one Confederate line and heading toward the earthworks of the Stonewall Brigade.

"*Charge! But don't fire!* Wait for my signal, damn you!"

The brigade jumped from the earthworks and gave the Rebel

yell as they rushed down into the swampy part of the woods, passing a fallen officer who was wounded in the spine.

The captain put his fist in the air. *"Fire!"*

Libby aimed and pulled the trigger. A Yankee's eyes widened as he lost everything above his brow line. He went down jerking and twitching. This time it was not her imagination.

A loud cannonade landed to Libby's right, followed by the screams of the dying. She turned her head, and the soldiers were right in front of her, but she was ready, teeth clenched and blood boiling and Arden not near her but inside her. She would avenge him; she would express love as a burning hatred; she was not afraid — they were fearless together, ghost and survivor, man and wife. A bluecoat pointed his gun at her, and she shot him, his throat exploding perfectly, as though its seams had been designed in the womb to burst that way. She watched him fall, his white breath pouring out through the hole in his throat, and she fought on, firing, reloading, minie balls falling around her and making hot pits in the snow. She saw another bluecoat taking aim, and she killed him, too; suddenly another was leaping at her, and she pushed the blade of her bayonet to his chest, and he was killed by his own momentum, his eyes shocked and a slight smile on his face he'd worn somewhere as a boy and was wearing now to heaven. Lewis had the regimental flag of the enemy in his hands, and he was running back to his line showing no fear at all on his face, just a joy so transcendent he looked like he was coming back from an altar call.

"Give 'em hell, boys!" the captain shouted. "Give 'em hell, give 'em —"

A whistling sound interrupted his command as a minie ball took off his right arm. His body hit the ground with a thump.

The Federals began to retreat, but the Confederates pursued them. There was no captain left to scream at them. The line of Rebels was in chaos, splitting into separate grudges and prayers, chasing the Yankees back into the woods. So many soldiers whose blue uniforms had been spotless were piled up dead, blood pulsing out, steaming as it melted the snow. Libby found herself caught between the lines, heat at her back and heat at her front. Only the top of her head was cold.

The fighting was hand to hand now, so close that rifles were being used as clubs. Another Yankee rushed toward Libby, and she swung her gun like a club. He went down, and she speared him in the back; the number *six* came out of her mouth in a cloud of spiteful mist.

Josephine stood frozen, gun unfired and senses overwhelmed. She had the feeling of standing in the center of some insatiable stampede. The screams around her didn't sound human, and the odor of sweat was of a more ghastly intensity than any found on a work shirt or neck of a mule. Even if she had been capable of shooting someone, she could not distinguish enemy from friend.

"Libby!" she called. "Libby, Libby!" Her mad sister was off somewhere, counting and possibly being counted.

A figure rushed toward her through the clearing smoke.

It was Wesley.

"Give me your rifle!" he ordered. "Give it to me!" He took her cold gun and shoved his hot one into her hands.

Because the South held the field, certain amenities were provided for the Rebel corpses. They were handled gently and were the first to be buried. Wounded men lay on the ground, waiting for the field surgeons. Unbearably thirsty from the loss of blood, they cupped their hands to drink from gory pools of melted snow. Some of them had torn at their clothes, searching for the place the bullet entered. Josephine, unharmed and in a post-battle daze, wandered the field looking for Libby, past Rebel dead who had fought like demons in battle but in death had turned back into men, or boys. Pranksters, dog lovers, virgins, duck hunters, gamblers, teachers, tillers of the earth. The fabric of their long underwear showed through the holes in their pants. A Rebel sat motionless against a fallen tree, his rifle still in his hand, one leg taken off by a Coehorn shell. On the ground next to him, two Union soldiers embraced, their death wounds matching. Josephine began perspiring, trying not to absorb any more of the sights. She had had enough of it a hundred yards before, but still more awaited her.

She found Libby calmly sitting cross-legged on the ground, still holding her gun, her eyes blank. Josephine knelt beside her. "Libby, are you wounded?"

Libby looked at her. "I killed eight of them." She held up her fingers to show Josephine, as though they were reinforcements coming in to bolster the spoken words.

"That's good, Libby. That's what you wanted, isn't it?"

Libby stared at her a moment.

"I have to find my stick."

"What stick?"

"The one I put notches on for Arden. I'll have eight new notches now."

Josephine didn't like the sound of her voice. It did not have an echo in their childhood or church. It had been at a lower register for weeks now, but at this moment, it sounded like someone entirely different, very close in cadence and tone to that of her dead husband. Josephine found herself repelled by it. She unscrewed the cap of her drum canteen and handed it to Libby.

"Drink some water."

"I'm fine."

"Please."

She watched as Libby gulped and handed it back to her. "Thank you," Libby said, but Arden's ghost had not left her voice.

"Have you seen Wesley?" Josephine asked.

"Over there."

She rose and followed in the direction Libby had pointed, past more of the dead and wounded. She kept her gaze steady and straight. She could no longer follow the story made up of bodies on frozen ground, a blue-and-gray tale whose ending was too sad to bear.

Lewis sat on an ammunition box, his legs dangling, the laces of his moccasins double knotted on his feet, his rifle resting on his lap. Wesley stood a few feet from him, looking at him. Neither man moved as Josephine approached. Smoky breath came out of Wesley's mouth, but no such breath emerged from the mouth of his brother. Lewis wore a quiet smile. Josephine stood between the two of them, her gaze moving from one man to the other, trying to solve the puzzle of the scene.

"Wesley," she said. When he made no answer, she reached out and touched Lewis's cheek, a knot of cold stone that held the smile in place. He did not blink when she passed her hand before his face, and the mystery — not a mark on him — took over her body, replacing the shock of the loss and concern for the survivor. This separation of scene and explanation vexed her. Her eyes moved down his body once again, and as she took a step and began to move around him, she saw that something — a bullet or a shell — had taken away the back of his skull and its contents, starting at the line of his ear, leaving some brain matter and a rime of frozen blood. Lewis still had a part in his hair, straight as an arrow and two inches long.

22

A heavy, windy rain began to fall that Sunday night, protecting the retreat of the Union army across the Rappahannock and driving the victors to shelter. No fires, just the relentless downpour and men determined to celebrate. The battle and its horrors could haunt them later. That night they would drink until they could achieve a kind of owl sleep in which the eyes don't move, in which dreams are banished but the dead are beckoned forth as a living presence, eyes bright and death wounds covered.

As the retreating army pulled up their pontoon boats, an aurora borealis undulated across the sky. Sheets of celestial color wrinkled like curtains and cloaked the trees, giving the illusion they could be touched and tasted. Blue, red, green, and violet lingered in the black of night. To the drunken men, it meant something they could not quite define. A blessing or a curse, a visitation, proof of God or a quirk of the cosmos. Some of the men had lost faith in miracles. They had lost everything, and that destitution followed them everywhere they went, even down the muscular forgetfulness found inside a bottle.

Libby sat alone under an evergreen. She had emptied the remainder of a bottle of Old Crow someone had passed her earlier. The branches sheltered her for the most part, but her journey into this clearing had left her soaking wet. The rain stripped away the grass and drummed into mud. Rivulets of water started fruitless treks to the Rappahannock and disappeared into snake holes. She leaned against the tree trunk and listened to the booming thunder.

She thought she heard footsteps, but her heart didn't skip a beat. She straightened, listening.

The footsteps came closer.

Arden said her name, or perhaps she said it herself. So hard to tell after all her time mimicking him. He emerged from the curtains of the rain and stood in front of her in his shell jacket and jersey pants. He ducked under the shelter of branches and knelt in front of her, so close that she could see water dripping from his eyelashes.

She reached out and touched his cool face, letting her fingers run down his cheek and across his mouth, then up to his wet hair. Every detail was true. Had she held a candle to his ear, she would have seen a small patch of freckles just above the lobe. The expression he wore was tender and sad, like that of someone watching a childhood forest cleared for lumber. He said nothing but whistled out quantities of smoky breath. The sharpest of memories could not replicate this vision. She touched his throat, the ridge of each vocal cord. When a drop of water rolled down his face and into his mouth, she felt the lump of his involuntary swallow.

His pupils shrank as lightning flashed. He took her hand. "You fought like a devil," he said, his voice sounding kinder than it had in recent dreams. "You killed eight Yankees. You honored me eight times. Aren't you proud?"

"Yes."

Her voice imitated his so faithfully, it sounded as though he had answered his own question.

"Then, why are you crying? You don't feel sorry for them, do you?"

"Arden, some of them were just boys."

"Old enough to kill."

"But the looks on their faces . . ."

"How about the look on my face?"

"One of them asked for his mother."

"I didn't ask for my mother. I asked for you."

"It was so different than what I imagined. I could hear the bullets hit them. And their screams sounded so much louder directed at me. Their eyes . . ."

"That's war, Libby. Most women only bathe what it leaves behind. But you had the strength to fight. Tell me you had no choice. Come on, say it."

"I had no choice."

"Them or you."

"Them or me."

"North or South."

"North or South."

"Now tell me you love me. Oh, there you go, crying again. We should be laughing like we always did. Want to see something funny?"

He opened his jacket.

"Look, Libby. Flies in winter."

December 17, 1862

Dear Pa and Ma,

I cant hardly write this for my hands shaking so bad at telling you that our Lewis is killed. It was at the terrible battle we fought at Fredericksburg a few days past.

Know that he had no time to suffer, and met Jesus in no pain. I buried him myself proper and marked it good so someday we can come take him home to our family place. It is right that he should lie next to Grandpa, Aunt Eliza, and Sarah.

He died protecting me — like he did every day of this war, like you told him to when we left. He oftentimes went barefooted so that my feet would be covered. He would eat little supper so that I could have extra. He kept me well and safe even when I fought him over it. You should be proud of your boy, who loved us all so.

No doubt you will fret even more over my safety now, but I am out of harm's way for the rest of the winter. We are to have more rations here than on the march, and I have shoes and a warm coat. There are many good men here with me and we aid one another. Floyd is the old rooster of our bunch and looks out for us, although we give him a terrible time. And two young cousins have joined us and I have become great friends with the older one, Joseph.

I know your hearts are broke with this news and I have no heart to go on soldiering without Lewis, but I know he would want me to continue the fight.

I will come back.

Your loving son,
Wesley

January 1863

Camp Winder

Near Fredericksburg, Virginia

Moss Neck. That place of bad water and sheltering pine. Stonewall Jackson moved into a manor whose furnishings stood out in stark contrast to the man himself. Bearskin couches, stuffed birds, and portraits of dogs all spoke gleefully of a life beyond the quest. But he had work to do, and these quarters itched of leisure. Jackson moved out the next morning.

There would be no more fighting that winter. While Jackson planned his spring campaign, his men had time to celebrate Christmas and build log shelters, complete with fireplaces and chimneys. Beds were bunk style, and any soft material — hay, leaves, or cloth — could find its place in a mattress. Chairs were made of barrel staves, and the outside walls were packed with dirt to shield against the bite of the wind. Now a soldier finally had time to rest and take stock in himself. Was that his face in the mirror? It couldn't be.

The hut that the sisters shared with Wesley could have housed six men. But Lewis and Matthew were dead, and Floyd was still coughing up fluids in the hospital tent. The luxury of space seemed to mock them. Wesley had gotten in a fistfight with a barefooted Rebel who had tried to take the moccasins off his brother's corpse. His lip was split, and he had a black eye. He wouldn't sing or play his thawed guitar, and when he spoke his voice was flat as though it, too, had fared badly in the cold. When he wasn't nursing Floyd, he sat in a corner of the hut and stared into space. His devastation moved Josephine, who wanted to join with him in that shared grief, and shower him with motherly comforts, and move her hands down the sides of his face, and press her lips to the top of his head. Once she found him standing under a tree, crying. He embraced her suddenly but wrenched himself free before she could warm him. Josephine herself could not tear free of the sight of Lewis, so calm and smiling and dead.

But even as Wesley withdrew and quieted and slowed in winter sunlight, Josephine saw encouraging signs in another loved one. The day after the battle, Arden's voice left Libby and she began talking in the familiar lower register of her false identity; to Josephine, this was a blessing. Libby put her oak stick with its nine notches under her cot and didn't take it out again. She seemed to be using the winter rest to draw on her reservoirs of strength, and slowly the color returned to her face. And though she still walked like a man, her feet coming down hard and her arms swinging wild, as though free of the memory of silk, her eyes had cleared and her expression had softened. She had worked tirelessly on the building of the hut, and once it was complete, she threw herself into her soldierly duties, drilling with precision, hunting rabbits, hewing logs, and helping to lay paths of split timber through the quagmire of mud that soon enveloped the camp.

But here and there cracks of her true self still showed. Something girlish in the way she folded a shirt in the darkness of the hut when they were alone together or moved her fingertips to her lips while listening to a story.

Once, Josephine woke up in the middle of the night to find that Wesley had not yet returned from his hospital vigil; Libby had sat down on her cot and was stroking her hair.

"Josephine," she whispered, "how do you know for sure?"

"Know what?"

"About what you're supposed to do."

"Do about what?"

But Libby didn't answer the question. Instead she told Josephine, "Say my name."

"Libby."

"Say it again."

"Libby."

"I like that," she murmured. She leaned over until her body lay next to Josephine's and fell asleep. Libby slept like a woman did, breathed like one, and was perhaps somewhere dreaming like one. This was the Libby who once lingered naked in deep water and remembered herself.

Like most wars, it started from a small thing, a seed of discontent that quickly grew and spread. The remaining pamphlets of *Les Misérables* had finally reached the camp, but before the readings could begin, they vanished. Accusations flew. Brother against brother. Friend against friend. Eyes filled with suspicion. Fingers pointed by firelight. The brigade had plenty of dried meat and even the occasional canned peach, but they did not have enough printed material to stave off the unrelenting boredom, and this dishonorable theft roused their warrior spirits.

In the midst of this tension, snow began to fall, at first turning brown in the mud and then piling up white.

The next morning, the fighting began.

"I tell you," one soldier said to another, "I don't blame that police inspector, Javert. Some say he was obsessed with his mission to capture Jean Valjean. But I think it was less a case of misguided passion, and more a case of a man trying to do his job."

"Bullshit. He was motivated by hatred and jealousy. I could prove that to you, if I had the damn book, which your company stole."

"Liar."

"Thief."

The first man packed a snowball and threw it at the second. It hit him clean in the face and exploded, leaving a red nose in its aftermath. The second man packed his own snowball and inflicted equal damage. Each man's friends rushed to his side, and then were joined by their companies, then their regiments, then their corps. A civil war within a civil war. Earthworks of white powder appeared magically, and to loud swearing and Rebel yells, the men tensed for the fight.

Libby and Josephine had crafted their snowballs with a woman's precision. Wesley joined them, still packing his snowball, his face red from running.

"Where have you been?" Josephine asked.

"With Floyd."

"How is he?"

Wesley gave her the shrug of unchanging news.

"Hold your fire!" the captain ordered. His right arm had been shot off in the battle of Fredericksburg, and he now gave signals with the other. "Wait until they get in range. Thieving bastards left us nothing to read. I've been reading a *woman's magazine!*"

The drummer boy of the rival corps came marching toward them with his line, rallying the enemy. He played so loud that snow fell off the roofs of the cabins.

The first snowball soared through the air, unleashed by a nervous new conscript who jumped the gun before the order, earning a rebuke from the captain. It landed ten feet in front of the other line and sank whole into the snow.

"Sissy!" someone called, and then snowballs filled the air in stark defiance of the officers, who muttered but could not court-martial.

"I got one!" Josephine cried, then received a hard missile in return that hit her shoulder bone and made her gasp.

Libby avenged her.

Wesley let the enemy snowballs hit him but did not throw his own, instead keeping it cocked in one hand as he marched toward the other line. He climbed up on the rooftop of a cabin and stood with his two feet planted and the original snowball poised in his hand, searching the teeming armies below him as Josephine paused in the battle to watch him from a low angle. The snow had turned to mud in places, and men were rolling in it, suddenly rising up with mud balls. One of the missiles hit Wesley in the knee, but he didn't even change expression.

He found the object of his vendetta and threw the snowball in a perfect downward trajectory. The rival drummer boy looked up in time to catch it full in the face. He fell in slow motion and landed arms akimbo on his back. His drumsticks fell like spears into the snow and stuck there. The force of gravity caused his drum to fly up and land behind him with a muffled thump. He flailed a snow angel as he tried to extract his arms from the straps.

"That's for Floyd!" Wesley called. He dusted off his hands, slid off the roof, landed in the position of a cat, and took off in the direction of the hospital tent.

Josephine scored hit after hit, making gains with the rest of her line, loving the way the eyes of her enemy widened when a snowball hit home. She found herself smiling. This was not grim work but the scuffling of children, half anger and half joy, then three-quarters joy, then joy full-on. She and Libby had fought like this against the neighbor children one epic winter after a gorgeous snowfall, tree by tree in the orchard, ambushes from the branches, advances into open land, sudden detente at the border of the cornfield. Sounds of a clean battle, whoops and shouts and exaggerated cries over timid pains.

She slipped in the snow and fell down, tried to rise and fell again. Libby stopped and helped her up.

"I got him," Josephine said.

"Good for you."

The other line broke and retreated, but were pursued mercilessly and struck in the back at close range. Some turned for a desperate last stand, fighting guerrilla style from hut to hut. In the midst of that battle, that happy chaos, that bloodless grudgesettling that should have spread throughout the war and left both sides stained with spheres of cold water but otherwise untouched, Josephine heard a sound. A sound lost in the din but as clear as a bell to her. Just for a moment and it was gone.

Libby's laughter.

Not the laughter of a man but a burst of feminine laughter, unguarded and true, evocative of everything pre-war and even pre-Arden. In the same way that a low-throated rattle is indisputable evidence that death is near, that burst of high-pitched laughter could not have come from anything but life. Josephine could not help but imagine the day could come when that laughter would rise again, multiply, show itself, and her sister would come back to her with Arden's ghost split like a locust shell and left clinging to a tree.

During a break in the battle, *Les Misérables* suddenly appeared in the hands of a prime suspect.

"Oh, looky here. I must have forgotten I borrowed this."

"You bastard!"

The battle was over. Brother returned to brother and friend to friend. Flasks appeared and were drained, and drill was canceled because the one-armed captain was lying drunk in the snow. Stonewall Jackson was a god left behind as liquor washed away the tendency to worship and fear. Day turned into evening, and evening, night, and the reading of *Les Misérables,* instigator of the war, was canceled because so many of the soldiers were by now unconscious.

Libby and Josephine lay together, bodies entangled on a single cot, warm with liquor despite the continuing snowfall outside the shaky walls of their hut.

"I fought well today," Josephine said. Her mouth was inches from Libby's, her breath sweet with brandy.

"If only you could fight the Yankees with equal ferocity," Libby said, but her voice was dreamy and forgiving.

"I could never kill a man, Libby."

"Are you sure?"

Josephine blinked. Through her hazy drunkenness, a certain tone had broken through, like the slight reek of tar in cheap whiskey. "What do you mean?" she asked. Her heart began to beat faster.

"That day in the woods at Sharpsburg . . ."

Josephine's breath caught. Her sober self was rising up to listen. That clarity brought by dread and fear.

"Yes?"

"I heard your voice calling me. And then it stopped. I rushed through the woods, looking for you. And then I finally saw you in the distance. The air was full of smoke, and there was such confusion. But as I approached you . . . I thought I saw you pressing something down on Arden's face as if you were smothering him."

Josephine knew she must answer, she must explain herself quickly with the version of the truth she had once found believable, but suddenly the truth was lost. She had spent the war burying it, and now in her molasses-slow brain she could not find its location.

"I have told myself many times that I was just seeing things," Libby continued. "As I've told you before, I saw many impossible sights that day. But this one will not be banished, and it tortures me. Tell me, Josephine, surely you could not have hated him that much, to cause his death?"

"No, Libby," she said. Her voice felt strange to her ears. Disembodied as though it belonged to someone else, half-man, half-woman, sober and drunk and truthful and lying and too young to know the things it knew. "Your eyes were playing tricks on you. I had no love for Arden, but I did not kill him. I told you. He was dead when I found him."

"But he was still warm!"

"Then death must have taken him very shortly before I came upon him." Her voice was calm, certain.

No answer in return but Libby's slow breathing. The angle of her body or an incipient cold made a slightly whistling sound come out of her throat.

The next morning they both awoke with pounding headaches. Josephine had only vague memories of the night before, but that troubling accusation remained.

Tell me, Josephine, surely you could not have hated him that much, to cause his death?

She looked at Libby and could read nothing on her face but the pain of harsh light and loud noises. She must have misunderstood. Libby could not possibly have said that. Perhaps she should revisit the subject. A little hair of the dog that bit them. But she didn't dare.

Had Lewis still been alive, he would have chastised his brother. "Damn it, boy. I told you to keep your distance from that old man. Now he's better, and you're sick."

It started with a cough that would not go away. Later the weakness and the fever took over, and soon Wesley was in the hospital tent with the other sick men who thought they had escaped the worst of the war only to find that the enemy was inside them, not blue but the sickly yellow of a rogue infection. Wesley lay shivering under a thin blanket, his arms crossed, as Floyd paced around his cot.

"Come on, boy. Get up and play that infernal thawed guitar

of yours," he begged him, but instead Wesley grew worse. Floyd made the mistake of abandoning his post by Wesley's cot to relieve himself in the woods, and when he returned, Josephine was in his place, applying a mustard plaster.

"Okay, then, Joseph. You can go. I'm here now," Floyd said.

"You shouldn't be in this tent. You almost died, and you could catch something again."

"No, the boy took care of me, and I'm going to take care of him. You get gone. Go pretend to shave or something."

But Josephine refused to leave, and eventually the old man gave up and relinquished the rickety wooden chair by Wesley's cot to her, although he did return at all hours of the day to check on him.

"Ah, Joseph," Wesley said weakly. "You ought to be playing poker or drinking somewhere. There's nothing to do in this tent."

But Josephine didn't want to be anywhere else. Libby could not pry her away from Wesley's side and began taking supper to her on a tin plate as Josephine administered Dover's powder and more mustard plasters in a vain attempt to mollify whatever force was inside him, moving through a feverish body already wracked by the scourges of the war. The nurses had removed his clothes, and when the blanket slipped and she saw his bare chest, the heavy toll of his tribulations was obvious. Starved flesh, evidence of scurvy, old scars, and a surface wound, still healing, that he'd mentioned to no one. She dipped a wet rag in water and bathed his face as Floyd returned.

"Camp fever, probably," he murmured. "Or the influenza. Or God knows what. I'll go scout up some dogwood bark. It's good for fevers. And put warm lard on his skin. Keeps it from itching."

Wesley spent most of his hours asleep. The nurses had seen other men go through these stages, and they began avoiding Wesley's cot and let Josephine do the work. "If you want to help," one of the nurses told her, "you could lend us a hand with the other men."

"I must stay with my friend."

"You're wasting your time. He's going to die. Direct your efforts to the ones who might recover."

Josephine recoiled from the woman who had said so bluntly what Floyd had said in the way he circled the cot, sighing, and Libby had said with the look she gave her when she brought in her supper.

"He is not going to die," Josephine replied in such a gruff and masculine anger that the nurse turned away. Later in the afternoon, Josephine left Wesley's side just long enough to rifle through her haversack and find some cigarettes she'd recovered on the battlefield of Fredericksburg and was saving to use for trade. She headed over to F Company and returned to the hospital with the two last volumes of *Les Misérables* tucked under her arm. That night she read by candlelight the scene where Valjean has volunteered to execute Javert, who has been exposed as a spy. Valjean approaches Javert, who is tied and blindfolded. He aims his gun . . .

Josephine closed the pamphlet.

Wesley's eyes fluttered, then opened. Slowly he moved his arm out from under the blanket and touched her arm. "Go on," he whispered. "Tell me what happened."

"I'll tell you in the morning."

And so she continued that way, with the only medicine she had left at her disposal: that of the suddenly disconnected plot line. She could only hope that Wesley's desperate curiosity to find out what happened next would cause him to live through another night.

Four days later, Floyd touched her arm. She moved her gaze away from his wet eyes and fought the urge to cover her ears and protect them from his quavering voice.

"You know I lost a boy in Kernstown," he said. "But he wasn't the first. I lost my youngest to typhoid fever. You're gonna hear a rattle . . ."

"Stop talking, Floyd. Go away."

"You're gonna hear a rattle, and it's not gonna sound pretty, Joseph. But when I heard my boy's rattle, I knew it was the sound of a soul shaking out of its earthly chains before it flew to heaven. That's what I told myself. Maybe it will help you, too."

Near midnight. A single candle burning. Mutterings in the hospital tent of the recovering and the dying, two sides of the story told and retold all through that winter. She leaned forward, stroking Wesley's hair. This was the moment she had chosen to tell him, in a voice so quiet only he could hear, something that had been running through her mind, again and again and again, the words chosen so carefully, like the words spoken at a wedding or a funeral or in the dead of night when the air is calm and pure and cold.

Wesley, remember when you told me that no woman would want to love you because you are scrawny and your toes are crossed? Well, I am here to say that yes, you are scrawny, but only because the war has starved you, and when they removed your shoes in the hospital tent, I saw that your toes were not crossed, merely bruised and gray from the cold. And you are handsome, as handsome as a man can be. And a woman does love you. And I am that woman. I am not Joseph. I am Josephine, and I love you. If you must die, then die knowing that a woman who longed to be your wife was by your side.

And yet she could not do it. Some nascent hope, wild in her body and eluding capture, would not let her speak the words that were only safe to say if death were certain. She could not welcome death that way. And so instead, she opened the pamphlet, leaned forward, and whispered into his ear:

It occurred to Jean Valjean that the grating which he had caught sight of under the flag-stones, might also catch the eye of the soldiery, and that everything hung upon this chance. They also might descend into that well and search it. There was not a minute to be lost. He had deposited Marius on the ground, he picked him up again, — that is the real word for it, — placed him on his shoulders once more, and set out. He plunged resolutely into the gloom . . .

Camp Winder, Virginia
February 4, 1863

To the Father and Mother of Pvt. Wesley Abeline,
My dear Sir and Madam,

It is with great regret that I write to tell you of the terrible loss of your son, Wesley, to the devastation of camp fever.

I had the honor to serve with Wesley and Lewis after losing my own son at Kernstown and joining their ranks.

Wesley had a lively soul and it spilled out when he played his guitar. He was ever kind and looked out for his fellow soldiers. I myself grew ill earlier in the winter, and Wesley tended to me and brought me back to health. I loved him like a son and am brokenhearted at his loss.

I felt duty bound to write to you of his passing. He was a fine boy and his actions, at all times, would have made you proud.

My sincerest condolences,
Floyd Cooper

Spring 1863

Camp Winder

Near Fredericksburg, Virginia

Violets had arrived, and white clover was coming. Colors blooming everywhere. Redbud, wild mustard, trillium. Dandelions
spreading over the hills. The aroma of honeysuckle awakened
the soldiers in a piercing way, reminding them they had survived
to smell that honeysuckle and others had not. Now was the time,
though, to heal. To assemble oneself back into the soldier barely
remembered from the fall.

Josephine missed herself in the same aching way the men
missed their wives. Somehow it had seemed tolerable to let her
true essence be lost under snow during the winter months. But
now that the snow had receded and the air had warmed and the
birds had returned, she found herself dwelling on that carefully
detailed fantasy. On this day she had realized that the time was
right, even if the deed was wrong, outrageous, crazy, and after
what happened with Wesley, she was not going to wait a moment
longer. And so she gave into the mad thought, let her actions carry
her away as she walked, that calm late afternoon, across a field
overgrown with clover and down a gentle slope. At the bottom
lay a gurgling creek short on frogs but sparkling with minnows.
The stones covering its bed were clean as though scrubbed that
way. The light of the lowering sun played upon the currents and

caused the color of the stones to change from pink to lavender and then to a brief powder shade of blue. Shaded by white oak branches, the bathing hole was only ten feet in diameter; but on this early evening it was empty, for the rest of the camp was at supper. Josephine expected no companions here but one.

Love grass lined the banks of this creek, so lush and soft as to invite a never-ending nap. Josephine sat in the grass, the slope of the hill kept her hidden from sight. She took off her filthy shoes and socks and put her feet in the water. Two bees flew by in their quest for pink trillium, but their buzz was gone and they were quiet as ladybugs. A band of silvery minnows lingered in a slow-moving eddy before making a sudden departure. She unbuttoned her jacket and pulled it off, then removed her shirt and sat there, bare from the waist up except for her cotton binding. It came off slowly, revealing breasts that were pale but still full. The months of privation had not taken them from her.

The wind brushed at her skin. A single bee came back and circled one aureole before flying away. She pulled off her trousers and drawers and settled back naked on the grass. A cloud of gnats appeared, drawn by the scent of sweat or perhaps just the sudden appearance of a body so pale and warm. They settled on her private hair, scattering as she waved her hand.

A few minutes later, she eased herself down to the creek until she stood in water that came to her navel. Immediately she felt the hidden currents that came swirling from different angles, tickling the backs of her knees and the insides of her wrist as she balanced herself. She sank into the creek until only her head was left uncovered. She looked toward the hill, watching the clover and a single rogue dandelion waving within it. She could not hear the sounds of camp. She heard nothing. It was as if camp did not exist, nor did the war, that this creek was an extension of her homestead lot back in Winchester, and this day, the sun easing down, was like any other spring day.

She could have rushed from the water and put on her clothes and gone back to camp as though nothing had ever happened. But she did not. Instead she watched the hill and waited.

Ghost. He hated that nickname. The old man, Floyd, had taken to calling him that, and the other soldiers had picked it up. Now when they glanced at him from their faro games and card playing, that's what he heard. With winks and cackles of laughter, as though coming back from the dead was a thing of merriment. Somehow, Wesley had survived when others hadn't. He was past the point where the nurses had given up, and, he learned later, Floyd had even penned a letter of consolation to his parents. Somehow he'd turned around and come back again. He remembered patches of time, but others just collapsed into some unaccountable space, like the air between dreams. He remembered the old man circling his bed, and Joseph sitting by his side, reading from *Les Misérables,* stopping those passages at their most urgent and tantalizing points.

He did feel like a ghost. Coughed out by a winter that should have held him forever. By all rights, he should have gone the way of his guitar, silent even when thawed. And yet, here he was. Alive, in the spring. Without his brother. And more of the ugly war still out in front of him.

When his fever was at his highest, he could swear his brother was leaning down to him, whispering in his ear, "Ain't so bad. Get up, boy, get up, get up." And he was comforted by that hallucination. The worst part of getting better was the realization that Lewis was gone forever. Wesley could picture him perfectly as a boy, twelve years old, back when his laugh was free and his scowl reserved for cats and math. Doing some pointless thing. Adding an empty can to a trash fire, or digging a hole in the ground with the end of a stick. Nothing a boy could do back then had huge repercussions. No passion was demanded of him, no depth of commitment. That was before Harpers Ferry and Fort Sumter. The South and the North rarely crossed paths, and when they did, they wanted less from each other. Wesley insisted on remembering Lewis this way. He could not stand to think of him sitting there with a smile on his face and nothing but eternity behind it, and would have given anything to see that smile change into something darker, or angrier, or more selfish, and then back into a smile again, the turbulent moods of a living man.

Grief, he thought, would have an ending, but it was a black cat that ran across life, through good conversations and orange firelight and endless drills. It sat on his shoulders and made his knees creak when he stood up. It balanced in the crook of his arm as he cleaned his rifle. And he could not banish it; it was loyal as a dog.

He wanted to tell Joseph all of this. Every now and then, he would muster his courage and approach the slender boy, his soul aching for a friend, but as soon as he entered Joseph's proximity, new pangs entered him. Confusion, self-consciousness, and an ache reserved for the gentler sex. Strange notes of pleasure and pain, guilt and redemption. Girls had made him feel like that, and sometimes whiskey, but never a fellow soldier. To love this way was like trying to paint with a slingshot. It wasn't just wrong — it was impossible. He looked at the other soldiers and wondered if they knew. Wondered if Lewis had known.

Wondered if Joseph felt it, too.

The night before Fredericksburg, Wesley had taken a drink to steady himself and asked him to dance, because all the men were dancing, and on this night such a proposition was normal and proper. Spinning around with Joseph in his arms, he had felt something that went beyond drunkenness and celebration and defiance and the false bravery men feel around fire, drums, and whiskey. What he felt, in fact, had nothing to do with war. Then the sudden death of Lewis and the drudgery of winter camp before the illness dragged him down. He lay on the floor of the hut on his blanket and longed for two souls out of reach — one in heaven, and one breathing from the cot across the room.

Lewis and Joseph: a knees-on-the-ground devastation and a hands-in-the-air bewilderment.

And he had thought, perhaps, that he would emerge from his long and ferocious illness cured of his alarming fondness for Joseph, and that this young soldier would turn back into a mere companion. And yet, despite his best efforts, his gaze still lingered when he looked at the boy and found himself wanting to touch him. Not a friendly punch in the shoulder but to stroke the side of his face, to come closer, to breathe the odor of his neck, and this filled Wesley, in a springtime teeming with flowers and birds, with the shame of the November before, when he had, for reasons unknown, allowed this boy to drunkenly kiss him in a smokehouse and then spent the rest of the march in a circling, angry interrogation of himself. *Why did you do that? Why?*

And yet he could not find another single reason for going forward into the next march and the next battle, because now that Lewis was dead, every part of his body yearned for escape. He was not like the others. He did not believe in Stonewall Jackson or his plans, and did not see himself as an angel in his avenging army. He was simply a fighting cock, doomed to slash and peck at his opponent — who looked just like him — as North and South placed bets. He did not want to kill anymore. He wanted to find another guitar and stun the enemy with song. He wanted to keep the springtime for himself and what was left of his family and not share it with this war. He was weary beyond belief, too weary to even bathe, as Floyd had pointed out over breakfast.

"Ghost, when's the last time you bathed that filthy hide of yours? October? Get on down to the creek and get yourself a bath before some digger wasp tries to build a nest on you."

Joseph, who was darning his haversack nearby, had glanced at him but said nothing.

"I don't feel like bathing," Wesley said. "And stop calling me ghost. It's not like you don't have one foot in the grave yourself."

Floyd tossed him the remains of a cake of soap. "Come on. Gonna be a nice spring day. You'll feel better."

Wesley caught the soap. "All right then, old man, just to shut you up. But I'll bathe later on, when everyone's at supper. Don't want no one to see how scrawny I've gotten."

"Ain't that the truth," Floyd said, his eyes softening. "You weren't but skin and bones lying on that cot. I still say it's a miracle you're still with us."

Now Wesley made his way down the hill as the sun began to fail and his own shadow lay out in front of him, moving through the clover. He was not looking forward to his bath. Lewis always used to tease him about moving into cold water one inch at a time, holding his breath, when Lewis would simply belly-flop in with a holler. He did not wish to cry today, here in this stolen moment of spring, by evoking that memory of Lewis in midair, that silly smile on his face, but here it came anyway, and Wesley felt his eyes grow wet and his heart hurt fiercely; as he stood a moment to let the feeling pass, he thought he saw something in the creek below. Something that moved in the shadows.

He came closer. He reached the bottom of the hill and glimpsed, in the mud of the creek bank, a pair of footprints that led to the water. He moved to the water's edge and found himself looking into the face of Joseph, who was silent, in water up to his neck.

"Joseph?"

"No." Something was strange about the voice, causing Wesley to move forward so that the toes of his moccasins dampened in the cool water of the creek.

"No?" he asked. The air was charged with something, a before-battle or after-kiss prickle that warns of silence.

Joseph rose, his pale neck revealing itself, then the shoulders . . .

Wesley's eyes widened . . .

Then the breasts . . .

Then the smooth belly . . .

Wesley's jaw fell open. His heart stopped.

The brush of light hair where the legs met. Proof of something he'd felt in his bones and beyond but that his mind had refused to confirm.

And it was not Joseph but some other creature that stood dripping in the creek as the mystery split like the last crack of a tree before it falls, and Wesley felt dizzy and pure as the answers to his questions flooded him. Of course, of course, of course. His body seemed to have lost itself. His hat fell out of his hand, and he plunged into the creek, the chill of the water unfelt as it moved up his trousers. He reached her and put his arms around her, holding her, kissing her mouth, his hands moving up to her breasts, affirming the solution and then moving around to her bare, wet back. This could not be what it was. Tears filled his eyes and fell down his face for what he'd found, what had been given him by a merciful God after all this time. Finally what he felt and what was true matched up like a green lizard on a green leaf, and he held and stroked the soft wet skin as the shadows moved around them.

"What is your name?" he whispered.

"Josephine."

He looked into her eyes and saw her there. "Of course," he said. "Of course."

April had arrived, and a new secret lived in the camp. A masquerade within a disguise. Love as the uninvited third party invading this war. Passion, silent and covert but growing every day. Josephine, revealed as a woman to the only person who mattered, now found that freedom raging within her, and it took all her strength to climb into those filthy, manly clothes, to lower her voice, and to breathe beneath her bindings. Only on certain occasions, when she used the excuse, late at night, of the call of nature, could she meet Wesley in the darkness of the woods, to be held and known.

"I can't sleep," Wesley said, stroking her face, "knowing you are so close by. This is torture for me."

"We're together now, though," she said, kissing his lips.

"It's not enough, Josephine. I love you. This is not how we were meant to be."

"I have no option."

She had recounted the tale of the sisters' deception to Wesley, shocking herself when remembering exactly how they'd managed to fool everyone around them. In those dark woods, the story seemed ludicrous.

Libby wasn't stupid. Her eyes narrowed when she looked at the two soldiers, the real one and the fraud, leaning toward each other and whispering. Even on opposite sides of the drill, their eyes would find each other. Wesley stopped teasing Josephine about her continued confusion about the proper way to clean a gun. And once, Libby caught Josephine brushing something off Wesley's jacket. They seemed to be caught in their own world, some kind of time out of keeping with the others in camp, untouched by the limbo that spring imposed while they waited for Jackson to find their next burial ground.

Libby had come so far and accomplished so much. Her cause was in danger.

"Josephine," she said in the darkness of the log hut, modulating her voice so as to rise above the crickets but preserve discretion, "why have you been spending so much time with Wesley?"

"His brother died. He's sad."

"Oh, for heaven's sake, his brother died months ago."

"He can still grieve, can't he? Don't you still grieve?"

"Don't compare my loss to his. Arden was a brave, noble man, and Lewis was a dirty, shifty piece of vermin."

"He was Wesley's brother, and just as brave and beloved."

"Ridiculous," Libby murmured, and then fell silent for a moment before speaking again. "Wesley might discover who you are. Then what will happen to us?"

"He wouldn't tell, even if he knew."

"Don't talk that way. As if you're preparing for the possibility."

"Please let me have him as a friend, Libby. I've been so lonely."

"Lonely? How could you have possibly been lonely? I've been right here by your side."

The men were rested, and a spring run of Rappahannock shad kept the hunger at bay. But the camp, once a sanctuary, was feeling more like a swamp that held them firm. Rumors began to swirl of an impending march eastward. Occasionally Stonewall Jackson was seen, his brow knit in concentration. Peace felt like soggy bread to him. He was a man who lived for battle. Libby wasn't sure of his plans, but she craved movement. The languor of camp was drawing her sister and Wesley ever closer. A new, hard march might shake them loose from each other.

As the drills and the rumors intensified, Libby began to once again sense Arden's presence. He spoke to her in dreams, or even those times between dreaming and waking, just before morning reveille put an end to him, shattering his words of love and hatred as she was jolted from sleep. Nights of full moonlight strengthened his presence, as did the smell of a hickory fire, and she could not move from the light of one campfire to another without feeling the brush of his hand. Libby had fought no battles since Fredericksburg, and the number of dead men stood at nine. Arden needed blood. He was growing impatient. He was whispering things about her sister. Terrible things.

Josephine and Wesley sat cross-legged, facing each other in the shade of two oaks that grew so close together that the elder of the two was slowly choking the younger one. For now, though, the intertwining branches and broad, flat leaves formed a canopy that held the sunlight out and provided the kind of dusky gloom that makes lovers speak true. "Josephine," he said, and she drank in her name as he continued. "You are so beautiful, even with that haircut. Even in that uniform. How could I not have known?"

"You knew in the smokehouse. We were both drunk and somehow you knew. Somehow you saw me. And believe it or not, that gave me the strength to get through that terrible march."

He stroked her hair, kissed her again.

"I have to leave now," Josephine said. "My sister will wonder where I am, and I believe she already suspects I have revealed myself to you."

"So what if you did?"

"You know that means betrayal to her. She is terrified of being caught and sent home before her quest is complete."

"Her quest is crazy. This war is no place for a woman. You both should be home taking care of your ma and pa. I'll bet they're worried sick about you."

"Let's not argue."

"Ain't no argument going on. Just two people talking."

In these shadows, removed from sun or campfire light, his features looked darker, and his voice had a deeper tone. Wesley leaned back against the tree, and she thought the matter was settled until he added: "It ain't your job to fight."

"Libby needs me. I'm her guardian."

"Guard yourself, Josephine. Just go into the captain's tent and tell him the truth. He'd send you home in the blink of an eye."

"If I reveal myself, my sister will be discovered, too. As you know, it's obvious who we are once the case is made."

"Would it be so bad for her to be found out? I think it would do her good to go back home. She's not looking well."

"It would kill her to leave now. The only thing that has kept her alive since Arden's death is carrying on his cause. You should have seen her in September. She wouldn't eat. She was wasting away, and no one could help her, not even me. She would have died, had she not saved herself with this mad plan."

His expression changed from thoughtful to longing, as though considering her story and then his own aching need for a kiss.

"You should have seen those two together," Josephine said. "They were one person. Everyone thought so."

"Maybe that's not such a good thing. Especially 'cause one of 'em is dead now. You tell me your heart is in this, and I'll be quiet."

She sighed and pushed herself off the ground to leave.

He caught her arm. "Let's go, then. You and me."

She sank back down.

"Both of us?"

"Lewis is dead. I've put in my time fighting. I've done my job. We can find ourselves a place in the middle of nowhere and hole up together. Remember the smokehouse? Hell, we could live out the war in some smokehouse, eating cracklings and smoked pig and applejack. We could get nice and fat and drunk, and sleep in hickory ashes."

"They'll find us."

"No, they won't."

"You know what happens to deserters."

"Nothing's going to happen to us."

"I thought you didn't want to be yellow."

"I'm not a coward. I'm not afraid of dying. I just think we have to take what's ours, because no one is going to give it to us. And if that makes me yellow, fine. I'll be yellow as a pound cake, yellow as lemonade. Yellow as a field of daisies. Let the cows graze on me, damn it. I don't care."

"I've told you over and over, Wesley. I can't leave my sister. God will take her if I leave."

"What if God takes you?"

"Did you know that she wakes up in the middle of the night and talks to Arden as if he's sitting there? She seemed better over the winter, but now she's losing herself. She needs me."

"You have your own life. She has no right to take it. And she has no right to take you from me. I love you. Please, Josephine. Say it back."

It was time to march again. Stonewall Jackson had put his fingertip somewhere on a map where the ground would soon be bloody, and it was no man's call to question him, only to follow him blindly. The men gathered their haversacks, oilcloths, and rations, and prepared to move. Josephine felt shaken out of her beautiful spring with her secret love. Somehow it seemed as though this season would never end and she could live like this — half-soldier, half-darling — speaking in her true voice to Wesley in the darkness of the woods. She had almost forgotten this war, so full of crazy soldiers and their crazy motivations, their crazy ghosts and their crazy gods. Just a sea of delusion: blue at high tide, gray at low.

When the long roll sounded one morning, she nodded goodbye to the escalating warmth of the hut and started the march. Libby was astonished, this time, by the weight of her gear. She had no idea how she'd carried such a burden over the Blue Ridge Mountains in freezing snow. Once she paused by the side of the road and threw away her blanket before continuing on. When the order to rest finally came, she lay down where she stopped without taking off her haversack. Over those few months, the road had turned to ice, then to mud, and then had dried partially in the sun. She smoothed out the dirt with the flat of her hand, breaking the crust and exposing a cool shade of brown, and fell asleep with her gun by her side.

On the third day, they reached Hamilton's Crossing and camped. Men on horseback with various messages for the officers came in and out of camp, and supper was a subdued affair, each man caught up in his own mortality again, the thought of loved ones at home and in heaven. The long respite was over.

Before she went on picket duty, Josephine found Libby sitting in her tent, holding her stick and gazing off into space.

"At last," Libby murmured. "I thought another battle would never come."

"Would that have been so terrible?" Josephine asked.

Libby glanced at her. "Yes, of course it would have been. I would ask you if you have forgotten your loyalties, but I'm afraid of the answer."

"My loyalties are the same. They are to you. They are what keep me here."

"And Wesley," Libby said. "He keeps you here too, doesn't he?"

The night was too beautiful for picket duty, or any duty at all. Josephine looked at Wesley out of the corner of her eye. They were standing picket together for the first time in weeks, under such a dominant moon that torches weren't necessary. Owls hooted, and frogs croaked from a stream that ran through a low place in the woods. Wesley had finally had a haircut; his ears glowed in moonlight. He had been so quiet at supper, and even now he said nothing, simply looking off into the woods, leaving her bewildered as to what had changed between them.

He caught her staring, and she looked away.

"It's warm tonight," he said at last. "Hot, in fact."

"The frogs are so loud."

"Maybe they smell the battle coming." His neck looked longer now, an illusion common to men whose haircuts had been overdue. She wanted to put her gun down, go to him, and hold his thin body. She was terrified of the coming battle. In every battle, she had lost someone. Who would be next?

Wesley was looking at her now, his face so boyish by moonlight. He stepped closer to her so he could say her real name.

"Josephine, do you remember when I told you about that feeling that I had right before Mechanicsville that I was gonna die? And Lewis broke my arm so I couldn't fight?"

"Yes, I remember."

"Well, I got that feeling again."

Josephine felt a sudden pain in her chest. "You think you're going to die?"

He shook his head. "I think you are gonna die, Josephine." He touched the side of her face and left his hand there. "You are."

"Don't be silly, Wesley," she managed. "I don't believe in those superstitions. How can anyone know?"

"I know. And you know what? I'm not gonna let you. Here I was marching today, thinking I'll just protect you. Shoot down every Yankee who even looks your way. But you know what? I can't stop nothing. I couldn't keep Lewis from dying, and I expect I'll have just as much luck keeping you alive. But then I realized something. I can keep you alive. All I have to do is tell the captain who you are."

Josephine drew in her breath. "You can't do that! You know that once I am discovered, Libby will be discovered, too. You know that I cannot let that happen."

"Then you have only one more choice left. Leave. Desert with me."

"No!"

"Then, I'm going to tell on you, Josephine. I know you'll hate me for it, and maybe you'll never talk to me again. But if something happened to you, I'd never forgive myself."

Early the next morning, Josephine saw it with her own eyes. That curiously formal way Wesley walked as he headed toward the captain's tent. She followed him at a close distance, unable to believe that he was actually going through with his threat.

Just before he reached the tent, Josephine caught up with him and grabbed his arm.

"Very well," she said. "You win."

He looked at her and stepped close to her. Too close for one man to speak to another man, but just right for them. "I have won, all right, if it means I keep you alive."

She lowered her voice as the camp swirled around them in its morning activity. "But even if we get past the pickets, we don't know the roads."

"We'll just have to take our chances."

"But Libby will . . ."

"No!" he shouted, and she was taken aback by the ferocity in his voice. "Stop thinking of her! Think of yourself. Think of me."

Libby stepped back from the crackle of torch light and nearly lost her footing in the damp grass of the meadow. Cows were vague shapes in the dark. She rubbed her eyes. Wesley and Josephine had roused her from sleep and brought her here. Libby's eyes moved down and saw that they were holding hands.

Josephine spoke first. "You're right, Libby. He did know."

Tiny bugs had gathered around the flare of the torch.

"I knew you were trouble," Libby told Wesley.

"I haven't told anyone."

Libby crossed her arms. Something landed on her neck and drew blood. She let it live.

"Wesley and I are leaving," Josephine said.

"Deserting."

"Yes."

"You're a traitor. Lower than a dog. You both are crawling yellow dogs, and I would shoot you if I'd brought my gun."

"I'm the crawling yellow dog," Wesley said. "Not your sister. She's only going with me because I told her I was gonna tell the captain she was a woman, and she knew if I did that you'd be found out, too. This is on me, not her."

Libby glared at him. "She could have avoided this entirely if she had not revealed herself to you. She put us both in danger. If my sister is shot as a deserter or killed by the Yankees, I know who to blame."

"Maybe you are the one to blame," Wesley said, "On account of this whole crazy idea was yours to start with."

Libby took a step toward Wesley. Josephine moved between the two of them.

"Libby. Come with us. We could all be happy. We can all go home. And live. You don't belong here, any more than we do."

"Arden is here to keep me strong. He speaks to me nightly. And you know what he keeps saying? That you killed him."

"That is only your delusion. I did no such thing."

"I don't want to believe it, but he keeps insisting. Maybe you want me to die, too? Is that what it is?"

"No. But I have no control over that. Whether you live or die is God's will, not mine. Wesley made me see that."

"Of course. Wesley has made you see so much."

Libby stepped back, leaving the other two in the circle of light. "Go," she said. "I hope they hunt you down. I hope they kill you."

"Libby . . ."

"Don't come any closer, or I'll call the guards."

"It's no use," Wesley said. "We should go before it gets light."

Josephine gazed at her sister. "Please forgive me. I'll pray for you every night. I'll ask God to watch over you."

Wesley picked up the torch. He took Josephine's hand and began to walk away. Her arm straightened, stopping him, but he pulled on her until she moved.

"You're a traitor!" Libby called as they walked away. "God will punish you!"

"Let them go," Arden said.

27

Wesley had traded some good whiskey for a compass and decided they would find their way through the forest and go west, parallel to the Orange Plank road, and then turn north. His plan extended no further, and there was nothing Josephine could add as a supplement. They moved like ghosts through the trees that night, hand in hand, the torchlight between them. Josephine had wanted to leave her rifle, but Wesley said, "No, don't do that. We still might need it," and his voice had carried the warning of danger. Wesley had told her to be very careful where she stepped and stay light on her toes should any crackling reveal their location.

They walked in silence, each with their own thoughts. Josephine felt a nausea sweep over her every time she thought of Libby. Could she live through another battle? What would happen to her without her older sister there to take care of her? But what choice had Wesley left Josephine but to flee? And yet she could not bring herself to be angry with him. In her bones she knew that she didn't belong in this war, and that the ruse would lead nowhere but to a violent end. Still, she worried terribly about Libby. The war was dangerous enough for a soldier of sound mind. Perhaps she should have turned herself in, and Libby too. But she couldn't bring herself to carry through with it.

The moon was half-full and sometimes could be glimpsed in the branches of the oaks. A hoot owl startled them and then went quiet. The crickets of summer were not out yet.

An hour into their journey, Wesley suddenly stopped.

"What is it?" she asked.

"Shhh." He pulled her into the middle of a clump of shrubs. "Lie down," he whispered, and covered her with his body.

It was then, face-down on the cool earth, she heard the voices. Soldiers were coming toward them.

"Ours or theirs?" she whispered.

"Shhh. Don't matter no more."

She felt his heart beating and the shivering of his body as the men came closer.

"Want a smoke, Christopher?" one of them asked.

"Sure, why not?"

The sound of a match striking and an inhalation. They were very close now.

"Warm tonight."

"Yeah."

"Tired."

"Yeah."

"Think there's gonna be a battle?"

"Hell yeah."

"I try not to think about it till I'm right upon it."

"I was twist-legged drunk during Fredericksburg."

"You're joking."

"Best way to fight."

Josephine hardly breathed. The footsteps passed the bush and stopped. Nothing now but sounds that designated tobacco being drawn into the lungs and exhaled again. A peaceful sound, just men and their habit.

"Ever tell you about my old dog back home?"

"Don't think so."

"Barney was his name. Crazy dog loved to pull up things. Weeds, flowers, bushes. Anything with roots. Well, my old grandma had this peach tree sapling. For a year she'd been watering it and fussing over it. She built this little wire fence around it to protect it. Well, one day we were having breakfast, and there's

Barney standing there in the grass, and he's got her peach sapling pulled up by the roots, and he's got it in his mouth, the leaves pointing one way and the roots the other."

Josephine felt Wesley's body stiffen and begin to shake. After several moments, she realized Wesley was silently laughing. She squeezed his hand hard in warning and finally the shaking subsided, and they waited for the men to walk away.

But the soldier wasn't done with his story. "Well, Grandma was a God-fearing churchgoing woman, but something came over her. The devil I guess. That old lady ran out there and yanked that peach tree out of his mouth and started chasing him around trying to beat him with it."

Wesley was shaking again. His body rocking with silent laughter. Josephine dug her nails in his hand, but he couldn't seem to stop himself. The bush began to rustle around them.

"And she kept swinging that peach tree, but that old dog just kept scooting out of the way . . ."

The branches of the bushes around her sounded deafening in her ears. Frantically she dug her nails harder.

"Hey, Clay, what's that sound?"

"I don't hear nothing."

Wesley had finally managed to control his body. Josephine felt the tension of his held breath.

"It's coming from over there. Probably some critter."

"Well, shoot it."

Josephine felt Wesley's body seize and then the other voice said, "Naw. Tired of shooting things."

Their footsteps faded into the brush. Wesley and Josephine disentangled themselves, and then he started laughing again.

"Wesley! What's wrong with you? You could have gotten us killed."

"I'm sorry . . . It was just so funny . . . that old lady chasing around that crazy dog. Made me think about the time our dog stole Lewis's drawers off the line and Lewis chased that old dog for an hour." Josephine's anger faded, and she wished for that laughter to leap from his body and into hers, banishing terrible sights and healing guilt and regrets. Washing out the blue, washing out the gray. Until she was left, peach-colored flesh and green eyes and red heart, just the colors belonging to her.

Eventually they found a river and followed it along. They rested in a cypress copse the next day, hidden from the sight of both Union and Confederate soldiers, now an enemy to both. Here they spoke in whispers.

"How far do you think we've come?" Josephine asked.

"Not far enough. You hungry?"

Wesley had brought along some tinned meat and hardtack. Josephine shook her head but accepted a swallow from his drum canteen.

"Why do you look so sad?" he asked.

"I can't forget the look on her face. She looked so betrayed. I've betrayed her, Wesley."

"It was you or her, Josephine." He slapped at his own face. "Something's biting me. Couldn't be a skeeter so early in the year, could it?" He looked over at her. "What did she mean, when she said you killed her husband? I thought the Yankees killed him."

Josephine had never spoken of that day to Wesley. So much time had passed, it could easily be folded into a dream, put with those other dreams that fade in the morning and take their meaning with them. "They did kill him. Shot him. Arden could not possibly have recovered from his wound, Wesley. He'd been shot in the stomach."

"Then, what did she mean?"

Josephine didn't answer for a moment. Without such a question, she could almost forget she was a deserter and concentrate on the immediate discomforts of the forest: the heat and the itching and the buzzing.

"My sister is quite mad," she said at last. "I imagined that the seeds of this madness were brought about by Arden's death, but looking back, I think it started earlier. It's as though Arden came in and took over her soul. Even before he died, I felt as though I'd lost her. And I suppose I hated Arden."

Wesley didn't say a word. Gently scratched his face as he listened.

"I suppose I hated him, Wesley. I've never hated anyone, but if you could just have seen the way he treated her . . . He took her away from us. I thought once he was dead, he'd let her go, but he never did."

On the second night, they reached the edge of the forest, which opened onto a vast meadow. No Yankees in sight. No Rebels. The war had missed this place. This field seemed to go on endlessly, the middle of nowhere that people talk about, nothing but goldenrod, sheep sorrel, high grass, and sunflowers. Grasshoppers jumped away from the sound of footsteps. An apocalypse could start on some distant battlefield, and it would not affect a fawn's curiosity or a bee's satisfaction. They kept walking, heading west, hiding during the day. Even out in this wilderness, a few homesteads had established themselves. At night they trespassed onto these properties if the dogs didn't warn them away. They drank from the wells and broke into smokehouses. They ate wild strawberries, experimented with dandelion leaves and cattail tubers. One night Wesley shot a wild turkey, and they cooked it on a spit. The weather stayed fair.

As the days passed, their startle reflex softened, until even the sudden flight of a covey of quails jangled not a single nerve. One night Wesley flopped into the grass and pulled her down next to him. They lay there together, on their backs, looking at the stars.

"Do you feel yellow?" she asked.

"Yes. But it bothers me less and less." A cloud appeared in the sky, suddenly, as though it had been thrown there by someone done with it. They fell asleep under its cover and didn't move until the stars were bright. Wesley sat up and took off his jacket and tied it around his waist.

"You always claimed to be scrawny," Josephine said. "That's not true."

"And you always claimed to be a boy."

"We should be walking. It's nighttime."

"What's the hurry?"

He made a small fire, using a pack of Federal matches and cupping his hand against the breeze until the kindling crackled. There was nothing to cook, and so they ate the last of the hardtack and fed the fire lazily. She studied Wesley's face in the light. He had looked so boyish when they first met. Now he looked like a man.

"What are you thinking about?" Wesley asked.

"Things."

"Happy things?"

"Some."

"At last." He plucked a piece of blooming grass and chewed on the starchy end of it. He had rolled up his sleeves, and Josephine ran her fingers over his wrist and then up his arm, finding the bump and checking to see if his new life had softened it.

"Lewis loved you," she said.

"Libby loved you, too."

"She did once. But she'll never love me again."

"You can't just banish love out of anger. It's hardier than that."

They lay down together, abandoning the fire and its dwindling rations. Overhead the Big Dipper hung low, the same Big Dipper of their youth, their marches, their battles, and their birth. It had claimed its fixed place, and there it lingered.

"I wish you had your guitar now," Josephine said. "Although it always made me sad to hear you sing."

"Really?"

"It made everyone sad."

"I didn't know that."

He put his arms around her and kissed the underside of her chin. His lips were soft for a man who had walked through freezing winters and bitten a thousand cartridges. "You belong with me," he said. She lowered her lips to his, and he kissed her fully on the mouth. Josephine felt the strain of a tiny muscle in her neck and a shiver through the rest of her body. The tiny fire swallowed itself and plumed with sweet smoke. Night birds called out from their roosting places — locust trees and half-grown beeches.

He removed her jacket. She said, "Wesley," very softly, but it seemed natural, under these stars, to be without jackets, and then without a shirt. Her white flesh amazed him. A secret purity lying under this war.

Kisses. The crackle of firelight. She was less a boy every second, and more a woman. And suddenly there was not enough time to get free of that cloth. She helped him until she was only Josephine.

He was naked, too. She couldn't remember how he'd gotten that way.

They lay down together in the grass. He held her in the circle of his arms.

"Does it hurt?" he said.

"So much less than other things."

By the time the last embers of the fire died, it didn't hurt at all. They fell asleep.

Josephine woke up crying.

"Oh, Wesley. What have I done?"

"You've done nothing wrong. We're in love."

"I meant, what have I done to Libby?"

28

May 1863

Chancellorsville. A battle that began in late afternoon and continued into the night. Libby was one of those ghosts who howled in the forest in those evening shadows. Libby killed a man, reloaded, and killed another as a tree burst near her head. She turned to make sure Josephine was untouched by the blast, but then remembered that her sister was gone, that vanished traitor. Even in the midst of the battle, screams and shots and the trampling of fallen men and dry leaves, she could not divorce her thoughts from her. Even though she was too tired and too afraid and too filled with rage to form the accurate sentences that spoke to her betrayal, the name *Josephine* stayed inside her.

Arden, though, was more than a name. He was a presence, an exhortation, the heaving breaths of his spirit keeping up with her, his voice shouting that unearthly Rebel yell right along with her. She shot the fleeing Yankees in the back. Twelve, thirteen, fourteen. And as the sun set, the gift of fifteen. The air filled with the scent of pine pulp and gun smoke and the smoke of the arrested fires. She stepped into a fallen Rebel's chest, the toe of her boot emerging bloody from his death wound as she rushed onward. She could not say she was a woman or even a man. Just a killing, counting force.

The next day the battle resumed. Sixteen, seventeen, eighteen.

By afternoon the woods began to burn. The smoke was so thick Libby's eyes streamed tears, and she held her shirttail over her mouth, trying to breathe. She heard a loud crack and looked just in time to see a man's head crushed by a falling limb. Smoke covered over the scene and left the man's death throes to the imagination, and Libby pressed on, leaves crackling under her feet. She came upon two Union prisoners, sitting tied back to back.

Arden appeared in the clearing smoke, his face black with powder. "Shoot them," he said.

"What?"

"You heard me."

"I can't do that, Arden! They're prisoners!"

"What difference does it make? Nineteen, twenty! They are merely blue numbers. Shoot them, Libby. Shoot them!"

Arden held his hands out to her. His red eyes filled with tears. "What is left of me but the cause? Are you going to abandon it, now?"

When the battle was over, Libby lay at last in the peaceful darkness of her tent, which had been set up on top of a patch of clover. She scratched her ankle and felt one of the blisters pop, splattering her skin with cool juice. A hickory log sputtered in a campfire, briefly scalding the song of nearby crickets. A soldier muttered something in his sleep. A dog padded by on three legs, from the sound of it.

Footsteps approached her tent and a voice called out.

"Libby . . . Libby . . ."

She sat up but didn't answer.

"Libby, why did you not kill those Yankee prisoners? Don't you see that they are devils? And should you not desire to kill them, since you are a soldier in the army of God? Do you think our wounded general, Stonewall Jackson, would have had mercy on them? What am I to think about that?"

Campfire light glowed through the tent, throwing a shadow across the cotton twilling as he spoke again.

"I'm so thirsty."

"I have killed eighteen Yankees, Arden."

"That is not enough."

Libby opened her mouth, but no sound came out. Arden's footsteps came closer. His shadow grew. He pressed his face against the cotton twilling. The shape of his features bulged into the tent.

She was afraid to sleep now. She spent her evenings huddled on one side of the tent, careful where she moved her eyes, lest she see a darting shadow or the imprint of a face. She traded food for candles and kept one lit every night, using her bayonet ring as a holder. In the mornings the wax had dripped down the length of the bayonet blade, and she had to scrape it off with a knife before she could pass inspection.

She had been questioned about Josephine's and Wesley's desertion, but claimed ignorance and seemed to be believed. The memory of her sister came back to her constantly, seeming soft and pre-traitorous at times, but hardening like a prism when Libby thought of what she'd done. She still felt shocked by the final conversation by torch light. She had never dreamed it would have come to this, Josephine and that boy skulking off like cowards for the homeland. And yet, when the first puff of smoke from expired candlelight woke her up in pitch darkness, she reached for her.

The men were camped at Guiney's Station. Chancellorsville had skinned them good, but they had won the battle anyway, and now the bounties of summer had restored them. They ate wild raspberries and trapped squirrels. They grasped the pungent shoots of wild onions and yanked them out of the ground. As potholes grew from that plundering, the taste of soup improved.

This was the season of letters. Ink was hot in the wells, and a group of Quaker women had sent a large supply of stationery, as well as a box of new gloves whose trigger fingers had been sewn closed. The soldiers laughed at the crazy, unwearable gloves, and at the crazy women who hated war. They did use the stationery, writing slim books to their loved ones by the light of Confederate candles, spilling endearments that would dry up forever once they came home.

On May 10, word swept through the camp that Stonewall Jackson had died after being shot by his own picket. Men wept in each other's arms and swore revenge. Their God was dead, and they struggled to put their cause back together knowing he would never ride his sorrel among them again. The mad cause was absent its mad general, and the men did not know what to do, and so they drank.

Late that night, Libby came upon a trio of new recruits, squatting around Wesley's old guitar. One of them poured kerosene on the useless instrument as the other watched and clapped. Their drunken cheers attracted the attention of the old drummer, Floyd, who hobbled over and asked their business.

"We're burning the guitar of that yellow dog who deserted with his friend," one of them explained, "in honor of our fallen general. Old Jack would not have emptied his pipe out on such a coward."

"You listen here," Floyd said. "You didn't know that soldier. You boys ain't but two weeks off the farm. Your mama probably gave you your last bath. You think you went through one battle and you're soldiers now? I saw that boy fight for his cause. I saw him sicken and almost die for it. He sang around that fire when he had nothing left to sing. He sang for us. That boy gave everything, and then he up and left, and I say, 'God bless him.' And, yes, I'm an old man. But I'm telling you now, the next one of you that touches his guitar, I'm gonna kick your ass from here to Sunday."

Floyd took the guitar, and Libby saw him late that night, fast asleep on his oilcloth, holding the guitar on his chest. The old man was snoring, reeking of kerosene and love.

29

Saltbox houses sat on scarred land, surrounded by old threshing machinery and cranky dogs and scratching chickens. Wesley and Josephine stole milk from patient cattle, squeezing it into their tin cups, and in one outbuilding they opened a barrel full of molasses and licked it from their fingers until they got spooked and ran away.

"Why don't we just find a place to hole up now?" Josephine said. "I'm tired of walking."

"That's not what we planned."

"Why does it matter? We should have stayed in that empty farmhouse we found yesterday."

"You know why no one lived in it. It smelled like death."

One morning they woke up in a barn and found themselves staring up into the barrel of a Springfield musket, the old-fashioned kind that went off on a whim. An old woman aimed it at them with shaky hands.

"Please don't shoot us!" Josephine cried.

"She's a woman!" Wesley added.

The old woman stared at him. "What did you say?"

"She's a woman." He said it proudly and with great definition, as though Josephine's gender was a pass that allowed them every consideration.

The old woman lowered the gun slightly and peered at Josephine. Light poured through the slats in the barn roof. Dust covered her spectacles.

"Women don't wear pants," she said.

"I'm pretending to be a man," Josephine said.

The old woman began to laugh. One of her front teeth was folded over the other, giving her the appearance of a rabbit. Her cheeks turned red. Dust blew away from her face. "You are no more a woman," she said, "than I am a billy goat."

She raised the gun again. Her cheeks paled and her mouth closed. The friendly rabbit vanished.

"We weren't gonna steal anything!" Wesley said. "Honest! We just wanted to find a place to sleep!"

The old woman didn't move. A dragonfly landed on the barrel and must have pleaded for mercy, because although she kept the gun pointed at them, she exhaled slowly and rolled her eyes. "A place to sleep, huh? Why aren't you out finding a place to fight?"

"We're not deserters, if that's what you mean," Wesley said.

"I wasn't born stupid, and God gave me a few more smarts during my life. You are chicken for sure. Got a whole yellow trickle moving the wrong direction down these parts, and a trickle of black folks going the other way. Black and yellow, like a bumblebee. My husband would have shot you for sure, if out of nothing but disgust. He died of a bad heart before there was ever talk of Secession, but he was a man, through and through."

"All right, then," Wesley said. "We're deserters. Please don't turn us in. We have some money. We'll give it to you."

She snorted. "Confederate dollars go a long way these days, don't they? Might as well give me a soiled handkerchief cut up in squares. No, I'm not going to turn you in. Truth is, I'm not such a fan of the Confederacy anymore. Their soldiers came through here a while back, took our last pig, and gave us all scarlet fever. I'm sure it won't be long before the Yankees come from the opposite direction with their own bad intentions. So, you just pick a color and stay that way. Makes no matter to me. You two got scarlet fever?"

"No," Wesley said.

"Typhoid?"

"No."

"Syphilis?"

"What?"

"Ah, I guess there's only one way to catch that." She lowered the gun. "You boys get inside the house. I got a jar of pickles I can't open."

The house was made of poplar logs; the gaps between them had been shanked with pine boards. The aroma of sassafras and mildew permeated the interior. Hickory sticks crackled in a stone fireplace; an old horsehair sofa sat against the wall, bordered by a spinning wheel and a stack of carver chairs.

Wesley and Josephine sat on the sofa and studied the room. A sway-backed dog came padding in from another room, made a sudden dash for Wesley, and shoved its muzzle into his crotch before he could close his legs.

"That's old Hank," the woman said. "Just push him away. He's fourteen years old, and he don't insist on nothing. Of course, he ain't good for nothing, either. I'd begrudge feeding him, but my boy's gonna want to see him when he gets back from the war."

"What's your son's name?" asked Josephine.

"Randolph. Haven't heard from him since winter, and he's usually good about writing. But I've learned not to draw conclusions about nothing."

She went into the kitchen, returned with an iron kettle full of water, and hung it over the fireplace. "Lucky for you, I was just about to boil me some eggs for breakfast. I got a little bacon left too, and some crackers and molasses." She eased herself into a rocking chair. It creaked as it caught her. The dog waddled toward the sound.

"You know," she said, "the farm looks like hell, but I got more than most folks. When the Rebels came through, we took every-thing from the smokehouse and hid it in the loft. They couldn't get the door open on the drying house, and they never found the root cellar. All they got of any value was a couple of chickens and a pig we were planning to slaughter come winter."

"Wait," Wesley said, "you keep saying *we*."

"Ah. I wasn't alone back then. My son's wife and little boy lived with me. He wasn't but eight years old. When we all got sick, I thought I'd die first, being the oldest. Not true. The woman went first. My grandson and I dug her grave together. Took us most of the day. Two weeks later the boy died, and I tried to bury him myself. But I just didn't have the strength. We'd had the first frost. The ground was hard as a rock. Finally I gave up scratching around with the hoe and laid him down under an oak tree and covered him with his coat. I piled some old chestnut rails on top of his body to keep the wolves away. That's all I could do for him."

She pointed out the window. "You see that pile of rails there, under that tree? That's where he lies. His mama's between the peach trees and the tool shed."

Wesley stood up. "That tool shed open?"

"Never had a lock. Rebs don't eat hammers."

Wesley walked out the back door without saying another word. As Josephine and the old woman watched him, he entered the tool shed, came out with a shovel, and carried it to the pile of rails. He set it down and began to roll up his sleeves.

The old woman looked at Josephine. "What's your chicken friend doing?"

"I think he plans to bury that boy good and proper."

The old woman watched him work. When he reached the lower rails, she closed the curtain and sat down in the rocking chair.

"I prayed so long for help," she said. "It got to where I didn't think God was listening. And then he up and sent me down a yellow angel. Why aren't you out there helping him?"

"Wesley wouldn't want me to."

"Why not?"

"I told you, I'm a woman."

The old woman didn't laugh this time. She squinted at Josephine for a long time, her eyebrows twitching. "Now that I look at you," she said at last, "I can see that possibility. But I still don't believe it."

Josephine took her jacket off. She unbuttoned her shirt and opened it. The old woman leaned forward in her rocking chair.

"I'll be damned."

Night had fallen. The old woman, whose name was Eleanor, opened the curtains to gaze outside. She'd been admiring her grandson's new grave since Wesley had finished it. "Yep. Yep. Yep. Looks so much better. Just wanted to see how it looks at night. It's got a nice shape." She let the curtain go, sat back in her rocking chair, and studied her visitors.

"Well, what a day, huh? When you woke up, I was pointing a gun at you. And now I just made you supper. Of course, in between that time, one of you buried my grandson, and one of you turned into a woman." Eleanor glanced at Josephine. "A very strange woman. Now that I know, I can't believe I was ever fooled for a second. But you never told me what you were doing in the army to start with."

"I followed someone," Josephine said.

Eleanor pointed at Wesley. "You mean, this idiot?"

"No. My sister, Libby. She joined the Stonewall Brigade to carry on her dead husband's cause. She was crazy with grief, and I was afraid something terrible would happen to her. And so I went with her."

"Mmm. I've heard of women sneaking into the ranks, but never quite —"

"Let's not talk about this anymore," Wesley interrupted.

Eleanor ignored him. "Why didn't you bring your sister with you?" she asked Josephine.

"Libby wouldn't leave. She's turned into someone else. I think she no longer knows right from wrong. Her mind isn't the same."

Wesley stood up. "For God's sake, stop it!"

He walked out the back door and slammed it behind him.

Eleanor raised her eyebrows. The dog laid his head on her knee.

Josephine sighed. "Wesley doesn't like it when I talk about my sister."

The old woman turned her palms heavenward. "How can you help that? She's your sister."

Later that night, Eleanor made Wesley drag the bathtub in from the backyard and set it up in the kitchen.

"If you two are gonna sleep here, you're gonna bathe. Tomorrow we'll boil those creepy-crawling garments of yours. Tonight we'll boil you."

Wesley filled the tub with water heated over the fire. Steam rose to the beams of the ceiling.

"All right, then," Eleanor said when Wesley was finished. "You, boy, go make yourself scarce until it's your turn. Go outside. And you, girl, get in the tub."

She handed Josephine a bar of bayberry soap and said, "Poor Pauline was saving this for when my son came home. She had a nice dress she was gonna wear for him, too. I almost buried her in that dress, but I just couldn't do it. You get yourself a bath and put that dress on. You ain't a boy no more. You got no reason to be."

Once she was alone in the kitchen, Josephine took off her

clothes and sank into the tub. The fragrance of the soap seemed foreign at first as she began to bathe, but by the time she reached her feet, her body had adjusted. She was softening. Field capabilities were leaving her, knowledge of the route step, tolerance for hardtack, texture of blood, desire to swear, lust for fire, instinct for the yell. She lathered herself again, washed her hair, and rinsed it clean. Her face and skin felt smooth. Creatures she would never have to wear again sank into the water.

When she was finished, Eleanor came in and handed her a linen robe. "Put that on," she said, "and come to the back bedroom. The one on the left."

A few minutes later, Josephine stood in the doorway of a room that was furnished only by a maple chest, a cord bed, a Sheraton mirror, and a stool. Eleanor held up a kerosene lantern and motioned her in.

A cream-colored dress lay across the bed. Decorative buttons had been sewn to the bodice. Josephine touched the fabric.

"Silk," she said.

"Naw. Not silk. Some kind of fancy cotton. But it feels like silk, don't it? Pauline remade it into something modern by following a pattern she found in *Godey's Lady's Book*. She was a bit taller than you, but it might fit otherwise. Sorry there ain't no petticoats. I had to tear them up for poultices when she got sick. She died in this room, you know. So did the boy. But it feels peaceful in here, don't it? Sometimes I sleep in this room when the other one keeps me awake. My husband died in that one. Too many rooms used for dying these days."

Eleanor put the kerosene lamp on the stool. "Now go on. Put that dress on and enjoy it. I've seen enough girlie things wasted in this war. Like you."

The door closed behind her. Josephine took off her robe and stood naked in the lamplight. One would have to look close for effects of the war. A thickening of skin in certain places, the elbows and the feet. Old scars and slightly sunken ribs. Tanned skin on the face and the back of the hands. She put the dress over her head and felt the cloth brush down her skin. She hooked the skirt and bodice up the front and adjusted the collar. The sleeves were a bit too long, and the hem of the dress brushed the floor. She held the lamp to the mirror and studied herself, amazed at how quickly the transformation had occurred, as though a magician had been called to rush the trick through. Joseph was gone. Josephine was back in the room. She looked a little bit more like Libby now, the angles of her face a little sharper and the eyes more intense, and she felt a rush of grief for her lost sister.

When they were young girls, the sisters used to look at themselves and move ahead in time to imagine their own maturity, the swell of breast and the widening of hips. Paling of throat, gentling of brow, fullness of mouth. In strong lights, they could even see themselves as mothers, each cradling a child.

The door opened. Wesley stood in the doorway. He wore a long nightshirt. His hair was wet and slicked back over his ears.

"My God, Josephine," he whispered. "How could I ever have seen anyone else?"

Josephine woke up shouting, "Libby, Libby!"
"No," Wesley said. "It's me."

Libby bolted upright in the tent.
"Josephine!"
"No," Arden said. "It's me."

The dirt had crusted over the little boy's grave, hardening like a shell. Eleanor knelt and patted it. "Yep, that boy did a fine job," she told Josephine, and looked over at Wesley, who was feeding the chickens with handfuls of millet. "You love him, don't you?"

Josephine followed her gaze. Wesley caught her eye and waved.

"I can't help it," Josephine said.

"Nor should you. Look. The hem of your dress is touching the ground."

Josephine pulled on the dress until it slid up her calf and fluttered just below the knee.

"We'll hem that today," Eleanor said. "It's been almost a week, and you shouldn't have to keep tripping on it." She picked up her spade and turned back to the grave. She had almost finished digging holes around the grave's perimeter. Josephine held a bag of sunflower seeds, waiting.

"That boy loved sunflowers," Eleanor said. "I remember when the tall ones came up to his chest."

She smiled, exposing her rabbit teeth to the memory.

"That's when he was but a little thing. His papa hadn't left for war yet. His mama was alive. Then all of a sudden, his papa was gone, his mama was dead, and so were the sunflowers. He died before they came back in bloom."

"You did all you could for him."

"And more. No one could say I didn't do everything I could think of trying to save that boy." Eleanor stopped digging. "I didn't have no quinine, no nothing. His chest felt like sandpaper, and his tongue turned white as snow. I tried every tone of prayer. Hand me those seeds."

"My sister had blackwater fever when she was thirteen years old," Josephine said. "Everyone thought she was going to die. My father even bought a coffin and kept it in the shed. He thought no one saw it, but I did. I can still smell the pine of it. When I opened the lid, it didn't creak at all. That's how well it was made."

Eleanor gathered some dirt with the side of her hand and brushed it into the first hole.

Josephine kept talking. "I was only fourteen. But I'm a natural nurse. Everybody says so. I could do everything my father and mother could do for Libby. She wouldn't take the quinine from anyone but me. After a while, my parents just let me nurse her alone. I saved her. Not them. I wasn't going to let her die."

Eleanor let some seeds slide from her hand into another hole.

"You're a good sister."

The bedroom was quiet but for the whispery sound the hem of Josephine's dress made when it dragged on the floor. The old woman was in the kitchen, making dinner. Outside in the backyard, lumps of red earth circled the boy's grave. Another week and green leaves would shoot out of the lumps. By August long-stemmed shadows would move across the dirt. Josephine stopped pacing and stood with her back to the mirror, looking at the bed and imagining a little boy on it, knitting his brow as he tried to decipher a fever dream. He could smell the dust in this room, the lingering varnish of a chest polished years ago. The shadows of late afternoon slid up the walls when his fever broke. Sweat coated his eyelashes. He sighed in his sleep.

Josephine could imagine him perfectly, drawing on the memory of her sister, who took the little boy's place on the bed each time Josephine blinked. Now Libby sighed in her sleep and frowned at the chill of the wet compress. Now the shadows were hers. Now she coughed, and a half-swallowed sip of blackberry cordial sprayed out of her mouth. Out in the backyard, a tin shed held her coffin.

"I won't let you die," Josephine told the child on the bed.

"I won't let you."

Wesley was knocking on the door.

"Please, Josephine," he begged. "Answer me."

Supper came late that night. The old woman kept changing her mind, withdrawing jars from the cupboards, muttering to herself, and then putting them back. Finally she had Josephine bring some dried fish in from the smokehouse and boiled some turnips. They ate around the fire, and then she disappeared outside and returned a few minutes later with a bottle of whiskey. She said, "I've been keeping it in the root cellar for a special occasion."

"It's half-drunk already," Wesley said.

"I've had a sip every now and again. I'm an old lady, and I've got a lot of aches and pains." She took off the cap and tipped the bottle back, stiffened as she tasted whiskey, gulped, and sat breathing out her nose. The firelight moved down her dress, exposing stains of different kinds. Her eyelids slowly closed. For a moment she seemed to have fallen asleep, but she opened her eyes and passed the bottle to Wesley.

"Sing something," she said after he'd taken a sip. "Go on. I hear you got a good voice. Your friend here told me when you were feeding the chickens today."

"And what did you tell *her?*" Wesley asked Eleanor.

"Wesley!" Josephine said.

Eleanor blinked. "About what?"

"I don't know. But she locked herself in the room all afternoon and wouldn't talk to me."

"She was just telling me about her grandson," Josephine said. "That's all."

Wesley wiped his mouth with the back of his sleeve. "Did any other names come up?"

"I don't know what you're talking about," Josephine said.

"*Libby,*" he said, leaning on the word. "What else would make you lock me out of the room? You blame me, don't you, for making you leave her?"

"Wesley—"

"I *saved* you!"

"Stop it," Eleanor said. "God's sakes, if I wanted this racket, I'd invite the chickens in. Just sing, boy. You'd be surprised how much that helps just about anything."

Wesley scowled.

"That's the face my grandson used to make when his taffy burnt. Now, go on. Earn your supper."

Wesley sighed and handed the bottle to Josephine. He took a breath and began to sing, moving his left hand as though reaching for the neck of a guitar and then catching himself. Josephine and the old woman listened as his voice caught its power and deepened in the crannies of the house. He stopped singing abruptly and put his head in his hands.

"Well," Eleanor said at last. "Time for bed, I guess."

The moon flushed light down into the room. Wesley and Josephine faced each other in a loose embrace, a dreamer's reassurance that a lover remains. That very first night, Eleanor had said, "This morning one of you was a boy. Now I suppose you're married. I don't care. I'm not here to remind you of the laws of God. Sleep in there together if you want. I know nothing."

Wesley moved. His eyelids fluttered. Josephine had been doz-
ing, but now she awoke and watched him. His face was smooth.
It had turned so rough and red on the long winter march. His
lips had cracked, as had the back of his hands. And now all traces
of privation were gone from his face, except for the dark circles
under his eyes, which had appeared late in December and hadn't
faded in the spring. He seemed to have thrived the past week on
the old woman's peculiar brand of insults and corn bread, and
already she saw in his face a different understanding of the hours.
He was on picnic time now, kite-flyer's time, whittler's time. He
did not have to march madly over the ice until he found the dead-
line of a battle, he didn't have to hurry to reload, or to duck, or to
pray, and if he had any conflict about deserting, it didn't show on
his face.

Wesley murmured something and turned to the wall, but Josephine could not close her eyes. She saw sunflower seeds drop-
ping in fresh holes. She saw the sick boy sleeping. She saw the
old woman washing his face. Perhaps the armies would never
again come out this far to ruin things, but love had made it out
here, long ago, and had never died. She imagined Libby standing
in the room with sunken eyes and a uniform that hung on her like
a sack. And Josephine, who had never felt the crisp outline of her
own character, realized it now. She had been put on this earth to
live her own life but also to love and protect, and that was something crafted and real and wild, like the texture of a nest. Take
away the love and she would have been translucent, just a ghost
in the shadows who aches to be alive.

"I won't forget you, Wesley," she whispered, and slid from
the bed.

She paused in Eleanor's doorway. The room smelled of an
herbal indistinction that pointed to folk remedies. The old
woman lay curled up in her nightgown, her covers kicked off and
her bare feet exposed. She was unguarded now, her face slack-

ened into a dreamer's acceptance of a twisting narrative. Without her heavy shoes and her piercing looks, she was just another child too young for war. Josephine wanted to kiss her face or cover her feet, but was afraid she would step on a creaky place had she entered the room.

The dog was sleeping by the spinning wheel in the main room. He lifted his head but did not rise as she passed by. She knelt in front of the sugar chest near the kitchen and opened the bottom drawer, where Eleanor had put her uniform after it had been cleaned and folded. "We'll need it for something," she said. "Maybe some neighbor boy will want it."

She found a long cloth in a kitchen drawer, suitable for binding her breasts. She slipped out of her nightgown and began to dress herself, gritting her teeth as she stepped into the old trousers. The uniform felt filthy, despite being boiled. Tears filled her eyes as she fastened the buttons.

Her brogans sat outside by the back door. Eleanor had been using them when she gardened. Josephine put them on and stood in the yard. She thought of the dress, folded back on the hope chest. She looked into the window of her bedroom, and a wave of love for Wesley overwhelmed her, a staggering amount that threatened to pull her down to a praying position. Her uniform itched. Her shoes felt heavy on her feet.

She was back in the army.

Wesley had taught her how to find her general direction by using stars and landmarks. She had a vague sense of where the army had last camped, and since they had been gone less than ten days, she figured the men were still resting and had not yet moved toward another battle. The cows in the fields paid her no mind, but lay like stones and slept as she navigated around them. Their lack of urgency calmed her. She was afraid to plunder storehouses by herself and had to be content with barely ripe cherries and anything that could be pulled out of the ground or taken from the edge of the woods. Once in a low valley she came to a streambed and found a little boy trying to catch minnows with a jar. She approached him cautiously and said, "Hello."

"Where you going, mister?" the boy asked.

Libby had haunted her as she moved toward the mountains. Now, walking away from them, Wesley was the ghost, his voice always within reach, his laughter substantial among the lowing of cattle in the fields she trespassed. She could not revisit the memory of his song or his sleeping face. When either of these threatened to come forth, she concentrated on something else, the antics of a squirrel on a fence or the quack-sneeze call of some roosting bird. She slept in a field of low wheat one night and felt something heavy on her legs when she awakened. An enormous corn snake had coiled up on her shins. She screamed and it slithered away.

Sometimes, as she walked alone by night and the weariness of her lonely journey affected her, she imagined herself marching with her former comrades: Floyd, Wesley, Lewis, Matthew, and even Libby. Wesley told a joke, and the others laughed. Suddenly the ghost laughter vanished, leaving a breathing sound in its place.

32

May 1863

Hamilton's Crossing, Virginia

The low branch of a sycamore tree was playing havoc with the new recruit. Each time the wind blew and the branch rustled, he would jump. Libby and he were standing picket together. She had stopped eating. Skin loose on ribs, pants loose on waist, vocal cords standing out in her throat. Feet numb, eyes weak and playing tricks on her. The torch listed, sending light into a stand of ferns, and suddenly before her eyes was a sight she'd seen in Chancellorsville, of a fallen Union soldier pulling up those same ferns to pack the wound in his thigh. The battles had returned to her that way, dead men suddenly appearing along a fence, the smoke of a fire dissipating and revealing a stack of severed arms. Screams and then silence in the middle of the day. Floyd had asked if she was ill, and she had shaken her head. Illness implied a cure, and there was no cure for this but another battle.

The smell of honeysuckle grew stronger in the heat. Crickets sang, locusts rattled, birds called, that peculiar form of orchestra emerging from its narrow season to cover the sound of the other soldier's breathing. She did not speak to him. Didn't care what he had to say or what he believed.

A voice called her name out of the darkness. It was difficult for her to see if the voice was real, and so she looked to her companion, who, unconcerned, rolled a cigarette.

The voice came again. "Libby." Just a little louder now.

Libby moved into the forest, her rifle raised, leaving her torch behind her, farther until the shadows covered her. Farther still until, in a place where moonlight came down in a sheet in a small clearing, her sister stood.

Libby's rifle did not dip in response to the recognition. It held steady, pointing at her. Libby's heart was beating faster, and her body was chilled. She had not seen Arden all night, but she knew that the tension of this meeting would summon him. It was only a matter of time before his body was next to hers and his voice was in her ear.

"Why did you come back?" Libby asked her. In the disguise of the man, Joseph, Libby had trouble seeing her sister. It was as though Josephine and all the love Libby had for her had disappeared.

"I came back for you," Josephine replied, her own gun loose at her side. "I love you, Libby. I thought I could leave you, but I couldn't. You're my little sister."

"You are not my sister anymore," Libby said. "You're a traitor to the South. You'll be arrested and shot, as will Wesley." Libby peered into the darkness, trying to see him. "Where is he?"

"I left him behind."

Libby was shocked at the thought that Josephine had done such a thing for her. "You did?" she whispered. But then Arden was there, his elbow brushing her arm. "She's come back to destroy us. She's a traitor. She's no better than a Yankee. In fact, she is a Yankee. Shoot her, Libby."

"Shoot her? I cannot shoot her!"

"Libby?" Josephine said. "Who are you talking to?"

"Do it for me," said Arden. "Do it for Stonewall Jackson. Do it for love and for justice."

"But she's my sister."

"She is number nineteen, Libby. An enemy soldier. Ask her if she killed me, Libby. Ask her one more time."

"Libby," said Josephine. "Please put the gun down. You are frightening me."

Libby did not move. Her aim was true. Her finger moved to the trigger, and it didn't feel like her finger at all. Perhaps Arden was right. Who was right and wrong anyway, at this angle of darkness, at this fraction of war, and in this moment in time?

"I'm asking you one more time, Josephine. Did you kill Arden?"

Josephine set her gun down and let it fall into the leaves. She held her hands at her sides. The moonlight scattered her shadow behind her. It did not fit her anymore.

"Yes," she said. "I killed him."

Arden, death-wounded and crack-lipped, stared up into Josephine's eyes. "Where . . . is my wife? I have to say goodbye."

"I'll go find her." Josephine started to rise to her feet, but Arden grabbed her wrist. "Wait," he said, then paused to ride out a wave of pulsing agony before he could speak again. His grip weakened. "I have changed my mind. I cannot make her watch me die."

"She would want to nurse you."

"You know how the gut-shot die. It would kill her, too. Do it, Josephine. Finish me. Hurry."

"Arden, no!" Josephine cried. "I could never kill a man."

"Even one you hate?"

Josephine couldn't answer.

"Please. You know that your sister isn't strong."

"She is only not strong because of you!" Josephine was immediately horrified by her own words, but Arden nodded.

"Then, do it because you hate me." His breath was coming hard and fast. His teeth were clenched, and his body seized in agony.

"I don't hate you, Arden."

"Then, do it because you love her. Please, please."

With no time to think further on the subject, with just a moment to obey whichever side of her soul was winning an argument whose points were fragmented and shooting out in all directions like bees from a broken hive, Josephine picked up the leather haversack lying near his side and held it over his face as his eyes registered pain and fear and gratitude. Only toward the end, after his eyes had rolled into the back of his head, did he suddenly begin to struggle, one hand jerking up to scratch her face, but she grimly held on and finally his body slackened and he lay there motionless, calm, and warm. That is the way Libby found them. That was the beginning of the lie and the secret. And she was going to take this to her grave, but now, in this moment, facing her sister and her pointed gun, she just spoke the truth. She wanted some kind of true thing with her there in that clearing. Even if it was her own worst deed.

"I know you don't believe me, Libby. But I did it out of mercy. So shoot me, if you must. But you should know that at the moment I felt Arden's life draining away, I didn't hate him. I loved him. Because, for the first time, I realized that he loved you."

Libby felt stunned by the confession, as though a cannonade had blown her all the way back to Sharpsburg and now she was touching her dead husband's cooling face as his death wound poured its hot scent into her nostrils.

"I told you," Arden whispered in her ear, and she was back in the woods around Chancellorsville. "She killed me. She admitted it."

"She chose me," Libby said. "She chose me on that battlefield. She chose me when I went to war. And now she has chosen me a third time, when she has come back for me."

Libby lowered her rifle.

"And I choose her."

"No!" said Arden. But he was fading, dissolving.

"Libby," said Josephine, her real voice breaking, "I came all this —"

An explosion rocked the woods, and Libby felt a searing burn on her face and a rush of hot liquid. Her knees collapsed and she fell to the ground. As more shots were fired and shouting filled the woods, she lost consciousness.

When she came to her senses, Josephine was leaning over her. "Libby! Libby!"

Libby opened her eyes. "What happened?"

"Yankees ambushed us."

She looked over to where Rebel pickets bent over the body of a Union soldier. Josephine tore the sleeve off her shirt and pressed it against Libby's face. "One of them shot you, Libby."

"Who shot him?"

"I did."

The pickets had turned to them. One of them peered at Josephine. "You're the deserter!" he exclaimed, and seized her gun. Two of the other pickets took her by the arms.

"We got you now," one of them said.

"Take him to the captain," another ordered, and they began to drag her away.

Libby was still dizzy and blood still ran from her wound, but she managed to raise her head and say the only words she could. The words that would save her sister and damn herself. The words that would end her quest forever.

"Stop. She's no deserter. She's a woman."

Brigade Headquarters
Hamilton's Crossing
May 20, 1863

Dr. James Beale
Dear Sir,

I write to inform you that your daughters, Josephine and Libby, are made safe and in transit to you presently. I ask you to collect them at Manassas Junction by month's end, as the Army can escort them no further.

I understand you must be fraught with worry, and hope my assurances of their safety can ease your mind and that of your family.

Their experiences throughout the past several months I cannot begin to adequately convey, but will leave to them to express.

Suffice it to say that I have never encountered two young ladies such as your daughters. And while I cannot officially condone their actions, I would be dishonest to say that they have not earned my deepest regard.

Yours truly,
Gen. James A. Walker

Josephine rode on the buckboard of the horse-drawn wagon next to her sister. Two officers' wives had volunteered dresses for them to wear, acting out of their strong belief that women, no matter how mad, should not be seen in pants. After the revelations of the night before, the other soldiers had treated them with confusion and awe, mystified by the fact that two members of the weaker sex had survived eight months of a brutal war with no one the wiser about their true identity.

How strange that the same soldiers who had eaten and drunk and swore and fought beside them now offered them their hands to help them into the wagon. Their eyes taking them in, shocked to the core. The astonished captain had escorted them to the new brigade commander, who had ordered them sent back home immediately, and word was being sent by horseman at this very moment to Dr. and Violet Beale. Libby's wound had been cleaned and an isinglass plaster applied.

Floyd came up with his hat over his chest. "I'll be damned," he said. "If this don't just beat all. I didn't know you were of the female persuasion, and I suppose that is a compliment to your skills. I'm just happy to see you leaving this war with all your arms and legs. It's terrible enough for a man but unholy for a woman to be here."

Then he moved close to Josephine and said into her ear: "I'm not saying you know where that boy is, but you tell that boy he ain't yellow any more than he's purple. Tell him I'm gonna find him after the war. Tell him I got his guitar and I'm treating it with all the respect a wounded veteran deserves."

They were on their way to Manassas Junction, where their father would meet them to take them back to Winchester. The horses were subdued, the driver quiet. The road was deserted. Nothing but early summer here on this section of Virginia the war hadn't bitten. In fact, war was nowhere. Not in the fields, not along the wormwood fence that existed in fragments, not in the dust or the heat or the sky. It was as though the war was a puddle and a gentleman had laid his coat down on it so they could pass.

Libby had not spoken a word since the ambush in the woods, neither in her false voice or her true one. She had simply stood before the general, eyes on the ground, as Josephine spoke for both of them. One of the field nurses had examined the women and confirmed that what was claimed was true. Unfathomable, but true. Now Libby rode next to her in a borrowed dress, and Josephine wondered if the sensation of the soft cambric chamois next to her skin even reached her, or if her mind was still only capable of feeling roughness of cotton and canvas and twill. Arden's ghost had left her, and perhaps it would be later in the summer or the fall when Libby could reassemble the pieces of herself into the girl she had once been long ago. But for now, Josephine was content to ride beside her on the road that would eventually connect to another, then another, and lead them back to Winchester.

She turned her thoughts to Wesley, and the memory of his sleeping face the night she left him filled her with such overbearing love as to take her out of her immediate circumstances and put her on a road made entirely of that feeling. She wondered where he was, if she was ever going to see him again. If he had made his way back to their unit and been arrested as a deserter. Or if he was still out in the world somewhere, living off the land, waiting for her. She knew, though, that she could not align circumstances herself, and that no amount of worrying could stand up next to what fate had in store for her. Still, she could not help thinking of him each time her thoughts wandered from her sister. Couldn't help going back to the smokehouse where their first kiss had taken place as they hid there together, on that day that was still there, across the fields and through the woods and past this moment. Waiting for her.

35

Late September 1863

Winchester, Virginia

Josephine poured the tea into the china cup and reached for the jar of honey.

Her mother came into the kitchen, nodded at the tea, and said, "Is that for Libby?"

She nodded.

"Make sure she doesn't spill it on herself," she said, in a voice that had softened over the past year. After Josephine and Libby were sent home from the war, their parents had met them at the train station, and the looks on their faces as the train neared the station had broken her heart.

Josephine stirred some honey in the tea.

Dr. Beale was in his parlor. A boy had shown up with not a tooth problem but a broken arm, and her father had gone about trying to set it with a hickory splint and the strips from a torn-up sheet. She'd been tempted to help. But she had another patient who needed attention.

Weeks had passed before Libby had said anything at all. Their mother thought the problem lay in the terrible diet she'd been forced to subsist on. Fresh fruit would take care of her, she believed. Beef stew and boiled potatoes. "We need to get some weight on her," she said, as though Libby's true self would fatten back into shape.

Dr. Beale, though, had the keen and sober vision of a veteran, and he recognized the look, a starker version of the one he still saw in the mirror. He took Libby to a doctor in Frederick who shook his head and said, "I've seen men like this. But never a woman." He gave Libby a tonic for her nerves and sent her home. And there was nothing to do but wait.

As the summer faded, Libby had started talking again, but she still spent hours alone in the backyard, sitting on a wicker chair and staring into the orchard. Josephine understood more than anyone the sacrifice that Libby, three Yankees shy of her goal, had made for her. She shadowed Libby, reading her dime novels and brushing her hair. She hunted down every color of flower she could find and laid them in her lap. Libby pulled the blooms off, one by one, and let the wind carry them away, watching them in that way the bereaved do, fixing unknown meanings to small and colorful things.

Josephine left the spoon in the teacup and stepped into the backyard, careful not to spill a drop as she approached her sister.

"Don't burn yourself. It's hot."

Libby's hands were steady when she took the cup. "Thank you," she said. Over the past few weeks, the register of her voice had risen incrementally, and now she only sounded like Arden on her saddest days.

"Can I get you anything else?"

Libby set the cup and saucer down in her lap and fixated on something in the middle distance. There was every chance the cup would be full of cold tea when Josephine returned to her. She stroked Libby's hair and caught her fingers on a tangle. "See? You're hair's getting longer."

She was walking back to the house when she heard Libby's voice.

"You're a good sister."

· · ·

Josephine passed the stables on the way to the woods, carrying a basket filled with bread, apples, and a jar of honey. Her lazy brother, Stephen, had left his horse half-curried to whittle on a stick. He looked up as she approached.

"Where you going?" he asked.

"None of your business."

She cut across the back lot and began the long walk, happy for a chance to think of Wesley and remember some incident shared between them. Nothing too significant. Just the way his neck looked after a haircut or the way his fingers moved on the strings of his guitar. Anything would bring him back, his face in sharp relief, and she would have to stop what she was doing because the love for him played havoc on her chores, causing her to spill the water in mop buckets and mismanage the fluted edges of dough.

When she reached the snake fence, she ducked under it and found herself in the gloom of the forest. She followed a familiar path down a bluff and continued her descent until she reached her destination. Before she ducked into the cave, she looked around to make sure she hadn't been followed. A red-tailed hawk watched her from the branch of a nearby tree. But there were no other witnesses.

The air inside the cave was cool. She followed a streak of lantern light.

Wesley rose to meet her.

"No one saw me," she said.

They kissed.

Libby blew on the surface of the tea, watched it move, and then poured the tea onto the lawn. A dog came up to investigate, and then walked away with a snort. Stephen ambled in from the stables, still whittling on a stick. Somewhere, she knew, was a horse half-fed or a wall half-painted. She appreciated that quality in him now, that open-ended sense of time that defied attempts to rush it.

He found a chair and sat next to her. He folded his pocket-knife, put it away, and tapped his knee with the stick.

"Where did Josephine go?" she asked.

"That way," he said, pointing. "She ran off with a jar of honey and a basket of bread, and wouldn't say where she was going."

Libby nodded but held fast to Josephine's secret. Stephen tried to talk some more, gave up, and left the conversation half-finished. He dragged his chair away and left her alone. She held the near-empty cup to her lips, tilted back her head, and caught a warm drop of tea, sparking a tiny remembrance, which led to a bigger one, then a bigger one, and then she had to drop the cup and break her concentration. Slowly she was coming back to herself. Filling in with her own thoughts and longings and beliefs and dreams. She didn't remember much of the war, but it still came back in fragments. Out of nowhere, a decapitated hand, a man's screaming face. And she would have to stop and feel herself in her own yard, and in her own skin. Repeat her name, Libby. Smell or see something familiar, like brewing coffee or a bird turning its head in that quick, impatient way that birds do. The nightmares, at least, had stopped. When Arden came to her in dreams now, he was sweet again, and talked no more of flies and Yankees, and insisted no more that Josephine had murdered him in cold blood on that battlefield. No, these dreams of Arden were small dreams, ordinary dreams. He reached high for something in the cabinet. He petted a dog. He came through the front door. He said things like "We need more bailing wire." She woke up in tears most days. Good tears. Normal tears. The tears of so many women across this land as the dead piled up. Brandy Station, Upperville, Gettysburg, Manassas Gap, Chickamauga. So many women were dreaming now of their men back at home, ordinary, alive.

Separating from Arden allowed her to mourn him, the husband he was and was not. The man who could sometimes be tender but also critical and short-tempered. Not a devil. Not a saint. Simply a man who had loved her in his own way, too hard, too much, too all-encompassing. He'd breathed her up inside him like a summer breath and refused to exhale, and she'd been lost.

Arden would disappear now for days, and that was all right with her, because he was always with her, a presence growing lighter, as memories do, puffed up by the passing hours and made into something comforting again.

There were times when she imagined he was angry and still blamed her for leaving the quest, but he would reassure her, calling to her from the orchard in the voice of a boy.

I love you, I love you, I love you.

Libby, say my name.

Acknowledgments

From Becky

My sister Kathy is the most generous person I have ever known and has supported and inspired me my entire life. She taught me some of my first words and has been encouraging me to find my voice ever since. "Beck, I want to write a book with you" were some of the most empowering words I've ever heard. She is the epitome of dedication and perseverance, and without her unshakable faith, this labor of love would never have been created or ultimately published. Kath, not only do I love you, but I love to be with you, too. I am honored to be your partner in this endeavor, and I hope there are many more to come. And, Michael, welcome to the family — I'm so thrilled to have you for a brother.

We began this book in the fall of 2002, and along the way we've met many people who helped shape it. Much thanks belongs to Dr. Stephen Potter of the National Park Service — we so appreciate your insight and expertise, and fondly remember our evenings together at the Piper Farm. We are also grateful for our time spent with Jerry Holsworth, local historian of Winchester, Virginia. Our deepest thanks go to the rangers and staff at the Chatham Manor Archives, the Fredericksburg and Spotsylvania National Military Park, Antietam National Battlefield Park, and to the staff at the Handley Regional Library and Archives in Winchester, Virginia.

Thank you to the amazing team championing this book: Jenna Johnson, Nina Barnett, Stephanie Kim, Ayesha Mirza, Chelsea Newbould, Michaela Sullivan, and Erin DeWitt at Houghton

Mifflin Harcourt. Thank you, Henry Dunow, agent extraordinaire and lover of baseball. Ro and Cory, thanks for making a mom of four feel like a supermodel for a day. Thank you to Dr. Donald C. Elder, Mrs. LaNelle Allee, and Mr. Randy Tumlinson for nurturing my love of history. Randy, Margie, and Sher — thanks for always letting me tag along and for putting up with my brattiness!

Finally, I must thank my fun and loving family. Jesse — thank you for our many adventures, and for indulging your history geek of a wife. I'm never happier than when we're traipsing across some battlefield or climbing in a ruin. I love you very much — and not just because you've got a smoking pair of legs. Abbey, Wesley, Katey, and Travis — you bring the sunshine to my life, and every day is a new crazy adventure. You all make me happy and so proud. And to my sweet Mommie, Polly Hepinstall — thank you for always believing in me. People tell me I'm just like you, and there could be no greater compliment.

From Kathy

Thanks first to Jenna Johnson, wonderful editor and faithful advocate of our book. Also thanks to Ayesha Mirza, Nina Barnett, Stephanie Kim, Michaela Sullivan, Chelsea Newbould, Erin DeWitt, Lisa Glover, and all the kind and supportive people of Houghton Mifflin Harcourt.

Henry "so good I hired him twice" Dunow took on the challenge of a second Hepinstall as a client, and for that he deserves many thanks and a new grill cleaner.

Polly "Sergeant Saintly" Hepinstall was, as usual, invaluable in correcting our grammar and logic mistakes, just like when we were kids.

And my blue-eyed unicorn of a husband, Michael Parks, mentioned one day that we should give the *Sisters of Shiloh* manuscript one more try after all these years and see what happened. I love you, Michael.

Thank you, Tom Gilmartin, for the advice and knowledge; and, Rob Schwartz, for giving me that short furlough to do research in Virginia all those years ago.

Thank you, Cousin Sheri Peddy, for cheering us on and always supporting our work. And J.D., Jack, Linki, Mark . . . and all our other cousins and second cousins, too numerous to name, who have always stood behind us.

Thank you, Cory and Ro, for making us look good and for being so darn lovable.

Thank you, Dawn and Randall, for the early interest.

And, Juan — remember when you had to leave because the Civil War research was taking all the space? I wish I could take that back. There will always be room for you.

Finally, thank you, Becky Hepinstall Hilliker. You're an amazing writer and collaborator, and I'm so happy we've finally realized that inspirational idea you had — was it twelve years ago? You know I'm bad at math. Thanks for never giving up and for your humor, good sportsmanship, and whip-sharp intelligence. The South may have lost, but having you as a sister is a daily win. I love you so much.